"It's been a long time, hasn't it, Cesca?"

A moose emerged from the trees near the cemetery. Its head swayed, surveying. Staring. Francesca pretended not to understand Charlie. "What has?"

"Since you and I were in Alaska together. In Talkeetna."

"Thirty-two years." She stepped toward the flight station, kicking puffs of snow. Glove on the door handle, she glanced at Charlie. "I don't intend to stand around reminiscing."

"Well, I'm sure glad to hear that." He peeled her fingers from the door and held both her hands as he kissed her on the mouth.

She jerked her head away, shook her hands loose. "How—how degrading," she whispered.

Mirth eclipsed any other expression in his eyes.

Francesca said, "This is Talkeetna. This is my hometown, and—"

"And you wanted to come home and make nice with people who don't deserve it, and that worthless pilot Charlie Marcus is kissing you at the airport. Something like that?"

"Just shut up, Charlie. Just shut up."

Br

CR

Dear Reader,

Stories unfold themselves to the author in unusual ways. From shortly after THE MIDWIVES series was conceived, I knew Francesca's story would be set in Alaska. In writing her story and Tara's, however, I realized that Francesca had grown up in Alaska, that her father was one of the famous glacier pilots of Talkeetna, flying climbers to Denali.

Talkeetna, Alaska, is a magical and fascinating town with its own real-life heroes and a more fascinating history than any fiction. The Fairview Inn is real—though not precisely as I have presented it—and I have taken artistic license with other features of the town. The characters are wholly mine—and their own.

I hope you enjoy revisiting the characters you met in *You Were on My Mind* and *Talking About My Baby,* and I hope you like Francesca's and Charlie's story—and like them as much as I do. Thank you so much for reading my books.

Sincerely,

Margot Early

THERE IS A SEASON
Margot
Early

HARLEQUIN®

TORONTO • NEW YORK • LONDON
AMSTERDAM • PARIS • SYDNEY • HAMBURG
STOCKHOLM • ATHENS • TOKYO • MILAN • MADRID
PRAGUE • WARSAW • BUDAPEST • AUCKLAND

ISBN 0-373-70878-5

THERE IS A SEASON

Copyright © 1999 by Margot Early.

This edition published by arrangement with Harlequin Books S.A.

Visit us at www.romance.net

Printed in U.S.A.

This book could not have been written without the generous help of many people and without information gleaned from some beautiful and insightful reference books.
Written references included but were not limited to
Achilles in Vietnam by Jonathan Shay, M.D. Ph.D.,
The Things They Carried by Tim O'Brien,
Firebirds by Chuck Carlock,
Wager with the Wind by James Greiner and
Heroes of the Horizon by Gerry Bruder.
Mary Buchmayr, Joe and Marty Creel, and especially Suzy Kellard patiently answered many questions about Talkeetna and Alaska. Marina Alzugaray has always been my inspiration for what it is to be a midwife. Jean Ewing, you are a wonderful friend and writer; thank you for being there.
Richard Dick of High Country Helicopters very kindly answered military questions, while Emarae Garcia, Karen Mortimer and my husband, Doug, talked to me about airplanes. Emarae also invited me to accompany her to prenatal visits with her midwife. Also, Doug, thanks for the music and for listening to all my stories;
I love you. Finally, thank you,
Gordon DeVries, for answering estate questions and for being so patient during my long conversations with Laura. Laura DeVries, thank you for the history lessons... and much more for your dear friendship.

All technical errors in this fictional work are mine.

PROLOGUE

CHARLIE MARCUS was using a pay phone in sight of Deadman's Wall in Talkeetna's historic Fairview Inn. In Talkeetna, everything not new was historic. In fact, he was history in the making. But, being too smart to climb Denali, he'd never be found on Deadman's Wall.

No Walls for Charlie Marcus.

That still left some ways to die. Like whatever way Mia had.

Francesca's voice had taken on a strident, piercing tone. He held the receiver away from his head as she shouted. "I am not scared! Stop saying I'm scared."

"Of course you are." Glasses banged behind him at the U-shaped bar, where off-season mountaineers from Italy toasted the gift of life, recently returned to them by Marcus Aviation. "Cesca, it's been thirty-two years since you've seen Talkeetna, and the only excuse for that is fear. You're chicken. Scared, scared, fraidy-cat."

"I cannot believe a fifty-four-year-old man is talking to me like this."

She was thousands of miles away, in Precipice, Colorado, where she practiced midwifery, but Charlie imagined his ex-wife's pale cheeks flushed beneath her auburn hair, maybe going gray. He'd turned gray a few years ago, second time he'd lost a plane, making his way down the glaciers, off Denali, after two weeks without being found.

She said, "I have no reason to be afraid. You may have forgotten why I left Talkeet—"

"No, Cesca, I haven't forgotten. I should add seeing your own flesh and blood to the list of things that frighten you."

"That old man does not frighten me! And neither do—"

"Probably not like the thought of his dying without your seeing him again, but—"

"He's not dying."

Yes, she sounded worried. Eighty was getting on. "Cesca, you know you should come up here and see about Mia, but the fact is you're scared." One of the Italians tried to hand him a beer, and Charlie shook his head, lifting his unopened Surge. "And I know why you're scared. Growing up with—"

"Oh, I get to be psychoanalyzed by the man who spent the first sixteen years of his life running cons with his father and the next twelve running away from his own wife and daughter."

"Don't forget the VC."

She ignored that. "One thing's for certain. If I come to Alaska, it will be for Mia—" Mia her friend, Mia her former apprentice, Mia who had vanished— "It will be to learn what happened to Mia. Not to see you. I'd prefer not to come within seeing distance of you."

And blood relatives who weren't dying didn't bear mention.

"Alas." With the toe of his boot, Charlie drew over a steel-leg cushioned stool, but someone had spilled a beer on it. He passed. "A woman like you is rare anywhere, but especially here. Men will queue up to hunt for you and sew your mukluks. You know what women say about finding partners in Alaska. 'The odds are good, but the goods are odd.'"

"I did find a partner in Alaska."

"Ah, Cesca. For those days we gathered berries in Denali, seeing our daughter, Tara, in each other's eyes...you can stay with me." He'd told her Talkeetna had changed, that now it was just like the place on *Northern Exposure*. It had changed since 1967—changed plenty. But it was still Talkeetna, launching point for Denali and famous for its annual Moose Dropping Festival. "You're talking to one of the few people in town who doesn't shower at the Laundromat. And my house is warm."

That should cinch it. In January of '68, when he'd rescued Francesca from a life of waiting tables in Anchorage and taken her to Hawaii, she'd shown her gratitude by marrying him in the most dire circumstances.

"You'll have to do better, Charlie. I grew up there. Remember?"

"Think running water. Think bathtub. Indoor plumbing. But maybe you could stay at Mia's. To look after the dogs. She's got a big dog-food cooker. You can melt snow for water." Before she could react—and before he could think too hard about Mia—he added, "Probably room for another midwife, too. I could fly you to nearby villages for births—"

"Like you did for Mia?"

A little jealous, Cesca? "Now and again."

Roy Walcott, Jr., Francesca's brother and the son of Talkeetna's oldest surviving bush pilot, entered the bar. Charlie turned his back. The day Roy Walcott Air Service closed its doors Charlie Marcus would declare an annual holiday in honor of the event.

Roy Jr. asked the bartender, "Haven't you got some air freshener, Spike? I smell *Charlie.*"

"'Scuse me, Cesca." Charlie dropped the receiver and strode six yards, making sure the can of Surge had a rough ride. "Well, if it isn't Roy Pilot-Error Walcott, Jr. How's tricks, Roy?" He opened the can.

From her phone in Colorado, Francesca Walcott heard the sound of a table crashing, wood splintering, glass breaking. Someone yelled, "TAKE IT OUTSIDE!"

She heard another explosion.

"YOU'RE PAYING FOR THAT TABLE, BOYS!"

"You've lived too long, Marcus, after you killed my—"

"MARCUS, FINISH YOUR CALL AND HANG UP MY PHONE! GET OUT OF HERE! YOU CAN KILL EACH OTHER IN THE STREET!"

A crack that was fist on flesh.

This does not attract me, Francesca told herself calmly. *Charlie Marcus is a barbarian, and he lives in a place filled with other barbarians. I know this better than anyone. I will eat this house before I return to Talkeetna, Alaska.*

CHAPTER ONE

Talkeetna, Alaska
June 16, 1963

''Not sure you should be seen with me, Francesca.''

Charlie Marcus is smoking a cigarette and checking down the railroad tracks toward Anchorage. He could pass for a movie star—Paul Newman, move over. His eyes are so dark brown they're almost black, and his eyebrows make him look like he's maybe Italian, and—okay, his lips, his mouth is wide and perfect—and any girl would die for that nose.

Oh, would the mosquitoes stop? How can you look good in a skirt with bites all over you?

''What's your daddy going to say when he sees you talking to me?''

Dad isn't going to say much, because once the train whistle blows, he and Charlie Marcus will be vying for passengers, and Dad'll have fits. Dad wants all the customers to fly with him, all the mountaineers and scientists bound for Mount McKinley and the photographers who just want to see Alaska, everyone—there's never enough to go around—and now here's Charlie, wanting the same thing.

I have a wife and three children to feed, a boy

to put through college! Dad says. *How'd a kid that age get a plane, anyhow? You watch, his story's not worth a dime, a rhyme or a second of your time.*

My brothers want to kill Charlie.

I tell him, "My dad says you don't look old enough to have a license, let alone fly passengers."

He winks at me. "I'm not. How old are you?"

Shivers down my spine. No point in lying. Everyone in Talkeetna knows everything. I'm tall, but I feel small, have felt small ever since we found out Mom is sick. "Fifteen next month."

The train whistle blows, and Charlie sees nothing but the train. Here comes Dad, hustling over from the airstrip.

"Slap me, Francesca," says Charlie. "He'll think I got fresh with you."

When I walk—no, run—away, I'm trying not to laugh. I hardly ever laugh lately. I see my best friend, Stormy, and I pretend I'm running to tell her something awful that Charlie did. I don't want Dad angry at me, but can I help it if Charlie Marcus steals all his customers? Dad has the personality of a tack.

Anchorage International Airport
Sikuvik—October—ice time—1999
30° F

HE WASN'T AT THE GATE.

Francesca didn't miss seeing him, but she would miss the free lift to Talkeetna. The easy way home, if there was one.

Flight announcements rang in her ears. She scanned the crowds on the concourse, searching in vain. Men with great furry beards. Eskimo and Athabaskans. Business people in suits. Booths and shops sold native art and espresso, natural skin care products and pizza.

She needed to claim her bags first thing. It was six o'clock and dark. The lights of Anchorage had winked yellow and white, reflecting off the water, as the plane banked toward the airport. Anchorage had come a long way. She couldn't conjure up the feelings of three decades before, Charlie popping into the diner where she was waiting tables, sweeping her into his arms... And leaving this cold land that had said its last words to Francesca Walcott.

Oil money had changed everything.

Good.

It would have changed Talkeetna and her family, too. Though both of those things were harder to imagine.

Francesca searched for overhead signs, found those directing her to the baggage claim and started in that direction, lugging her heavy tote. Her face tingled, warm, tears threatening—one of those hormonal rushes she'd begun to associate with impending menopause. But maybe it was terror instead. *Face it. You knew he wouldn't show.* And she'd be returning to Talkeetna alone.

Maybe it was better that way.

On the other hand, it wasn't too late to change her mind and go—where?

A blind man weaved toward her with an assistance dog—or one in training. The wolflike puppy tugged at his leash, dragging his owner behind him, as the poor gentleman tapped with his white cane. Sniffing at passing travelers, the dog circled his master with his leash.

Fortunately, the man carried no luggage.

No luggage.

That flight jacket.

Aviator sunglasses.

She strode toward him. "That is the worst disguise I ever saw. You should be ashamed of yourself, Charlie Marcus."

"Don't blow my cover, Cesca. I couldn't leave him. He's too valuable. Besides, he's Mia's."

"Did they find her?" Hope. Relief. Mia was fine, and she, Francesca, wouldn't have to go to Talkeetna. That meant she would've abandoned most of her possessions and come to Alaska for—

It didn't matter. Mia was safe.

But Charlie shook his head and tapped his cane convincingly as he tried to unwind himself from the leash.

"You're abominable. Impersonating someone with a disability."

"Save the lecture. You have bags? Let's get out of here, before someone notices this ain't no German shepherd. Sorry I can't offer to carry your luggage."

Hauling the bulging tote a pace behind and beside him, Francesca noted the changes in her ex-husband. It was years since she'd seen Charlie—at Tara's wedding to Danny Graine, the start of a marriage that had ended in divorce. Charlie's body seemed lean and trim as ever beneath his blue jeans. The mustache suited him now that his brown hair had turned gray. They both stood five-ten in their bare feet, but Francesca felt taller. Tall, wide-hipped, ungainly. Fifty had come and gone.

The dog set the pace. Catching up, Francesca said, "I thought her dogs were in Talkeetna." One of the faceless voices who'd phoned after Mia's disappearance had promised to care for them till Francesca's arrival.

"This is a new dog. Cute, isn't he?"

With his brindle coat and uneven mask, he was less

than cute. People stared as Charlie dragged him onto the escalator.

Francesca turned from the onlookers. "You take that animal outside the terminal, and I'll collect my bags."

Travelers flattened against the handrail, lifting tote bags clear as the dog raced up and down the moving steps, winding its leash around Charlie, sometimes cowering behind him.

"Sit," said Charlie. "Stay. Good King."

"King?"

He ignored her, as though she were a callous stranger.

How could she have left Tara to come here? Tara. Francesca practically shuddered as she thought of her grown daughter's plight in Colorado, something neither she nor Tara had shared with Charlie. And why tell him? Over the years, there'd been things about Tara's life that Charlie hadn't seen fit to share with *her*.

Anyhow, she was here, in part, for Tara. To settle a score.

And for Mia. *Where are you, Mia?*

Mia—Mia with her sled dogs and her airplane. Mia with her long-legged stride, her winning smile, her way of drawing the line when—

Mia Kammerlander, certified nurse-midwife, had disappeared from Talkeetna a week ago Monday night, a few hours after a birth. She'd gone on a snowmobile, leaving two of her dogs in burlap sacks at the Village Airstrip, ready to load on her Beechcraft for a race in Nome. Five more were staked nearby, and another had run off and come home alone. Mia had named Francesca as a contact person, in case of emergency, and she'd been contacted—first by the Alaska State Troopers via her local sheriff.

Then by Charlie.

They reached the baggage claim. Charlie pulled off his sunglasses, revealing the eyes Tara had inherited—and a shiner.

As Francesca traced the inside of her cheek with her tongue, he said, "Give me your claim checks and take the dog outside. What am I looking for? A steamer trunk, a full set of Gucci and what?"

"Two bags. I don't think that's unreasonable."

"Cesca, Cesca, not so touchy. Just want to make sure my plane will get off the ground."

His plane.

What have I done? Why am I here?

"A duffel bag, black with green straps. And a blue backpack." She handed him her baggage claim tickets and headed for the doors with the husky in front. The last thing she wanted was to be caught in the airport with this dog.

"MAKE SURE HE DOESN'T throw up in my car."

"How am I supposed to do that?" She wanted to throw up on the leather seats of his black Porsche 928 herself. She'd never seen the car before, and it accentuated her struggles of the last eighteen years. Not that Charlie hadn't helped out with child support. He had. But...

I don't want to be here, to be with him, to be having these thoughts, these feelings.

He headed south, and the road wound past Connors Lake. Francesca averted her head from King's wagging tail. She would arrive in Talkeetna smelling like this dog "Where are we going?"

"Friend's house. Hotels in Anchorage are outrageous."

"I thought we were going to Talkeetna." The seat

back sloped toward the rear windshield, and the shoulder strap forced her to recline. The relaxed posture was unnatural to her, especially now. "I expected to be there tonight, Charlie." *It's only a hundred miles away.*

"Surely you want to arrive home during daylight."

"It's not my home. I'll be staying at a hotel out on the Spur Road." She couldn't imagine a hotel on the Spur Road, but the new lodge had almost a hundred units. After all Charlie's talk about running water.

King wriggled from her lap to climb across Charlie's. "Oh, no, you don't. Hold him, Ces."

The street was snowpacked already, Halloween still days away; the lights of the cars reflected off the slick surface. *This is Anchorage?* Airport hotels replaced the open country she remembered. Everything developed, some things better than others. In the airline magazine, she'd seen some of what Prudhoe Bay had bought Anchorage. Performing arts center. Sports arena. A big city hardly twice the size of Grand Junction, Colorado.

Not far from the airport, Charlie turned up a side street and drove to a house at the end, against a forested hillside. The windows were unlit, but Francesca made out the shape of a real estate sign in the darkness. He reached for a garage-door opener over her head and pressed it.

"Is this your friend's car, too?"

"No, but I've been known to allow a trade. Tonight, we stay in the house."

Francesca decided the friend was female. "Whose house is this, Charlie?"

They were in the garage, the door going down. A truck with dog boxes sat in the other bay. No escape. King whined.

Charlie killed the engine, and she remembered his hands. Brown hands, strong hands. He patted the pockets of his jacket, checking for something, then removed the keys from the ignition. "It's Mia's place."

FRANCESCA'S LEGS WOBBLED on the steps from the garage up to the house. "Why did she keep a house in Anchorage?" *And why do you have a key?*

"Here, King." Charlie filled a food bowl and water dish.

"She wouldn't have come here often, not leaving her dogs."

"It was her ex-husband's place. He left it to her a few months ago—mainly, I think, because he forgot to change his will. But it's the kind of thing I might do for you someday, Cesca, in the event that you outlive me. No, don't move. I'll bring in your bags."

Francesca remembered when Mia had married—and divorced, an event casually reported by e-mail. But Francesca had never met Mia's husband. So much she didn't know of this woman, who had served as her apprentice in Colorado so long ago. Since then, they'd corresponded in fits and starts, met twice at midwifery conferences. But between her dogs and her plane and working as a midwife in Talkeetna—how stunned Francesca was by that choice, Talkeetna!—Mia had been tied to Alaska.

While the dog wolfed its food, Charlie slipped out to the garage. He returned and set her bags on the linoleum.

Francesca asked, "Why aren't you looking for her?"

Charlie closed the garage door, studied the keys in his hand before placing them on the counter and beginning to lock up for the night. "It's dark. And it snowed the night she was lost and has every day since. But seeing that you brought it up, we'll be leaving early."

Early. Before light? Francesca had suspected that line

about arriving home in daylight was bogus. Home... She concentrated on Mia.

Charlie had been searching—and planned to continue. Impossible to tell how he felt. All along, he'd treated Mia's disappearance more as an intriguing puzzle than the loss of a close friend. Mia was his next-door neighbor in Talkeetna.

Charlie had lost many friends.

He followed Francesca, at a distance, as she walked through the house turning on lights. A nice dwelling, presented to sell. The living room contained just a few pieces of furniture, possibly leased, a framed watercolor of a moose among birch trees and a Native American carving of a seal. The bathroom was immaculate.

Wanting, needing to know more about Mia, she opened drawers. A hair dryer. A comb with a few tawny hairs still in it. A fat novel that looked as though it had been read in the bath. Francesca felt a knot form in her throat. She picked up the book. She wanted to take it, to read it, to know what Mia had been reading before—

Missing isn't dead.

But what about when a woman left the Village Airstrip on a snowmobile and didn't come home? There wasn't anywhere to go but lost.

Other drawers yielded nothing, no sign of Mia's belongings—or her ex-husband. "You said he left her the house? He's dead?"

"It would have been premature otherwise."

Just a few more hours, Francesca promised herself. Less than twenty-four hours, and she'd be rid of Charlie Marcus. Except that Talkeetna was so small. And he and Mia had been neighbors. *And I can't avoid everyone I don't want to see.*

No, she'd come to face people, not to hide.

"You're a million miles away."

The rhythm of his voice touched old chords, chords to accompany simpler melodies, idealistic folk ballads and finally the blues of rock and roll, reaching into the vastness that was knowing. Ending innocence. It was the oldest chords that stirred her. She was years away, and his breath was at her shoulder, and she wanted life so different and wondered that, back then, the beautiful had held hands with the sad.

She'd traded it for an edgy contentment.

They were in the hallway, the hallway of an ordinary house in Anchorage, so how could it smell like Alaska? Trees and a certain earthy dampness.

She turned and saw his eyes. "Just—" She stopped. "We think—"

Nothing. No way to say a scent had paraded her choices past her.

Charlie tensed. She wouldn't have known that if she hadn't known him.

He was always singing to her, and in the dim anonymous hallway he sang the cruelest words that could be said by a woman to a man or a man to a woman, and Francesca had said them to him.

Just last week, on the way home from a birth, Tara had turned up that song on the radio, and Francesca's neck tendons had grown short and the seat of the old Subaru too stiff.

She turned to the next room. An office. A desktop PC. Empty closets. Computer manuals neatly arranged on the shelves above the computer. A framed print of a red Cessna flying near snow-laden peaks.

Finally, the bedroom, with an attached bath.

A wool spread in a rustic pattern covered the bed. No headboard. In the closet hung a few changes of clothes—

Mia's—and some shirts that must have belonged to her husband. Ex-husband.

Oh, ex-husbands.

Ignoring her own, Francesca knelt to peer under the bed. She opened drawers in the oak dresser. Three messages on the answering machine.

Francesca pushed Play.

"Wednesday, four-oh-one p.m. This is Joy Morrow calling for Mia Kammerlander. My number is..." *Beep.*

Francesca cast a look at Charlie, and her mouth felt hard and old. "Anyone you know?"

He shook his head. "Sounded like business."

"Tuesday, ten-oh-two p.m. Mia, it's John. If you're in Anchorage, call me. I want to talk about your picking up the pup." *Beep.*

"Saturday, eight-seventeen a.m. Mia, it's John. Couldn't make the race today. I guess you'll know that by the time you hear this. Bonnie has the pup. Hope he works out for you. Call me if there are any problems."

At least two weeks worth of messages. Francesca opened the lid of the machine and pressed Annc to hear Mia's message. "You've reached the home of Chris Clausson. I can't take your call right now but will return your message...."

Chris Clausson was her ex-husband. So Mia hadn't changed the tape after he died. Not so odd. Sometimes it took people a while. "How did he die?"

"Ah...pilot error. Took two fishermen from Arizona with him."

Nameless dread gripped her. She'd grown up in a flying family, walked away from them and married and divorced a pilot. Conscious of Charlie in the doorway, grave and sober, Francesca hurried to leave the bedroom without investigating the adjoining bath.

"Hey. What have you got there?" Charlie frowned at the puppy, who had come down the hall bearing an article of clothing. He caught the pup's harness-style collar. "Sit." He pulled up on the collar, pushed down on the puppy's rear while Francesca studied the animal's brindle fur and slanted amber eyes. "Drop it. Drop it. Francesca, open his mouth."

"I beg your pardon?"

Charlie lifted skeptical brown eyes. "You know, in twenty-four hours, you're going to be responsible for forty-two of these animals. Forty-three, counting King here."

Forty-three? She'd envisioned a dozen, twenty at most. Now she saw something else—memory. The neighbor's sled dogs when she was a teenager. Barking, barking, the year her mother died. Dog bite. "So this is the puppy mentioned on the answering machine?"

"Yes."

"How did you get him?"

"From Bonnie. When Mia didn't show in Nome, she brought King back to Anchorage."

"Is that his name?"

"You have a better idea?"

"I suppose we can call him that." Her throat went dry. "Until Mia returns."

Opening the dog's mouth himself and plucking free the garment, Charlie didn't answer.

THE REFRIGERATOR was at least partially stocked. Someone had shot a caribou that fall and given meat to Chris or Mia, or maybe one of them had gotten the animal. The idea of eating red meat made Francesca queasy. In Hawaii and Colorado, she'd sometimes eaten fish or free-range chicken, but red meat... It had been so long. "Just a little for me, Charlie."

"You'll have to get over that up here, honey, or you're gonna starve. And freeze."

"I've dressed out a bull moose, Charlie Marcus." Her diet wasn't his business. Anyway, by this time tomorrow—no Charlie. "What are the police doing?"

"Well, they're looking." He tossed scraps to King, who sat waiting.

With a vengeance, Francesca sliced some cracked and mushy carrots from the refrigerator. "Have they been here, the police? Have they searched the house?"

"Francesca, there's no evidence of a crime—or a death. She's missing. They're looking. That's what you do with missing people. Look for them."

"But it sounds so strange. Why would she leave her dogs like that, ready to get on her plane?"

"It looks like one of the dogs got away from her, and she jumped on a snowmobile to go find it." More scraps for King. "There were no tracks anymore, once people realized she was gone. It snowed, and the Village Airstrip isn't exactly hopping this time of year, especially after dark."

Francesca wheeled around. "Have the police questioned you?"

"Careful with that knife, Cesca. Me and every other single male in Talkeetna—and that's most of us. Actually, I was playing basketball that night."

It was on the tip of her tongue to snap, *That's right. In Alaska, they let short men play.* But Charlie was of average height—and the perfect build for a pilot.

That perfect build annoyed her. Men could pass fifty and not grow broader through the beam, and silver hair was so becoming to them. They went on being strong and handsome, frequently picking young and fertile mates. Life, at its most biological level, was unfair, and Charlie Marcus exemplified this fact.

He and Mia had probably— What were the police doing? "Have they asked why you have a key to this house?"

His lush eyebrows twitched attractively. "Not with such enthusiasm."

She brandished the knife.

"I told them what I told you. Now, now, Francesca, don't make assumptions. Imagine, after all these years…"

"It *is* your imagination. Tell me, what possessed you to send Tara—" She dropped the knife. "Tara. I have to call Tara."

"Great. I'd like to say hello, too. I have a bone to pick with her."

"Well, don't pick it now. She has enough on her plate." Francesca left the room, and he heard her shut the bedroom door behind her.

Tara had enough on her plate? Just what was on their daughter's plate?

Charlie frowned. A week ago, Tara had called and asked for money for a new car. A lot of money. She'd had a vehicle in mind—told him the mileage. Next he heard, she'd taken the money and gone off to Denver to car shop. With a man. His daughter's taste in men had never impressed Charlie Marcus.

And Francesca was holding out on him. What was this stuff about enough on her plate?

He went into the office, pressed the mute button on the extension there and lifted the receiver.

"Everything's fine, Mom. We're great."

What was that sound in the background? It sounded

like— Oh. Right. Tara had given him a story for this, too.

Charlie silently replaced the receiver and collided with his ex-wife outside the bedroom door. He meant to catch her arms, to steady her. He caught her waist.

With barely a movement, she brushed away his hands. "What were you doing?" Her eyes drifted suspiciously toward the office.

"Trying to find out why our daughter has a *baby* in her home."

Francesca backed into the doorjamb. "She's a midwife. It's a client's."

"You're a miserable liar."

She preceded him down the hall, her walk as strong and sultry as an eighteen-year-old's. "Yes, you're the pro in that department, Charlie."

"When have I lied to you?"

She wheeled. The words were there, loaded and ready to fire. But they were in the same room together, she and Charlie, and old habit kicked in. Charlie'd been home from Vietnam eighteen months and was skunk drunk when he'd said, "Enough 'You did this, and you did that,' Cesca. If you want to keep lists in your head, take up earth sciences. I know when I let you down."

She'd stopped counting his mistakes, right up to the day she'd said she didn't love him anymore.

"Forgive and forget" was pretty rusty from disuse. But Charlie had never really lied to her. Just…kept quiet. She could do the same. "If you want to know about Tara's life, ask her yourself."

He cocked an eyebrow. "Ivy? Do I get to ask about her life?"

"Ivy is not your daughter." She was Francesca's by adoption, adopted as an adult, a woman with no memory of her past and no family. Tara and Francesca had met Ivy at a midwifery conference, and Tara had dreamed up the idea of inviting her into their family. Since then, Ivy had been reconnected with her past—with her husband and her thirteen-year-old daughter. She and Cullen were expecting their second child December first.

"Well, now. She calls me Dad," Charlie pointed out, "just like she calls you Mom."

"Isn't one mutual child enough for you?" After the words, a splinter held her throat.

His eyes were clear and startlingly open. She knew he wouldn't speak, just leave the air humming with meaning.

Charlie began to wish Francesca had stayed in Colorado. Why had he wanted her to come back to Talkeetna? To talk to someone about Mia. Bad choice of someone. She came from a family of assholes, and she hated Alaska. Didn't even want to eat meat.

Shit.

He pushed past Francesca and strode toward the kitchen, but the puppy had vanished—with the main course.

SHE TOOK THE BEDROOM, leaving Charlie the couch—and King. She would get to know the dog, and Mia's others, when she must.

If only the bed wouldn't creak. Charlie would get satisfaction from her restlessness. Francesca didn't sleep well under the best circumstances. And with Tara's problems in Colorado, Mia missing—

Talkeetna.

The old man. What did he look like now? Thick silver hair, like her grandfather's, she'd bet. When she'd left, it had been the color hers was now. Seeing him would be like seeing photos of old rock stars and finding they'd aged, the way Jimi and Janis and Jim Morrison would've, had they lived.

Only he was her father.

Shivering in her long flannel nightgown, she poked through drawers in the second bathroom. Toothbrush, toothpaste, hair dryer, homeopathic remedies for insomnia, headache, anxiety... Another brush with blond hair in it. Mia.

Francesca pictured the woman she remembered. Six feet tall, curls bobbing around her pretty face, a strong, blunt competence, an intelligent restraint. Once, after watching two obstetricians at the local hospital draw circles on a mother's abdomen to track the progress of an abruptio placentae, Francesca had asked Mia, "Don't you ever get angry?"

Mia had thought briefly. "No. I just go away. Sometimes," she'd added, "forever."

Hard to forget that answer.

Mia, where have you gone now?

Talkeetna, Alaska

PAMMIE SUE WALCOTT watched her husband, Roy Jr., shut the door, wipe his feet and hang his plaid wool coat on a peg, just as he had every night of the thirty-eight years they'd been married. He surveyed his house and his youngest son. Tony was there a lot lately, which was fine with Pammie Sue. *There's always room for our kids in our house, as long as they live.*

Her husband kissed her. "Hi, Pammie Sue."

She had always appreciated the comfort of having some things the same, year after year—like the things Roy Jr. did when he came home from the airport each

evening. But comfort had left her two weeks before, left
forever. Her husband's bruised jaw had faded to sickly
yellow and green, the color Pammie Sue felt inside.

"Have they found her?" The raspy knot had formed
in her throat the night her first grandchild was born, the
night Mia Kammerlander was lost. Mia had guided baby
Kate Elin into the world, and it was so happy for a time.
Minutes.

Roy Jr. shook his head, no, she wasn't found, and Pammie Sue shut her eyes.

He rubbed his head, behind his ears, looking like his
father. "Francesca's coming home."

Pammie Sue's heart pounded, as though it meant
something. It didn't. But she must have winced, because
Roy Jr. glanced at Tony, watching TV. "Shall we take
a walk, Pammie Sue?"

Their twenty-eight-year-old son, their youngest,
stretched his arms behind his head and craned his neck
to see them. "Is this the Francesca I've never met? Aunt
Francesca?"

Roy Jr. just looked at him.

"Guess so." Tony returned to Beavis and Butthead.

Husband and wife walked in the snow, heading over
to the snowmobile trail beside the train tracks. They held
hands, as always, but Pammie Sue wondered if he sensed
something amiss. *I've never kept anything from him till
now, nothing important.*

Francesca was coming home. "Will she try to recon-
cile with your dad?"

He drew a breath. "Well, now, P.S.—" he called Pammie Sue that often "—I can't say. Not if she's hanging
out with that sly-faced slime from Kansas City, which
she is."

Charlie Marcus first came to Talkeetna in the early sixties, but he was from Kansas City.

Roy Jr. talked on. "He's flying her in, and it's because of Mia Kammerlander. Mia studied how to be a midwife with Francesca or something."

He sighed, and for once Pammie Sue couldn't guess his thoughts. *I married into a family of hate, and Charlie Marcus is what they hate.* But Francesca was her father's only daughter. Forgiveness could happen, and maybe it should. Maybe it should.

"This sounds awful to say—" yet it came from her mouth "—but I just wouldn't put it past Roy Sr., after all this stalling, to give her his half of the business."

When Roy Jr. said, "It's not half. It's fifty-one percent," Pammie Sue knew the same thing had occurred to him.

But she ceased thinking about Roy Walcott Air Service, thinking instead that Francesca had been her sister's friend, had been Stormy's friend. And Mia had studied with Francesca.

Pammie Sue clasped her husband's arm, and she almost told him, but instead she said, "I'm tired."

And never said she was afraid.

CHAPTER TWO

Talkeetna
November 22, 1963

It's almost dark but not snowing when school lets out. On the way home, Stormy asks, "Did Mel get in?"

"Last night." My middle brother, Mel, goes to the University of Alaska in Fairbanks. Dad flew up to get him because of Mom's doctor appointment in Anchorage today. I'm scared because Dad had Mel come home.

Stormy stops at her house, and her blue eyes tell me how sorry she is about my mother. "You want to come over tomorrow?"

She's sweet. She wants to come to my house and see guess who.

"Maybe you can come over, Stormy. I don't know yet."

At the airstrip, Charlie Marcus is unloading his plane, passing supplies to Mr. Frey from the store. Charlie hands a box to Mr. Frey, and Mr. Frey tells him something, and Charlie almost drops the box. It slides from his fingers, and he catches it again, lower. He stares at Mr. Frey, and I try not to stare at Charlie, in case my family's around.

My dad's plane isn't in his hangar.

"Boo!"

I jump a foot and slip on the ice, and my brother makes sure I don't go down.

"Mel! Don't do that!" He was hiding behind the shed next to the hangar, waiting to scare me. He smells like beer. He must have been messing around with his friend Dale, seeing that Roy Jr.'s so busy with Pammie Sue and the baby.

Our eyes meet. He says, "They're not back."

We go around front, and with Mel beside me it is not a good time to be ogling Charlie Marcus.

There's a radio on.

Charlie has pulled a transistor out of the cabin of his Cessna and is standing there in the snow, and he puts his head in his arm against the fuselage and his other hand over his face. Someone's talking on the radio, but I listen to the sky for my dad's plane and try not to watch Charlie looking so strange.

Mel is absolutely still, and suddenly he walks toward Charlie's plane on those long legs of his, and he stops and stares at the radio, and I hear it, too.

Their faces look identical, my brother's and Charlie's, and I see the picture of President Kennedy that Dad hung on our wall.

I want my mother to come home, want her to be well. Please. Please.

No one speaks, and I wish Mel or Charlie would. I talk to Charlie whenever I won't get caught, and I know he is wise. When I was afraid for my dad, flying in the mountains, landing on glaciers, he said, "You don't have time to sit around being scared, Francesca. This ain't no dress rehearsal."

Why doesn't he say something now?

Someone shot our President. I want to cry, but I can't.

There's a plane coming, and my brother and I look at each other. Mom's going to die, too, I think, and I know Mel's thinking it, as well. And I can't stand it. I just can't stand it.

It's not a dress rehearsal, and it's not a bad dream, and I wish it was.

Second day back

DENALI WAS OUT, unobscured by weather. The Alaska Range, the mountains of Francesca's childhood, filled the immaculate windshield of Charlie's Cessna 185. And the Talkeetnas, to the northeast—

Home.

No. She'd lived on the big island, lived in the San Juan Mountains of Colorado. This wasn't home. It had stopped being home on a summer day in '67, a month after her high school graduation.

Charlie's occasional guide commentary, pointing out the old and the new between communication with the towers, kept her from removing her headset and ending the constant static. She'd slept too little. But the headset, and flying north from Anchorage in a Cessna...

All so familiar.

King dozed in a burlap sack behind the seats. "He may as well get used to it," Charlie had said when he deposited the wriggling dog in the bag. "This is how sled dogs travel in the air. Keeps 'em from fighting."

Francesca knew that. Charlie had loaded the plane with supplies for Talkeetna and mining or surveying equipment and who knew what else. The Interior stretched ahead of them, familiar as a lover when the years had been kind. Seeing it left her with the same shaky feeling.

She didn't want to go back, and the Cessna was taking her there and couldn't take her there.

Mia had nothing to do with her past in Talkeetna.

Knowing the voice-activated headsets cut out the first sounds, Francesca said, "Annoying Charlie, how long has Mia's husband been dead?"

Static and the voice of another pilot filled the space. Codes.

He cleared his throat. "…was her ex-husband."

Why had he bothered to clarify that?

"…two, three months."

"That's all?" She had to repeat herself, having spoken too quickly. Had Mia grieved?

Would I grieve?

She knew the answer—for herself. "Why did they divorce?"

"…dogs. He didn't feed them for three days. She was doing births; he went hunting, and the weather turned nasty on him."

"But people don't divorce over one incident."

He made some sound that ignored her comment. "…it was three winters ago. Maybe four—no, three."

I just go away. Sometimes, forever. "They were living in Anchorage?"

"…in Talkeetna. He, uh, worked for me then. Not when he died."

The noise of the engine, the darkness and the distance provided by the headsets made talking safe. But not safe enough for her to ask about his relationship with Mia, ask what it had been. And she didn't care, truly. Charlie was attractive and sometimes funny. Nights past, he'd had her rolling with laughter till her sides ached, till she was filled with the euphoria that came only from laughter.

Sure, she still felt the spell.

But she knew better.

They'd been married more than a decade.

No, she didn't want to become involved again, and what if he *had* slept with Mia? Francesca was moving into a different phase of life—what Tara, with the oblivion of the young, called "the Crone years." Thank you, Tara.

In Colorado, she'd been living on tofu and yams, and the natural estrogen brought her body and emotions into precarious balance. Despite Mia, despite Charlie, despite Tara and dear little Laura.

His voice interrupted the static. "...the baby. Tell me about the baby."

Was he psychic? Time to take off this damned headset. But not before she said, "There is no baby."

"...must have come from the border."

Until recently, their daughter had worked as a midwife at Maternity House, a birth clinic on the Texas-Mexico border.

"...what did she do, adopt one of those babies?"

"In a manner of speaking." Francesca bit her tongue. Tight-lipped, she removed the headset.

He touched her arm and pointed toward her window. The river plain below shifted in the half-light of morning. No, the ground wasn't moving. She put on her headset and said, "Caribou."

"...so what did she really need the money for? Adoption?"

"She bought a Range Rover! With money she got from you and borrowed from Isaac."

"Who—" Charlie's voice darkened "—is Isaac?"

"A physician. He lived in Rwanda and was married to a Rwandan woman. He has three children."

Crackle, static. A tower interchange involving another plane.

"...what happened to his wife?"

"I don't know. She's dead."

"...and Tara borrowed money from him? For a Range Rover? Tara drives junkers.... Not buying this, Francesca. Where does the baby fit in?"

Why not let him have it? It was his fault as much as anyone's, his influence on Tara. His genes, for that matter. "Your daughter stole the baby."

The radio suddenly demanded his attention.

That wasn't fair to Tara, Francesca decided. When she could talk to him again, she said, "A Mexican teenager abandoned Laura in her car. Tara's car. They'd talked beforehand. Tara made some promise to take care of the baby if the mother died."

"...want to know where twenty-three thousand dollars and a Range Rover bought in Denver and Isaac fit in. 'Fess up, Cesca. Is he a loser? He is, isn't he?"

"He's a physician."

"...know, I told her before she married that last skunk, I told her, 'He's gonna walk out, he won't go the distance, Tara.'"

"The pot calling the kettle black. She must have been impressed."

"...of Earthly Delights, you're the one who filed. Who is this guy? Give me a last name. I'm going to check up on him."

"What? You think he has a record? Bad credit? You checking up on anyone—" Suddenly she was cut off, and he was talking to the tower in Talkeetna and they were coming in over trees, so many trees, in the shadow of the great mountains. The unfinished sentence grew stale in her mouth. *You checking up on anyone is the ultimate hypocrisy.*

Talkeetna.

Heavens. There really was a big, new hotel on the Spur Road.

She made out the streets arranged in a grid among the trees, traced the path of the train tracks. The ground was white. The Cessna would land on skis.

I won't be here long. Just till Mia comes back.

But she didn't believe it herself.

And Charlie had been right about one thing. She was scared shitless.

FROM THE SNOW-COVERED TARMAC, she studied the tower and the flight station, and she scanned the adjacent small hangars and planes, the nearby offices with familiar names.

Marcus Aviation.

Roy Walcott Air Service.

The office was new. The professionally lettered sign was new. The flight station was new. Yes, a lot had changed since August, 1967.

Fluorescent lights burned inside the Roy Walcott Air Service office, but the door remained shut. As Charlie jumped from the plane, she said, "Well, Dad should be enjoying a prosperous retirement."

"Not so's anyone would notice. All he enjoys is yanking people's chains, and your sorry eldest brother is his favorite dog. You can bet the old man's in there making sure the papers get pushed just right."

Charlie hefted a box from the plane, the green beneath his eye garish in daylight.

"Charlie, who did you slug it out with last week?"

"I walked into a kitchen cabinet."

The wind picked up, and the cold entered her like death. In Colorado, she'd always kept warm by layering. Here, the wind penetrated the hood of her parka. Even in her Sorel-style boots, her toes lost feeling. Another layer of socks would have helped. Charlie was messing around in the back of the plane again, so Francesca headed for the flight station to thaw.

HE WATCHED HER SKID on the ice as she made her way to the terminal building. Her recovery, her startled wobble, counted years and told independence. Zeke, one of the mechanics, abandoned a Cessna 185 and trailed after her. Art Turner of Art's Air Taxi tapped out a cigarette and beat him inside. Charlie laughed out loud and murmured, "Welcome home, Francesca."

But he, too, looked toward the office of Roy Walcott Air Service.

No one emerged.

By the time Charlie had taken care of the Cessna, loaded a pack with the clothes Francesca claimed not to need, staked, fed and watered King and gone inside, she was nowhere in sight.

Art Turner, filling a coffee cup, seemed not to see Charlie, and Charlie returned the favor. As owner of Marcus Aviation, he had nothing to say to his competitors, nor they to him or each other, and the world was better for it.

But Turner was sixty-two years old, and he'd been flying customers back when Francesca left home. Charlie figured he'd missed nothing.

Becka Knight, who had come out to marshal Charlie's plane, silently uncapped her thermos. Becka had won the Mountain Mother Contest the previous summer, competing against other Talkeetna women in the vital skills of chopping wood, building fires and hauling water.

Charlie had sat on the all-bachelor panel of judges. "You know, Becka, I think you've let that contest go to your head. Only October, and you don't have a word to say to me." He leaned against the counter, working up a smile. "Where did she go?"

Becka nodded toward the rear of the flight station. Francesca was outside.

"Nice to see you, Becka."

His hand touched the door, and Becka said, "Charlie."

He turned.

"They found Mia."

FROM BEHIND THE FLIGHT STATION, she could see two new roads, three more air taxi offices and the edge of the cemetery. She'd last seen her mother's grave with fresh earth on it and no headstone yet. There would be another grave near it now.

Francesca's throat constricted.

Behind her, someone sang "Trouble in Mind" in a fair impression of Janis Joplin. Francesca laughed as she turned, from cold toward the warmth. No one in sight to watch Charlie's antics. They were alone. Alone for miles, it looked like. Art Turner had disappeared. Even the mechanic who'd introduced himself was gone.

But the back windows of the air taxi offices faced them, Charlie and her. Revealed them.

"It's been a long time, hasn't it, Cesca?"

A moose emerged from the trees near the cemetery. Its head swayed, surveying. Staring. She pretended not to understand Charlie. "What has?"

"Since you and I were in Talkeetna together."

"Thirty-two years." With a last glance at the closed

back door of Roy Walcott Air Service, she strode toward the flight station, kicking puffs of snow. Glove on the door handle, she glanced at Charlie. "I don't intend to stand around reminiscing."

"Well, I'm sure glad to hear that." He peeled her right hand from the door and held both as he kissed her on the mouth, tickling her with his mustache and his warm, minty breath.

She jerked her head away, shook her hands loose.

"How—how degrading," she whispered.

Mirth eclipsed any other expression in his eyes.

"This is Talkeetna. This is my hometown, and—"

"And you wanted to come home and make nice with people who don't deserve it, and that worthless pilot Charlie Marcus is kissing you at the airport. Something like that?"

"You *are* worthless, and I didn't come home to make nice. My brother's body is over there—" She couldn't speak.

The humor fled his eyes.

"And, yes, my father might be inside that office. You may have forgotten why he and I haven't spoken in thirty-two years, but I haven't."

"As you're well aware, there's more than one reason."

"Just shut up, Charlie. Just shut up. Not one word."

She reached for the door again, and his chin lifted, cocky as ever. "You know, your loyalty is what convinces me you still love me, Cesca. Despite your decision to kick me out of our house, after taking up with—"

"Don't say it."

"Well, you did take up with another man, and while I don't go around saying it to other people and certainly have never said it to our daughter, I feel perfectly free to say so to you."

Francesca wanted to strike him. It wasn't the way he painted it. It never had been. "You left me. Repeatedly."

"A very good sign I was going to come back. You have a history of turning away from people who don't suit you. But why repound old poi, as they say on the big island?"

"No one ever says that but you, Charlie."

Oddly tense, Charlie nodded to the east and slightly north, indicating the direction of town. "Shall I bring the transportation around?"

All Francesca could see of Talkeetna was the Spur Road and massive trees flocked in white beyond it. *I should get out of here.* Rather than meet her father—or Roy Jr.—in front of whatever bystanders might be lounging about. "I need my bags."

"Of course. And the dog, don't forget." Charlie gestured to the path that led around the flight station. "He's over here."

KING STRETCHED to the end of his chain, trying to greet them. Francesca had forgotten what an Alaskan sight that was. Dogs chained to stakes. Did her father still have the cabin beside the village airstrip, or had he moved?

The glass door of Roy Walcott Air Service pushed outward, and Francesca started, almost slipping on the ice. But the man who emerged was a good twenty-five years younger than her and slender, with overlong black hair. Jackson Browne cute. Something in his face gave her a painful twinge as he said, "Hi," before ducking into the terminal.

Her breath caught, and her mind played irrelevant thoughts. Not a pilot. She could spot a pilot from five hundred yards. Anyhow, tourist season had ended with

September, any Denali climbs were long over, and the miners had already come in from the mountains.

"Your nephew, Tony." Charlie snapped a leash on King and coaxed him toward the snowmobile he'd pulled up, with a sled behind it. "No hands." Charlie meant for flying. "Climbs mountains and can't hold a job. When Tara and Ivy came up here back in 'ninety-four, Tony led them on half the walk-up climbs in the park before the old man and Puppet Boy caught on. Then it was 'sixty-seven all over again."

Francesca listened. Tara had never mentioned the Walcotts, which was enough for her mother. If Tara couldn't warm her grandfather's heart, then his heart was broken beyond repair.

Charlie finished hitching King to the front of the snowmobile and climbed on. "Get on the sled, Francesca."

A snowmobile and sled.

There were vehicles at the airport. Cars had passed on the Spur Road. She imagined how she would look riding into Talkeetna on a sled pulled by Charlie Marcus's snow machine.

Like fresh meat, brought home by a hunter.

What was pride worth? She climbed on the sled and didn't look at Roy Walcott Air Service as Charlie drove past. She held her head high, stretching her spine, and let the cold sting her until they were almost at the railroad crossing, and then she whipped her head around once more.

To see the cemetery.

"THE HOTEL IS ON the Spur Road," she yelled, above the wind and the snowmobile. "Where are you going?"

"Thought I'd take you by the airstrip!" As Charlie

pointed, King, in sled-dog heaven, pulled hard, trying to speed them along.

He meant the Village Airstrip, not the FAA airport where they'd landed; the latter was the launching point for Denali expeditions. But private pilots still used the old Village Airstrip. It had been the only strip in town when she'd left, and the Quonset huts and frame hangars remained, sandwiched between trailers and cabins with satellite dishes outside. A neighbor's house had become the Talkeetna Village Airstrip Gift Shop, now closed.

The cabin was there, though. Her childhood home, where her mother had died. No smoke came from the chimney.

He must be at the airport. He must have seen me.

The lumps in her stomach multiplied when she saw Marcus Aviation's old frame hangar.

Charlie hung a left on Main Street, beside the Fairview Inn—bless you for looking the same! So much had changed. She saw gift shops, now closed for the season, a basketry studio, the laundry and showers, the Garden Deli and Espresso Express hung with a banner reading, IT'S A GIRL!

Espresso in Talkeetna? And open for business.

But the trees, oh, heaven of beautiful woods with winter's skeletons of undergrowth still from every corner. Log cabins and frame houses she remembered. Empty flower boxes lined windows; hooks on porch roofs dangled pots in summer. There was a new prosperity that still allowed for a lean winter.

They swung down B Street. Well off Main sat a plywood shack nestled in the woods, with space cleared for a massive dog yard. Dogs howling and barking. So many dogs.

Charlie guided the snow machine up a path beside a

log house, trees and the Talkeetna River behind it. Tall roof peak, logs neatly stacked on the porch, heavy door with an ice ax for a handle. A rustic garage. Whistling, Charlie shut off the snowmobile.

This wasn't her hotel.

That place with the dogs—next door, through the alders and black spruce.

There was boyish pride in the way he hefted her duffel bag from the sled. Francesca grabbed for it.

He turned, brows tilted up, eyes wide, talking in silence.

"It's beautiful, Charlie. I'd like a tour. But I'm not staying." There. That was gracious. And assertive.

"Why, Francesca, no one's asked you to stay."

If she could just get out of this sled, she was going to kill him.

"Let me help you. Ah, you're the same feather-light maiden I stole from here three decades ago."

Shoving him in the waist-deep snow would be unladylike.

"Welcome to my home, Goddess of Earthly Delights. Unlike many of my esteemed neighbors—" his voice lowered oddly "—I decided to build to code. Figured I'd pay the tax and have the chance to resell and move to Hawaii when I'm old and gray."

"You are old and—"

"Though our twilight years are upon us, it's cruel of you to—" His eyes caught a movement on the far side of B Street. Swiftly he clasped her elbow to steer her toward the cabin. As she peered over her shoulder, he said, "Don't do that, Francesca. It's awkward for you and feeds his ego, which doesn't need it. You'll meet in due time."

She broke free. Across the street, a Brad Pitt type secured the door of his cabin and tossed long golden hair from beautiful, young, sun-kissed skin. *That's when you know you're getting old,* she reflected. *You see a thirty-year-old hunk and wish you had skin like his.*

As their neighbor flashed a mouthful of gorgeous teeth and went to tend to—yes, dogs—in his yard, Charlie sighed. "Cesca, Cesca, didn't I warn you? The odds are good, but the goods are—"

"He's a child!"

Charlie threw back his head, and his laugh was warm, soothing memories of Talkeetna. It was glacier picnics and summer camping and the taste of blueberries in Denali. He'd fed her fresh berries.

She rooted herself outside his door, near the firewood. "No."

"No, what?"

No Denali summers ever again. No.

"I need to go to my hotel, and the dog needs to be taken to his home." She gazed across B Street. "I don't suppose Brad Pitt would like to feed Mia's dogs."

"Alan and I have already discussed the subject, and he told me you spoke with him on the phone."

"So that's Alan."

"Francesca, your behavior is very dangerous. Don't wave back."

Francesca waved. "Hi, Alan!" Alan had phoned her after Charlie had called about Mia. He'd said he could feed the dogs for a short time but hoped to be reimbursed, preferably in advance. As he headed across the snowy road, she scrutinized his plywood shack and doghouses, then his long legs.

Charlie muttered something profane. "Whatever you do, don't offer to sponsor him. In any way."

Alan's skin was even more enviable up close. Up

close, you could see that he'd missed a few shaves, though, and smell that he hadn't bathed—well, in a while. "Eh, brah," he greeted Charlie and turned to her. "You must be Francesca." He held up a can of beans with a spoon stuck in it. "I was about to have lunch with my dogs. Want to join us?"

"Thank you, Alan. That's very kind. But Charlie was just going to take me—"

"Inside, to settle in."

Francesca opened her mouth to set things straight.

"Cool," Alan replied. "Then I'll see you soon, yeah?" He spoke directly to Francesca, blue eyes on hers. "Mia talked about you," he added, in an eerie past-tense way, made more true by the genuine grief in his eyes.

"Yes." Her stomach hollowed. Not from premonition that Mia was dead, she told herself. Mia wasn't dead.

Charlie's breath wisped warm on her neck.

"Ciao." Alan flashed her a peace sign and loped through the overgrown yard and across the road.

Charlie said, "Ciao," and slid one arm behind Francesca's back and the other beneath her knees. Groaning dramatically, he carried her into his cabin.

He set her on her feet inside the single room and shut the door. "You're blushing."

"It's called a hot flash."

"Does that mean you want to be kissed again?"

"I'd kiss all the dogs on this street if they would come up with some tofu or yams for lunch. Natural estrogen." She had been blushing, but she wasn't going to tell Charlie. She'd forgotten about Alaskan men.

Charlie ducked outside to lift packages off the sled. Returning, he said, "In anticipation of the exotic tastes of the Goddess of Earthly Delights, I have procured from

Anchorage a dozen packages of tofu. And if you run out, there's more at the trading post or the supermarket in Wasilla.''

She almost touched his arm. "Oh, Charlie."

His sober eyes delved into hers. "Let me bring in your bags."

For a moment Francesca tasted wild berries. Smelled deisel fuel and heard the intense roar of a Cessna engine flying low, low enough to lift her hair and make her crouch against the moist mosquito-buzzing earth. No. *No.*

Slowly, she shook her head.

His thumb grazed her lower lip. "Scaredy-cat." Turning away, he carried his packages to the small kitchen.

She remembered why she was in Talkeetna—and, disconcertingly, Alan's bleak gaze. *He's just worried about her,* she reasoned again.

Arms crossed over her chest, she watched Charlie light the woodstove. "Charlie, we have to talk."

"Winter's long. Can it wait till after lunch?"

"No. I have to say this. I came here to find out what happened to Mia. She's never had any family, and I feel that in naming me as the person to be called in case of emergency, she was asking for my help, asking that I see her as family."

He focused on the plank floor.

"I'm going to insist on meeting with the state troopers. I need to know exactly what they've done, what kind of search they're planning...."

He shut the door of the stove and sat on a cushioned log chair beside it. His eyes met hers over his steepled hands.

"What?"

"A state trooper's staying at the Fairview. They found her, Cesca."

Roy Walcott

Well, she has come, and she came with him, and Roy Jr. says it's all because of the dead girl, the midwife who delivered my first great-grandchild.

Nothing has changed. Maybe those two think we notice about as much as a bear in winter, or maybe they want to pain me, carrying on outside these windows. Or perhaps she's saying she doesn't care how any of us feel.

Well, I care, Missy, and I will never stop caring, onto my deathbed. You laid with him and married him and had his child, and it never looked pretty from the start. And that swindler you couldn't part with killed my boy, killed your brother, same as if he'd shot him. Play that on your phonograph and dance.

All right. Roy Jr. said I'm looking bad, not to get wrought up, and I'm sure he's right. Deep breath. When I go home, I'll chop some wood. I'm eighty years old, and my life won't be shortened a day by that sly cheat, though he's stolen two of my children, and one's as dead as the other.

There is no just reward on this earth for a man with no conscience.

Now, young Tony thought we should step outside and greet the two of them. ''If you don't forgive people,'' he said, ''it ruins you inside.''

I just looked at him, and then I told him he hadn't lived very long.

And he hasn't done much, for all he thinks he has, guiding senseless folks from everywhere but Mars up and down the West Buttress. But I'm not saying that to my grandson.

All the time Roy Jr. is sitting there, shuffling papers.

My grandson then said to me that at least he lives, as though the rest of us don't, and he walked out the door.

Sometimes there's nothing to do but turn the other way and pour another cup of coffee.

If she'd come alone, it might have been different.

Many times, I wish it was. I have always wished for that.

CAPTION ON A PHOTO at the Fairview Inn: *Roy Walcott founded his Talkeetna-based air service in 1949 and was among the first pilots in Alaska to attempt glacier landings. Roy and his son Roy Jr. built their new office at the FAA airport in the early seventies. While Roy Jr. now handles most of the flights, Roy Sr. still keeps his hand in the family business. His wisdom is valued by pilots and aviation buffs throughout Alaska.*

CHAPTER THREE

Talkeetna
July 22, 1964

It's my birthday, and I've already had the best present, last month. Mom's cancer is gone. Dad flew her to Seattle again, and the doctors can't find anything, and they're pretty sure she's cured. I wake up in the mornings and think it's a dream. She's been working in the garden with me. Mel and I did it all by ourselves last year.

Today, she and I weeded, and now Mom's resting, which is fine, because Charlie just landed from Anchorage and asked, "Want some ice cream, birthday girl?"

I can't believe he cares it's my birthday. Although I slipped the date into our conversation a week ago, we haven't talked since. It's hot out, and he scoops a big cone for me and one for him, too. I'm eating ice cream beside his plane and listening to the sky for Dad's when Charlie says, "Sweet sixteen and never been kissed."

Talk to me, baby! I've been waiting a year for this.

"Not like your friend Stormy," he adds.

It's not supposed to go this way. "Don't talk about Stormy."

Last week, Dad told my mom that Stormy's one loose caboose and I should find another friend. It's unfair. No one really knows what things are like for Stormy, though our family ought to. Just imagine having Pamela Sue for a sister. I've seen Pammie Sue bite Stormy. Before P.S. married Roy Jr., that is, bless his good taste. We call her the Bride of Dracula.

Charlie looks sorry and smacks the first mosquito I've seen him hit. He licks his ice cream cone and points out that mine's dripping on my shoes.

He treats me almost like Mel does. In the middle of a conversation about, say, civil rights, he suddenly starts acting as though I'm twelve. Or else he makes fun of me, saying I'm going to marry a boy from Indiana and become a happy homemaker.

Well, it's time to dispense with those ideas. I lick my ice cream cone. "Charlie, do you like me?"

The bottom of his cone breaks off, and then he eats the whole thing and wipes his mouth with his handkerchief. "Francesca, someday I plan to marry you, if only because your dad will never get over it."

My heart pounds, and when he climbs in his plane, I lean into the cabin, hoping he'll offer to take me with him, which he never has. He's hauling out a box, flipping through records. He never comes back to Talkeetna without new music, but this time I don't care what he's brought. Was he kidding?

He jumps down and hands me *Meet the Beatles!* "Happy birthday."

Okay. Now I care. Before I can thank him for making me the first owner of that album in Talkeetna, Alaska, he starts singing "I Want to Hold

Your Hand,'' and his eyes look different than they ever have.

We hear a plane, and Charlie nods at the album. ''Start thinking up a good story for your dad. It'll keep your mind off kissing.''

Charlie's house, Talkeetna
October 1999

''MIA?'' Francesca asked stupidly.

The rocking chair beside his stove grazed her leg as Charlie nudged it toward her. She sat, her boots near his. Neither had taken them off, though his running shoes lay on a rug near the door. ''What— Why—''

''I heard at the airport. I didn't want you to find out there.''

In full view of her father, her brother, her nephew. ''Tell me everything.''

''I don't know everything. I'm not sure the troopers do. Some teenagers were out snowmobiling and found her snow machine. Looked like she hit a tree. They didn't notice anything funny, but apparently the cops did. Anyhow, their detective has taken up residence at the Fairview, has a hobby of photographing snowmobile tracks and is eager to ask you some questions.''

''Me? I was in Colorado!''

He rose. ''Let's credit the Alaska State Troopers with understanding that much. I'll make us some lunch.''

Francesca sat numb on the edge of the rocker and noticed, in a daze, that Charlie was bringing in her bags.

The loft loomed overhead, unseen. ''I'll sleep on the couch, Charlie.''

He didn't answer.

ALASKA STATE TROOPER Peter Sheppard was lanky and attractive. Taller than Charlie, with shorter hair and clean-shaven. The gait of a runner, a life-long athlete. No wedding ring. She liked the decisive way he'd said, *You'll excuse us,* to Charlie.

The trooper settled her in an office above the historic tavern. Even here, photos of bush pilots, row upon row, lined the dark walls. Francesca had snuck up to this room with Mel and Stormy the summer she was seventeen. Mel, home from the U, had paid them a six-pack to steal Art Turner's slick flight-seeing ad—the first in town— from downstairs. He'd drawn a dress on Art, and a friend from school had reproduced the altered image. Two weeks later, the new ads papered Talkeetna.

Mel.

God.

Francesca pulled herself back. She was present once again, and suddenly numb. "May I see Mia?"

Trooper Sheppard's eyebrows shot up. "Her body's in Anchorage. But yes. And while I'm thinking of it—" he selected a card from a stack beside him and handed it to her "—keep it. These gentlemen are trying to get in touch with you."

Executors.

He moved on. "Where are you staying, Ms. Walcott?"

He asked casually, but Francesca had lived too long to believe any question from a cop was casual. "With my ex-husband."

"Who is?"

Good grief. Blushing—again. Oh, for a dignified hot flash. "Charlie Marcus. We were married a long time ago."

He nodded, glanced at his left hand. "I know how that feels. So—ten years, maybe?"

"It's been almost twenty." *And you don't know how it feels.* "Please tell me about Mia."

"You knew Mia when you lived Outside."

"Yes. Please tell me what happened to her."

"Can I get you a cup of coffee?"

She shook her head.

"I'm getting one myself. Can't live without the stuff."

He was gone a few minutes, and the photos on the wall beckoned. Standing, she traced out a grainy image of her father as she remembered him. Strange to know that he and Roy Jr. and Pammie Sue were in Talkeetna, and so was she, and she hadn't seen their faces yet.

The face I'd really like to see is Stormy's. But Stormy was still on Oahu, as far as Francesca knew. She'd been so brave, sticking it out in Hawaii after— Ghastly. What a sickening nightmare that had been. And so unnecessary...for the mother and for the children. Francesca could still see Stormy on the porch in a tropical downpour, playing "Who'll Stop the Rain?" on her guitar, over and over again.

I need to write her.

The door handle clicked, and she jumped.

The trooper. "I brought you some herbal tea. I don't know if it's—"

"Thank you."

Their hands brushed. Was she hyperaware of all men up here?

With his bare left hand, he gestured to the photo. "Your father?"

"Yes." Francesca found her chair again, a scarred walnut captain's chair that had somehow made its way to Talkeetna.

The trooper sat across from her and steepled his hands, the same gesture she'd seen Charlie use just an hour before, so that this time it seemed like an imitation. Peter Sheppard spoke abruptly. "We're having trouble finding Ms. Kammerlander's next of kin. Can you help us there?"

"She has no family." The room was drafty. Francesca sipped her tea. "Her parents are dead. No siblings. She was from Phoenix."

Peter ran a hand over his cropped hair. "Well, that's a start."

"You have no birth certificate?"

"Actually—no."

Impatient, Francesca repeated, "Please tell me what happened to Mia."

"A week ago Monday, Mia Kammerlander left seven dogs beside her plane and apparently set off in pursuit of an eighth, who'd run away. Tracks near the airstrip were obscured by bad weather, but the person who first discovered her dogs and plane saw a footprint in the vicinity. The print was obliterated before he had a chance to photograph it for us. Last night, two teenagers on snowmobiles discovered her machine in the woods east of the Spur Road. Her body was covered with snow, and it appeared that she'd hit a tree. However, when we investigated the scene, we found what seemed to be another set of snowmobile tracks made at the same time as hers. And indications that someone was with her when she died."

"But how could you tell?"

"That's what the CSU is for."

He knew more than he was saying, knew something he wouldn't say. It didn't matter what.

Mia mattered. Mia had hit a tree on her snowmobile. And she'd been with someone, someone who hadn't reported the accident.

"Do you think she was murdered?"

"I wouldn't jump to that conclusion. But you may be able to help us. Could you retrace for me your relationship with Mia? From the day you met."

Now? Is this what happens when someone— She had to talk about Mia to a stranger. Francesca winced.

"I'm sorry for your loss," he said, and she knew that in some way he was.

Eleven years earlier, she told Peter, she'd met Mia Kammerlander at a midwifery conference in Albuquerque. Mia had inquired about becoming her apprentice in Colorado, where Francesca practiced. "It was odd. Our conference badges said where we were from, and I'd sat on a panel about breech presentations, but..." How could she put this? "There are midwives whose names are known all over the country—all over the world. I'm not one of those. So I was surprised."

Trooper Sheppard's upper teeth rested on his slightly tensed bottom lip. Playing the angles, thinking. Francesca knew few things as attractive as intelligence behind a man's eyes.

More about Mia, more to tell. "But we spent time together at the conference and really hit it off. She came to Precipice to work with me, and after a few months I invited her to move in and share the rent, which she did. We lived together, oh, eighteen months. When her apprenticeship was done, she went to Anchorage to conclude her training. She got into sled dogs and flying and moved up here for good."

"Did she know your ex-husband Outside?"

"He already lived up here." Francesca searched her memory, then shook her head. "She didn't meet him through me. Why is this relevant? Charlie is a lot of things, but he's not a murderer. If he was out snowmobiling with someone and she ran into a tree, he'd certainly—'' She stopped. ''Did she die when she hit the tree?''

''The autopsy should tell us that. Tell me. Why do you think she picked Talkeetna? Had you spoken of it?''

''Never fondly.'' She bit her lips shut. He didn't need to know that.

He raised his eyebrows and watched her, waiting.

Francesca said, ''Is that all?''

Another long silence. He nodded and stood to get the door. Before the sun went down, he'd probably know everything there was to know about her relationship with Talkeetna.

And her family.

SHE MUST PLAN SOME KIND OF memorial service for Mia. Would the executors have instructions? When she came downstairs thinking about these things, Charlie held a can of something carbonated—and non-alcoholic. She noticed. He probably knew she noticed, but neither of them mentioned it. Supposedly, Charlie had been dry for seventeen years, ever since that summer— She didn't need to keep lists about some things. When a man failed so miserably as a father, once was enough.

She walked ahead of him past the U-shaped bar and out into the cold. She'd chosen to walk to the Fairview, and he'd come with her, hands in the pockets of his parka, flight jacket abandoned. They'd stopped briefly at Mia's to put King on a chain near an empty doghouse.

The day had gone gray. She saw her own breath and his. ''I'd like some time alone, Charlie.''

Hands in his pockets, he stepped back.

''I'm just going—'' she faltered ''—to take a walk.''

His eyes were flat and unemotional. He knew where she was going, and because she hadn't asked him along he was angry or hurt, which in a man looked just the same. An instant of seeing, and he'd known her plans. Charlie's brain wasn't wheels turning, working a problem, going somewhere. He'd already arrived.

And his barely stiff silence was vulnerable. "See you at home," he said at last.

She started east alone.

A snowmobile whined up the Village Airstrip to her right. The elderly man driving waved to someone outside a house bordering the strip. Francesca's mouth parted, and he stared through her before turning left on Main Street. He'd bought a new parka with a wolverine collar, but he wore the same or an identical faded denim cap with Roy Walcott Air Service on the front.

The sound of the engine passed and grew distant, and she did not look back, at her father, who'd wrinkled and grayed in the blink of an eye, or at Charlie.

MARY FRANCES WALCOTT
MAY 10, 1920-AUGUST 25, 1967
BELOVED WIFE AND MOTHER

WITH HER GLOVE, Francesca swept snow from the top of the headstone. Falling to her knees, she touched the snowy ground, trying to find the earth beneath, and could not. Mama.

Soul empty.

Memory was colored and clear, far away and close.

Hands on her thighs, she breathed deep.

The other marker was beside her mother's, and Francesca had only glanced at it so far, choosing instead to stare at the Mount McKinley Climber's Memorial and the bulletin board listing the names of the fallen mountaineers.

She remained by her mother's grave so long the snow penetrated her polypropylene tights, and still she was warm. Thoughts came and left with her breaths. They were the memories of Roy Jr. buzzing that patch of taiga in Denali and of her father's face with brand new lines around his mouth and eyes and bitterness and hatred on his tongue, and they were the feel of her mother's thin, cool hand and her soft voice saying, *Francesca,* with the love that is expressly a mother's. It was her brother Mel's mountaineering pack on her shoulders and her thumb out—hitching from the edge of the Spur Road.

Mel had been heading out of state to medical school in a week, but he'd said, *Don't do it, Franny. We're your family.* She'd never answered, and five minutes later he'd tossed his pack in her doorway.

Her eyes lifted, drifting over snow, crawling up granite.

MEL WALCOTT
MAY 24, 1946-JANUARY 9, 1969
YOU MADE US LAUGH

Sweat pressed from her forehead, and she unzipped her parka and got to her feet. So different from what she'd expected. Her father had flown for the Navy during World War II and believed certain things about war and military service.

"Mel Walcott," she whispered. "He got this one right, didn't he, Mel?" Someone else had said the rest on a long black Wall.

She cried.

FOOTSTEPS CRUNCHED on the snow, and she looked behind her.

Black hair in his eyes, he made his way through the markers, then lifted his head and flipped back his bangs just before he reached her.

God, how you look like Mel.

Not the black hair—only Roy Jr. had gotten that—and Mel had been taller, like her dad. It was the gesture. Tossing back long bangs, revealing that young face with hope in the cheekbones and jaw, a mouth that would hardly know how to frown.

He wore top-of-the-line outdoor gear, weathered by Denali. Frostbite scars whitened his nose and cheeks. "Hi. I'm Tony."

She held out her hand.

He shook it. He had calluses.

Standing a few feet to one side, he read Mel's marker.

The smell of wood smoke came off him, and steam breathed from him in wisps.

In one Hawaiian bonfire, Charlie had burned stacks of letters with foreign postmarks, and Mel's single postcard had been mixed in with the bunch. Crying drunkenly when he apologized, Charlie had told her, *They're letters. They aren't people.*

Mel's had said, *Hi, Franny—Lift a beer for me, and kiss the baby. Mel.*

She sighed and zipped her parka in the gathering dimness, the end of daylight. "Well, Tony. Can I buy you a beer?"

SHE LOOKED UP CHARLIE'S NUMBER in the phone book and called him from the pay phone at the Fairview Inn. When he answered, she said, "Hi. It's me."

"Hi."

His tone reminded her how they'd parted.

"I'm at the Fairview with Tony. I'll be—back—" not *home* "—in a while."

"Don't rush. Unless you'd like to feed the dogs and save paying Alan to do it."

She'd planned to keep the conversation short. Behind her, four old men, one vaguely familiar, argued about who was Talkeetna's best pilot. In the Walcott household, there'd been only one answer to that, and in the Marcus home it was the same song, second verse. "How did you know I was paying him?"

"Alan doesn't do anything without getting paid, and if he could get paid for doing nothing he would. But if you want to pay him, he probably needs the cash, and you're afraid of dogs, anyhow."

She was not afraid of dogs, nor would she rise to this bait.

But she hadn't come to Alaska with a lot of money. She didn't have a lot of money.

"I'll feed the dogs when I return."

"They'll be salivating."

She hung up and joined Tony at the table he'd picked, next to the old codgers and beneath the oil of Denali. He'd already got them a couple schooners of beer, and he nodded at an adjacent wall of photographs. "Have to keep my distance from Deadman's Wall."

She squinted in the semidarkness.

Climbers.

"Just don't you end up there," she said, and something in his look was part Pammie Sue. *He's Pammie Sue's son.* Her distaste and anger weren't something she could help.

Behind her, one of the denizens said, "So Marcus, he firewalled the throttle, and by God, he was out of there. Now, that storm last summer when that fellow was down in the crevasse, he dead reckoned those spires, and one moment of doubt—''

The sweating at her hairline resumed. She grabbed her beer and drank deep.

Tony said, ''Are you all right?''

''That's confidence!'' the voice behind her chortled.

No, Francesca wanted to say. *It's stupid.* Supremely stupid to fly for one minute to the west and turn and fly north for another prearranged length of time and then west again, keeping to some course you'd worked out in your head to squeeze between ice spires you couldn't see. Should she ask Tony if he'd be willing to move to another table? No. She'd bet that every one of those men knew she was there and knew her name, though they'd pretend not to.

''I'm fine. Tell me about yourself, Tony.''

He leaned forward, shoving his bangs away with his hand. ''Oh, I really wanted to hear about *you.* Hang out. Extend the olive branch.''

He was so young and so like his cousin Tara that she kept from saying he wasn't the person who could extend it. He was none of those people.

A voice she tried to stifle said, *But I am.*

IT WAS ALMOST SEVEN when Charlie led her into Mia's yard amid the dogs' clamor. Francesca had filled him in on what Trooper Sheppard had said.

A metal cooler loomed on stilts over the doghouses, to keep out bears and other predators. Charlie said, ''Her meat's in there. She keeps harnesses, sleds and other dog stuff in the shed.'' He indicated the flashlight he'd lent Francesca. ''She'll have a headlamp with the mushing gear.''

The dogs leaped against their chains, gnashing their

teeth and growling low as she attempted to pass. Keeping her distance from the snapping jaws, Francesca climbed the ladder outside the meat shed. Opening the door, she discovered dried strips of meat and whole haunches. The place smelled of meat, and it was nothing new—not really—but she grew dizzy in the cold night. Overwhelmed.

She had to feed these dogs. She had to feed them herself.

They howled.

She called to Charlie. "Did you say she has a dog-food cooker?"

"Inside. Alan's been using it. Oh, wait—"

He strode away, toward the shack, while Francesca examined the meat. Oh, here were buckets of— This must be for the dogs. Whatever it was.

"Here, Charlie, take this bucket."

"No, put it back. We've got to find the dry food. The troopers have put a lock on her door, and Alan's not home. He's running dogs—he'll be gone all night."

Mia hadn't locked her door? Francesca descended the ladder. In the snowy yard, a big husky jumped on her, knocking her against a fence, his breath warming her skin.

Dry food. And water bowls. Mushers always baited the water with meat, so the dogs would drink it before it froze.

Ignoring Charlie, trying to ignore white snapping teeth and barking that shook her skin, she hurried to the other shed. The cabin with its plywood exterior was so dark, so abandoned. The shed smelled of cold staleness and particleboard. She found the dry dog food and a headlamp hanging on the wall. *I can't wear her headlamp.* Only when she emerged without it and the flashlight picked up Charlie petting King did she realize how shallowly she was breathing.

She let herself inhale, and the air was distinctly like Talkeetna, like the frozen river and the spruce and tamarack and dampness and wood smoke.

The dogs were still barking, but somewhere she heard a plane.

FOR A MAN ALWAYS IN MOTION, Charlie had an outsize love of record albums. He'd gotten weepy over parting with the Doors and Bob Dylan and his Beatles collection when they'd first left Alaska, and he'd accumulated more albums in Hawaii, before and after Vietnam. Charlie hated the metallic sound of CDs.

Seeing him picking over the jackets as they prepared to make dinner, it was all Francesca could do to hold her tongue. The last thing she needed right now was a trip down memory lane, courtesy of Elektra or Apple Records. When he chose Bonnie Raitt, she relaxed. Music that had nothing to do with the two of them together.

But "Nick of Time" spoke to her.

Charlie sang tunefully along with occasional phrases and turned suddenly with a spoon he'd dipped in a jar of something Alaskan and promising. She opened her mouth and received a dab of blueberry jelly.

"Good?" he asked.

"Delicious."

"Mia's." He set the lid loosely on the jar. "Dessert."

Mia had been his neighbor, and she'd given him blueberry jelly, and there needn't be any more to it than that. But Francesca had to wonder...and she didn't notice him putting on the *White Album,* didn't hear a song before "Martha My Dear." Abruptly, the past reached her.

In Hawaii, Stormy had cried when she heard that song,

and Francesca had known that someone, somewhere, had called Martha Ann Storm "Martha My Dear." Francesca pictured Tony's face as she'd seen it in the Fairview. "Charlie, are the Storms still in town?"

Did he start, or was that her imagination?

"Just some scud," he answered. Scud. Dark, low clouds—pilot talk. He meant Pammie Sue. "Though I bet she's real happy now, with her new grandchild."

Francesca sat straight up. "What new grandchild? Roy Jr. has a grandchild?"

Charlie did things with his mouth.

"What? Out with it, Charlie."

"I'm sure I told you. That Mia was at a birth that night."

"Charlie! You did not say it was my brother's grandchild."

"I don't recall your wanting family news."

"Well, I want it now. She died that night."

"Ah, how the family feud brightens your eyes."

Francesca saw Mel's grave. "Not hardly."

The baby was Roy Jr.'s youngest girl's. "She and her husband run the deli and espresso place."

Thinking like a midwife, Francesca exclaimed, "But it wasn't a home birth, was it? Up here? There's not a hospital closer than Anchorage, is there? Or Wasilla? Who did the postpartum visits?"

"Mia had a partner. They worked out of the doctor's office on the Spur Road. Yes, we have a clinic, now, Francesca. But I think it was a home birth."

That's a very liberal-minded doctor, Charlie.

So much to absorb, and Francesca didn't want any more. She wanted something simpler, and what she saw was Denali in summer, a Cessna on a dime-size sandbar, a tent near the berries....

Beside Charlie on the couch, she spread jelly on home-made rolls, her contribution to the meal. The Beatles sang, and the jelly tasted like summer.

"Let me have some more of that, woman."

She passed him a roll, and he saw her eyes.

Charlie said, "Here, let me get that," and pretended to wipe jelly off her mouth. There was a heartbeat of not thinking, and then they were kissing.

It was different from what had happened outside the flight station that morning.

This was his cabin, and kissing was deadly serious or deadly playful. There was no future in it and a whole lot of past. The good parts were warmer than the lagoon where Tara had been born, before Charlie left to fly helicopters over a foreign jungle. The good parts were sweet as Denali berries, sweet as this kiss could be if she let herself believe.

There were worse things than believing, and she'd done them to him, and he'd never done them to her, except perhaps in Vietnam, which wasn't the same. No, it wasn't the same as growing tired of waiting for a man to get rid of his problems.

She pressed her hand to his chest, meaning to move him away.

How could so many years have passed, and his chest feel the same? Same wool shirts he used to wear. She took back her lips.

His eyes had a greedy look she remembered.

I should give thanks to see that look in any man's eyes.

Let alone Charlie's.

"Charlie—" she began.

But he kissed her again, threading his pilot's finger through her hair. Why don't we do it in the road?

I Will.

She reminded herself of things that justified turning her back on true love, and nothing did just then. Nothing did.

She wasn't going to say so to Charlie.

But she could kiss him back.

And let him guide her toward the ladder to the loft and to his bed.

Alan Smith

"Haw!" I have a lead dog who corners before I open my mouth. Why talk? Mushing's like surfing, and your mind goes away.

Almost always.

Life is shit, Mia! I'm going to run all night and all day tomorrow and miss Trooper Sheppard's next visit, if that's okay with you.

No. Can't. Your dogs need me. They need you! Sorry, your friend Francesca is not a dog woman. I guess anybody can get religion, but you'd rather I fed your dogs, believe me. They're out of it, Mia. Sometimes I think Sasha's going to die. Just die of a broken heart. I've had her sleep over, and so has Charlie. So much for "No dogs in my house." He brings her treats. I kid you not.

What do I tell this cop? Can cops keep things to themselves? This guy wants to know everything, and today I just didn't feel like telling him, and now I'm on his shit list.

Mia, he acts like someone murdered you.

Oh, shit.

Oh, shit.

Oh, that hurt. Did I break something? Okay, I won't get up yet. Where are you guys? Great, try to whistle and spit tree bark and blood. Basil, come on back, buddy. Bring 'em back.

They'll come. If people were dogs, what a world this would be.

Uew. Breathe.

Never took a tree like that before.

Never took a—

"Mia! Mia!" You can scream and scream out here and no one knows. "Mia!"

Why should I stop?

"Mia!"

"Mia!"

"Mia!"

People think you chant mantras, but you can scream them, too.

For a long time, for maybe an hour, till you feel your dogs' breath.

"Basil. Hi, Basil. There you are. Oh, thank you, Snip. Mona, sweetheart. There's a kiss. I knew you'd come back." Warm dogs feel so good, licking your cuts, making it better. Making it better. God, someone cares. "I'm okay." I have to tell them, because I've always told them what's worrying me, and they know what happened to you has got me worried. Not just sad but worried about my life. I tell them, "Everything's okay. This was my tree. I hit my tree, but I made it. I'm just half-dead, and it won't get worse."

It won't get worse than this.

You weren't murdered, Mia.

And I don't have to tell anything.

CHAPTER FOUR

Denali
August 23, 1965

Mud sucks at my boots, and the mosquitoes are thick. Mom and Dad are in Seattle, or I wouldn't be here. Charlie's edgy. He hands me a basket and scouts the river, scanning the country as far as we can see.

I say, "No bears." Last year, Mom and Dad and Mel and I camped near here together. A sow was teaching her two cubs to fish, and Dad and Mel had their twenty-twos, but we all just watched the bears until they waddled away. Their hair was gold and wet from the river.

That seems like a long time ago. I don't want to think about it now. Charlie and I are just picnicking. Tired, I ask him, "Do you have a rifle?" But he's loading one.

I learn what a wintry smile is.

We leave the plane and hike toward the carpet of reds and greens and golds, into grass and leaf and brambles and berries. Bearberries, cranberries, blueberries—I start on the blueberries, picking and eating and blinking away mosquitoes. They're nasty.

Charlie crouches, and he picks faster than I do.

We're so close, and I'm surreptitious about eating berries. My dad always tells me to leave something for the bears.

Charlie notices, too, and laughs. "You eat more than you pick. I could feed you and pick for both of us."

I open my mouth, because I know he won't really do it.

But we see each other for a second, and he puts a blueberry in my mouth.

And then another. His skin is smooth and tan, and there's a scar on the back of his hand. His fingers touch my lips this time, and I watch his hand because I'm afraid to see his eyes again, and I pray that it won't stop. Please don't stop, Charlie.

He is touching my mouth. He is touching my mouth.

Don't stop. Don't stop.

Mosquitoes bite my face, and they don't matter.

But he brushes them off, and there's blood on his hand and his hand is on my jaw and my mouth.

I thought a kiss would be something else.

He's not a boy, he never has been, and I don't feel like a girl but a woman, suddenly comfortable in the person I became when I learned my mother has cancer. I move my lips against his.

When he pulls back and I feel his breath, so close, he says, "Let's pick these berries and get out of the bugs."

We are completely silent, and we both pick fast.

Third day back in Alaska

SHE WAS IN CHARLIE'S BED.

He'd shaved before dinner last night. Now only a slight

shadow darkened his cheeks, and the whites of his dark brown eyes were milky clear. "Well, good morning there."

Francesca covered her face with her hand, then her whole head with the sheet.

"No excuses. You couldn't resist me."

His arm found her bare body. Not yet light outside, but she was afraid. Afraid of the heat and the tenderness of the night.

She must have tensed.

Charlie's kiss was sound and brief. "Thank you, Goddess." Releasing her, he got up.

Shutting her eyes, Francesca replayed the events that had led to her being in his bed.

Mia's dead.

Charlie pulled on clothes, singing "Piece of My Heart."

I really did not need to do that. Sleep with Charlie. Make love with Charlie.

She'd known him—she counted—thirty-six years, and she wasn't going to make up names for what had happened. It was familiar. Intimacy had changed when he went to war. Everything had. When he returned, it was as though she'd lost his operating instructions, a one-thousand-page owner's manual, and the company had gone out of business. Sex set other things in motion, and alcohol blurred the past's gentleness with new complication and intensity, all volatile and private. Men could cry uncontrollably and rage seemed bottomless, until she was glad he could drink and, God help her, wished he would. Then he drank, and the bottom disappeared from her own rage. She wanted damages. She wanted to make it better.

Last night, he was sober. Warm whisperings. *Like this, Cesca? Tell me. You can always tell me.* New and old gentleness blurred with complication and intensity, all volatile and private. Neither of them could be closer to each other; there was nowhere closer.

Remembering in the morning, she lay with her face in his pillow, scarcely breathing. *I should not have done that. I should not have done that.*

It was going to be very hard to undo.

SHAVED AND SHOWERED, Charlie brewed a pot of coffee and watched the bacon and eggs on the grill. Francesca. Women were like the weather, and he didn't like the forecast this morning.

I forget how fickle you are.

He switched on the radio, for the forecast on his current wife. More snow. Thirty-knot winds.

The wind was already bending the double panes.

He traded the radio for the Who. *Yeah, Cesca, I can't explain.* "Breakfast!" he called up to the loft.

He sang through the first ring of the telephone as he checked which line was blinking. Home. "Charlie here."

"Hi." Joe Burke, his sole winter employee. Mechanic and master of detail. And whenever Charlie found him with his feet up, staring out at the darkness, he knew where Joe had gone, in his mind, because Charlie'd been there, too. Joe said, "I'm at home, but there's something going on up near Gold Creek. I was at the store when they got a halfway radio transmission. No clue yet, but I said we're fueled up and ready."

"Thanks." He'd take his coffee and the pickup to the airport. He'd shoveled the drive last night while Cesca caroused with her nephew. "Anything else?"

''An e-mail from New Zealand, saying the expedition may be off.''

Charlie laughed.

Next month, three men and a woman would arrive from various places Outside for a first winter ascent of the West Rib of Denali, the kind of thing the park service hated but never stopped making exceptions for. The climbing party had first contacted Charlie a year ago, and cards and letters were still coming, from Kathmandu, Tyrol, Auckland and Seattle. Seattle had booked the reservation, but Nepal had written once, Austria had phoned, and New Zealand, who was female, had sent thirty-two e-mails. Not a cohesive group.

Joe was on e-mail and had begun to report irrelevancies. *She eats red meat, and she hates male Kiwis. She likes Americans.*

Charlie said, ''We'll be here all winter.''

''That's what I told her.''

Francesca came down the ladder in last night's clothes as he replaced the receiver. She looked shy, and he thought of things the two of them might never discuss.

No. Everything would come out. She'd brought up the Storms already.

My Generation and yours, Cesca. He sang to her, seeing the change of weather in her eyes, on her body, the whole time.

Chewing her bottom lip, she fingered a business card. ''I forgot. I'm supposed to call these guys.''

He read over her shoulder. Mia's lawyers. He whistled, whistled over the words that clanged in his mind. Mia Kammerlander was dead. *Kid. Kid. What happened?* ''The phone's over there.''

It rang before she could pick it up, and Charlie took the call.

"Hi," said Joe. "Enjoy your breakfast, and don't rush out. It's a baby, and you know who's got the midwife in their pockets. Sick about Mia, by the way."

"Yeah." That and a few other things. Mia's midwifery partner, Honeydew, had bid on Charlie at the 1996 Talkeetna Bachelor Ball and Auction. December was cold, and he could've got warm, but Honeydew preferred Shawn Colvin to Janis Joplin—*come on*—and one evening she'd said that women always remember their first time but men never do, taken one look at his face and walked out of his house, slamming the door. She consistently flew with Another Outfit.

Two hundred dollars going into Someone Else's pocket today.

Gritting his teeth, he gestured that Francesca could use the phone.

She tucked the attorney's card in her wallet. "It's too early. They won't be there." Her eyes sought the kitchen counter and found breakfast. "Oh, Charlie, that looks good. Thank you." Biting her lip again. "Look, I'll get out of your hair today."

Midwives.

SHE WASHED all the breakfast dishes. Charlie was doing something with a calculator and paperwork, and she said, "I'd better see about feeding those dogs. Do you think Alan's home?"

Charlie scraped back his chair in a gesture of exaggerated tolerance.

"You don't have to do anything, Charlie."

"Oh, I'll tag along."

Snowflakes flew horizontally down B Street. Alan released a dog whose paws he'd been examining and left the yard to greet Charlie and Francesca.

"Pretty," said Charlie. "What happened to you?"

A thousand-yard stare answered him. Snow gathered on Alan's eyebrows and the fur of his parka. The turquoise eyes in the cut and bruised face sought Francesca. "I hit a tree."

She felt Charlie move beside her. Turning his back to the wind.

Alan gazed past them. "I wish Mia had been with her dogs. Running them." When she hit a tree.

"One of them was running her," said Charlie.

"Yeah. Taxes. He always runs away. It's a game, yeah?"

Francesca blinked away snow—and something unexpected, out of place. Then, gone.

Alan shifted his weight, and he was magnificent, battered or not. Untouched by the cold. "I think I should feed her dogs. But, well—" Flushed, he stole a glance at Francesca. "I guess we should settle up."

"Settle what?" Charlie eased Francesca toward the edge of the road and nodded at a passing pickup, wipers swishing. "They aren't her dogs."

Alan looked thoughtfully blank. He faced Francesca and seemed pale and vulnerable and oddly alone. "Forget it."

There was a ten in her coat pocket, but as she fished for it, Charlie's hand caught hers and held it. "Cold, honey? Let's get out of this."

Chewing his bottom lip, Alan eyed her pocket.

"Write me up a bill," Francesca suggested.

As Charlie dropped her hand and swung away, Alan gave her a thumbs-up. "I'll run 'em, too, yeah?"

"WHY DO YOU HATE HIM SO MUCH?" Francesca shook snow off her parka and left it beside the door with Charlie's. "He's just a boy."

"He's the most insidious moocher I've ever met. I warned you, and admit it, Cesca—I'm nothing if not an excellent judge of character."

"Your father taught you well."

She immediately wished she hadn't said it.

But his expression was bland. "Almost as well as yours taught you."

Touché. Still, his cut was light. Her father had never used children to help defraud people the way Charlie's had. The way Charlie's had used him.

And Tara.

I have to call Tara. I must tell her about Mia. As she lifted the receiver and dialed her old number in Colorado, Francesca reminded herself to call Ivy and tell her, too.

But when she heard Tara's voice and little Laura mewing in the background, the thought fled. Francesca delivered the news about Mia as succinctly as possible. Tara said she was sorry, and Francesca asked her for news.

"Oh, Mom, I've got students, apprentices, coming out of the woodwork. Everything's coming together. It seems chaotic, but I know things are going to work out. Today I'm helping Isaac's kids make Halloween costumes."

An invisible burden seemed to shift from Francesca's shoulders to those of the tall, dark-haired physician who had been her landlord. If Tara was involved with his children, maybe he was serious about her after all. Maybe they could get married and adopt that baby. Isaac. *Solve this, Isaac. Make it right.*

Because Francesca could not.

"Where are you staying, Mom? Let me write down the number."

"Oh." Francesca froze. "I'm…not sure. You can always call your dad. I'd better go, sweetheart."

It was their shortest phone call on record, even shorter than when Tara was keeping things from her.

Charlie handed Francesca a copy of *Aviation History*. "Fan yourself, Cesca. You're looking warm."

He couldn't know what Tara had just asked her or that she'd been too embarrassed to tell her daughter she'd spent the night at his house.

In any event, Charlie's expression turned from speculative to grim. "So. Has Isaac started treating her like shit yet? I ought to go down there."

"No. Everything's fine, Charlie. She's looking after his children. He's not what you think. Stay out of it."

"I don't see why I should. Does the guy walk on water or something? If so, I'd like to go down there, shake his hand…and ask him a few questions."

Francesca let him finish. "Charlie, that trooper asked me about you and Mia yesterday. If he thinks you had something to do with—whatever happened, he'll see you leave, and the next thing you'll have led the police right to Tara and that baby."

He lifted his cup of coffee, grown cold. "The baby."

"Yes."

Charlie rubbed his forehead. "Why can't she adopt the baby? Someone left it in her car."

"Oh, wake up. The baby would be turned over to social services. And Tara's a single mother—woman. Charlie, she is nursing that child. Inducing lactation. In her head, this is *her* baby."

"I can see her point."

Charlie and Tara were picked from the same patch. The dissident radical midwife and Charlie, her father.

Francesca drew a long breath and released it. She had to trust Tara, trust her daughter, trust life.

Because of Mia.

"Is this affecting you, Charlie? That your next-door neighbor who gave you homemade blueberry jelly died in a senseless and suspicious way?"

He lounged against the refrigerator with dramatic ease. "Of course not. People believe red blood runs in my veins, but actually it's a blend of caffeine, diesel and rock and roll. O positive, the universal donor, and I would open a vein for you any day, Francesca."

"Were you lovers?"

"Oh, please. She's Tara's age." He looked like she'd suggested incest. But why wouldn't he meet her eyes?

And why—

Why wasn't he teasing? Why wasn't he twisting her words and making her feel like an idiot?

Her face wasn't hot and dry. Her chin was not uncertain. None of these things were happening, because if he and Mia had—well, it simply didn't matter. "You did, didn't you?"

"No. I didn't." His expression changed then, and he said, "Why, Francesca. You don't like the idea of my having slept with another woman."

That line would've worked with someone who knew him less.

Francesca saw a man in a too-tight suit. She saw another Charlie, whose weakness had chiseled off decency and left an unformed being, squirming to evade the eye of principle. But it was his father who'd become that unformed being. Not Charlie.

He was good. As though still trying to convince her family, she told herself so again. *He has always been good.*

And he'd gone to war and was changed forever.

She knew his stories but not all his stories, and from them she'd learned things she could never put into words. Men were human and fallible, and people might die because of mistakes that looked stupid and were and came from letting down one's guard or just trying to survive or from a second's pleasure or forgetting where you were or bad luck or exhaustion or indifference in circumstances laced with pervasive evil and betrayal and contempt and love, love between men; it was all so complicated that she could never find the right words, and Charlie was always frustrated because neither could he. She would tell him, *It's understandable,* and he would say, *You don't get it.*

She hadn't been there, and because of that she would never really get it. But she'd loved him desperately in those moments when she wasn't getting it, and she'd worried it and rearranged it in her mind, wondering if betrayal touched him less than others because he'd always expected so little from people. He saw through flaws and called them by name and knew that perception could lie. So all his rage at betrayal and deceit and illusion and chance and evil and hypocrisy concentrated instead on stupidity. Usually his own. His self-loathing and self-love were loathing and love for the human condition.

She told it to herself again and again, her story for who he was, and she failed. No words for it.

Dear Francesca, In future communications please avoid the use of my Christian name....

So her letters had begun "Man of My Heart," and when he came home for good, she'd carefully called him "Sweetheart" and "Babe" and even "Hey, Marcus," for three months, until in one night of trying to turn sex back into love his name slipped from her lips and he'd said, "Say it again. It feels good."

Charlie was not weak, and he was kind, and that was why he was bothering to tease her now.

He had slept with Mia.

I don't need a farce. "Charlie, we've been divorced almost two decades. I know you haven't been celibate. And now I guess I know your taste extends to very young women."

She swallowed, and he saw. Their eyes met, and his steady look was frankness and caress. His lips twitched.

Meditatively, he rubbed his jaw. "Well, they do like me, those college girls in their Birkenstocks and Earth First! T-shirts. Come June, you wouldn't believe the traffic through here—Mother Nature's nymphets flinging their backpacks on my doorstep and rinsing sprouts in my sink. Oh, now she laughs. A slow recovery from the thought of a beautiful young woman in my bed."

"Charlie, I don't care if—"

"Oh, skip that. Your jealousy is legend. And conspicuous. Now, tell me—barring your supreme lack of judgment at the time you rid yourself of me—have you invited any lucky men to your bed?"

"That's a very tacky question. I had a daughter to raise."

"That didn't stop you the first time. Come on, Cesca. It's not tacky; it's intimate. Tell me you couldn't let other men pollute your body. Tell me how much you love me."

The phone rang.

Twice.

He touched her cheek. "Hold that thought."

She put her hands to her head and noticed the sweat

in her hair. She yanked the refrigerator door open and went for the Tupperware container of tofu.

"Give us ten," said Charlie into the receiver and hung up the phone.

Francesca's mouth was full of raw tofu, and she covered it quickly and swallowed, then grabbed a paper towel to wipe her lips.

Charlie took the towel from her and dabbed at her more, needlessly, she was certain. "Get your birth bag. We're going flying."

Her birth bag? Her mind switched to midwife mode—and laws and ethics. As Tara liked to say, these were burning times. She folded her arms over her chest and waited, while fear of persecution faded and memories took over. Her father's radio crackling in the darkest and coldest of winter nights, the sound of his boots on the plank floor of the cabin, the door opening with a banshee wail of wind and shutting behind him. A baby on the way, a dog-bit child, a miner cut in a knife fight...

The wind cried.

Charlie traced the inside of his cheek with his tongue, then shifted his head. "Fine. She can have her baby in my plane. It's a breech, but I'll take Joe along to assist. I've seen him replace landing gear in six feet of powder at forty below and mend a cracked cylinder on a glacier, all with one arm. I'm sure he can catch a baby, too."

Francesca's jaw tensed. "Charlie, I don't even know the midwifery laws here. Where's Mia's partner?"

"In Fairbanks. And Dr. Bob's in Wasilla. You're it. It's a Good Samaritan thing. Now get your fetoscope and be one."

Only a second passed before she walked beyond him to her pack and began collecting her belongings. "When we return," she said, "you can drop me at the Fairview. I'm sure they'll have a room."

THERE WAS NO GETTING the last word with Charlie. He sang along with "You've Got to Hide Your Love Away" and "Ticket to Ride" in the pickup on the way to the airport, gazing into her eyes at every stop sign, reminding her of the last time she'd left him. Which wasn't the first.

He left her in the flight station while he spoke with his mechanic, a small, bearded, dark-haired, wiry man with a good right arm and a mechanical left. A bell rang in Francesca's mind. Could that be Joe Burke?

Possibly.

Behind the ticket counter, a young woman with a long blond braid that reminded Francesca of Ivy spoke on the radio to an incoming plane. Francesca was breaking her rule about a second cup of coffee when the side door opened and another woman entered.

A neat black bow gathered smooth hair colored golden to the roots. The fur ruff of her parka rubbed against heavy gold hoop earrings and mature skin blushed with pink, her clothes an ensemble of dark teal, her black boots cuffed with fur. She carried a metal thermos and utilitarian lunch box.

Catching her eye, Francesca smiled. "Hi."

The woman's smile was quick and small, and her blue eyes blinked and refocused.

Why is she looking at me that way?

Time and memory tricked and turned.

Heat coursed up Francesca's spine, up the back of her neck and down her arms and legs. Motionless, she watched Pamela Sue Storm Walcott straighten her back and shift the lunch box. Penciled eyebrows drew upward.

"Francesca."

"Hello, Pammie Sue." *Smile, Francesca. It won't kill you.* Her legs carried her two steps forward. "Congratulations on your new grandchild. And your own children. Tony seems very nice. I hope everyone's well."

"Yes. Yes." Her eyes flickered past Francesca to the pilot's lounge, separated from the rest of the station by a glass partition. "Well," murmured Pammie Sue, "enjoy your visit. Things have changed. We have several good restaurants, now. Debbie and Alex have the deli."

Francesca knew the names of Roy Jr. and Pammie Sue's children, had heard them over the years from Stormy, had even sent a gift from Hawaii when Debbie was born. The little crocheted hat had been returned unopened, and Francesca wondered if Pammie Sue was flushing because she remembered.

Another brittle smile signaled her sister-in-law's departure. "There's Roy Jr. He'll want his lunch."

Francesca wanted to catch her arm. Even a cool conversation with Pammie Sue was light through the iron curtain of her family's silence. Without any intention of taking down the wall, Francesca reached toward that light. Another pace closer to the woman moving past her. "Do you hear from Stormy?"

Pammie Sue's right boot skidded in a wet spot on the linoleum. Catching her balance, she flushed. "Of course."

She skirted the slippery area and walked on.

Francesca couldn't help but look past her, to the pilot's lounge. A tall gray man with her father's nose and chin and her mother's eyes gazed through the glass. She had known he would age like that. Proud and able to hate without end. When he turned his back, it scorched.

"THANK YOU, HONEY." Roy Jr. accepted his lunch, the same sort of lunch his wife had been making him for almost four decades. A sandwich with some meat and lettuce in it, a piece of fruit and a thermos of fresh coffee with plenty of milk. He'd left home without lunch today, hurrying to fly Honeydew out to the pregnant woman from Gold Creek. Canceled.

Next time Roy Jr. met him on the street, Marcus's ass was grass.

Pammie Sue kissed him. "I didn't expect you back yet, but Tony said the flight's off."

"Don't ask."

The door swung inward with a blast of bitter weather. Roy Jr. tensed. His father. First time he'd seen him today, which meant Dad had just heard about the Gold Creek flight.

"That sly-faced dandy would steal his own mother's hat pin." Roy Sr. glowered through the glass at the woman on the far side. "That's how he twisted their arms, him and Joe Burke. Burke tells the Macleans they've got a midwife, after all. Well, the chances of his setting down at Macleans' place in this wind are none to zero. I hope he tries, and God can have them both."

Pammie Sue sighed in the direction of her father-in-law. "You are really something. I have no affection for Marcus Aviation, but that's your daughter."

No reply, but there were things to be said. Roy Jr. would say them to Pammie Sue at home.

Another blast of wind.

Marcus came in.

Roy Jr. could still feel the man's neck in his hands, still feel the pulse of an artery. *I should have killed him when I had the chance.*

His father walked out, and Roy Jr. held the door for Pammie Sue while the wind blasted them. When his wife was outside, Roy Jr. told Marcus, "Next time I see you on the street, you're dead."

"Better wear a cup. You're walking better now, by the way."

Roy Jr. let the door swing closed and faced him. Marcus stood by the coffee. *I'd like to break that decanter on your head.* "How do you sleep nights, knowing you killed my brother, *Charlie?*"

The smart ass didn't have anything for that. Couldn't even keep the coffee off his mustache. Roy Jr. couldn't stand the sight of Charlie Marcus's weak rabbit face, and he left.

CHAPTER FIVE

Talkeetna
May 9, 1966

Six mountaineers have been sleeping in Dad's hangar all week. Now he's gone, flying the first two up to Kahiltna Glacier. Jean-Pierre is showing me a picture of a mountain in Chamonix when the radio crackles. "...November 2014 Foxtrot coming to Talkeetna Village Airstrip on final descent."

My legs are noodles, and I can't say anything intelligent to the French climber. His voice goes on as the plane gets closer, and then it's passing my window, a song of red and white. I've just about stopped breathing. "I've got to do something." I leave Dad's passengers.

Outside, it's steamy and thick for May, the ferns and high-bush cranberries beside the side door and the shed grabbing at my bell-bottoms and peasant blouse. There's a path behind the office next door, with no windows for Roy Jr. to see me; it goes past the Marcus Aviation office, which has been closed since last August.

When his feet touch the ground, I creep up behind him, but he glances over his shoulder. "Francesca." He starts to turn back to the plane, but he sees something and reaches up to touch my soft, straight hair, which Stormy ironed for me last night, then pulls his hand back, staring at my mouth.

My voice comes out too high. "Where have you been?"

"Ketchikan. Flying helicopters." He's all over my eyes. Checking for makeup? Not me. "And where have you been? You don't look like Talkeetna."

I don't want to talk about being in California with my parents while my mom saw new doctors and Mel visited Stanford University because he wants to be a doctor now. Like we have the money. But he's fishing on the coast to earn some. My parents only brought me along because Mom was so sick and because we could stay with Grandma and Grandpa. I don't want to talk about it, yet I do, because California changed me and I'll never change back.

"How's your mom?"

Charlie is straight and matter-of-fact. I tell him, and it could be worse. She helped me hoe yesterday.

Then, because he likes music, I say, "Mel and I saw Joan Baez." But she wasn't just singing. *Isn't the war awful, Charlie?* Mel's friend Dale enlisted, and Mel thinks he's crazy. I'm glad Mel's never going. Roy Jr. could still be drafted, though. Charlie is still looking at my eyes, like he's trying to read me. I tell him, "And we heard some Beats." At night, my brother and I would walk to the coffeehouse at Tressider Union and drink coffee and think about how my mother looked in pain, and someone would stand up and start reading or talking about the war or singing a Bob Dylan song.

His tongue is in his cheek. "I guess we'll have some conversations, won't we?"

I'm happy, really happy, for the first time since he left.

He climbs back up into the plane, and it's full, but I get in, too, in case Pammie Sue or someone comes by. From the seat, I watch him open a crate. When he comes back, he crouches beside me and says, "Well, here's something they didn't have in Palo Alto, California." He hands me a forty-five with a label I've never seen.

"I Can't Explain." The Who.

"Who are they?"

"British. Guy from England gave it to me."

I start to hand it back to him, but he says, "No. It's yours."

I feel pretty and older than when he left. I meet his eyes, and he must know what I'm thinking. "I'm not a child, Charlie."

He doesn't say anything for a minute. "Hasn't anyone ever told you that you can't go back to holding hands?"

I've been different since that day in Denali, since one kiss and a quick and quiet flight home.

"Because you can't." His jeans scrape mine, and he says, "Don't get me in trouble my first day home, Francesca."

Our fingers are touching, and I lean toward him first.

This time, he uses his tongue.

Near Gold Creek

"...CESCA, SEE IF YOU CAN HUSTLE them along, get 'em out to the plane. If she can't go, I've got to take off....

Come back when you radio.''

Snow pecked the windshield. Francesca's hands and feet had gone numb in the drafty cabin. It hadn't occurred to her until now that Charlie might leave her at Hawk and Susie Maclean's place, twenty miles from the village of Gold Creek.

It should have. This was Alaska, where bush pilots dropped you off and promised to return and remembered or forgot, and if they forgot, you were on your own. And where a pilot never shut off his engine if there was a chance he couldn't start it again. A familiar resignation, one step past terror, gripped her.

Today, not even the landscape invited. It was invisible, and wind buffeted the Cessna. Suddenly, shadows materialized and became the dark tips of trees, trying to tear off the wheel skis, and the Cessna dropped down into solid white. The plane skidded on snow, Charlie's hands steady, his eyes alert. They stopped moving, and a shape emerged from the blowing snow.

"Here's Hawk," said Charlie. "He's Susie's husband. Their place is a half mile up through the trees. Need help with those snowshoes?"

"No." Nor with the pack, though Hawk took it from Charlie's hands.

The bearded stranger blew clouds of steam that angled away horizontally as he exchanged a few words with Charlie. Adjusting her snowshoes, Francesca tried to hear over the airplane and the howling wind. Finally, Charlie caught her arm. "Hawk says she's been in labor since yesterday afternoon. She's close and doesn't want to risk giving birth in the air."

"Has her water broken?" Francesca had to yell.

Hawk shook his head.

Her lips tightened. No way of knowing if Susie was close or not, except that Charlie had told her they had other children. What if she didn't make it to Anchorage? A cabin without running water would make a better birthing room than a Cessna in flight—especially on a day like this. Still, Francesca had attended only two breech births outside a hospital or birth clinic—more than twenty years ago.

I didn't sign up for this.

But she was a midwife, and a woman in labor needed her.

Ice stung her face.

Charlie said, "Kiss me, and I'll come back for you."

How could he seem so vulnerable there in the blowing snow beside the rumbling Cessna? He wasn't, she told herself, but there was no not kissing him when he was going to take off in this, when his hand held the front of her parka. And his lips were so warm and...temporary, something she might lose forever in a moment. She had always felt this with Charlie and felt it now and gripped his parka, too.

Shivering, she left him. Don't die. Don't die.

But she mustn't start—mustn't begin feeling that way or pretending that any words could keep him safe.

Minutes later, breaking trail up to the house, Hawk told Francesca, "Thank you for coming. I'm sorry about what happened to Mia. I guess you knew her."

"Yes." The snowshoes gathered powder and grew heavy. Her face felt brittle, her mouth difficult to move. Alaska came back to her in another way, the cold woods and the sound of a plane taking off and knowing Charlie was in the air. Now wasn't the time to wonder who had been out with Mia the night she died or when she would face her own father and speak to him or if she would ever see Charlie Marcus alive again. She had come to attend a birth. "Tell me about Susie. Did Mia help with her other births?"

"No." Hawk shook his head. "She just came up this way to see about her mine."

Francesca's thoughts were on the breech, walking through possible scenarios, preparing for possible cord prolapse, hoping someone had boiled plenty of water so she could scrub and examine Susie without delay. But his comment distracted her. "A mine?"

In Gold Creek, Mia's ex-husband had worked it with her, before and during their marriage. They'd made some money, Hawk thought.

The feel of birth, the scent of birth, already filled the air in the cabin, mingling with the aroma of fresh-baked bread. There were magazines on a table as she walked in, *Mother Earth News, Organic Gardening, The Utne Reader,* beginning to tell about the family, as did the homemade wooden train on the floor, the half-eaten toast, the breakfast remains on the cheerful table.

Hawk and Susie and their three children lived in a rustic one-room house no larger than Charlie's place. They kept sled dogs and shot their own meat and grew their own vegetables and taught their own children. After just a few minutes in their home, with a three-year-old snuggling against her while she listened to fetal heart tones through a contraction, Francesca felt the family and their welfare resting with her. And Francesca had nowhere else to be. She could stay forty-eight hours postpartum and keep in touch by radio after that.

They're not my clients.

Reality silenced the voice. All winter, this family would be on her mind, though they wouldn't expect her to spare them a second thought. They knew that contract with the land that was uniquely Alaskan and built on self-reliance.

The older girls, ages seven and eleven, made up a bed for her in one corner with the sleeping bag Francesca had brought, and Francesca made sure Susie ate some bread and drank plenty of water to keep her strength up. Francesca dictated the notes to Callie, the eleven-year-old. "Station, plus three. Just use a plus sign. Dilation five centimeters. Put *cm* for centimeters." The birth might happen in an hour—or several. Francesca had learned not to guess.

Hawk had braided Susie's pale hair. Her flushed skin glowed, sweating in labor, her eyes luminous. As she groaned with contractions, Hawk stimulated an accupressure point behind her heel, and Francesca prepared a chair with a pillow on which she could rest her head and shoulders, to try a new position.

Callie quieted her younger sisters. "Mommy's okay. She's just having a baby."

In Precipice, Francesca had questioned Tara's choice to attend home births without physician backup. But with or without the support of the medical community, Tara was seldom more than a few minutes from a hospital. In wonder, Francesca watched snow white out the trees. *And here I am in a cabin in the Talkeetnas, attending a breech birth.*

Yet she seemed so far from civilization, Alaska so wild and accepting of people doing whatever they chose....

A notion came to her and startled her, a thought that seemed to accompany the lines on her face and her changing body.

I feel free.

She blinked at the glass, and the toddler climbed into her lap.

IT WAS DARK WHEN CHARLIE made it home. He'd run some errands in Anchorage and considered going to Mia's house there and booting up that computer. He wouldn't have done it while she was alive, and he decided, finally, that he wouldn't do it now that she was dead.

He let it rest. There was nothing he wanted to know except who had been with her when she died. To that end, he'd headed home and spent some time at the airport, sweet-talking Becka and trying to figure out who'd been in town the night Mia died.

Hopeless. Whoever it was could have driven into town—and driven out.

While Becka checked the computers, Roy Walcott had wandered in and poured a cup of coffee, and he and Charlie had ignored each other as they had for more than thirty years. When the old man left, Becka had said, "I've seen some things around this place that make no sense, but you flyboys about take the cake."

Charlie had said, "Check outgoing flights. See if anyone took off the next morning."

He'd learned nothing.

In darkness and still-falling snow, he'd driven home past the log cabins and clapboard businesses. Basketball practice began in an hour, but Alan was feeding Mia's dogs and Charlie walked over. He arrived as the musher was trying to get his head and shoulders out of Sasha's doghouse. Charlie knew Mia's lead dog was lonely; nonetheless, he longed to sweep the snow off the doghouse roof onto Alan.

He petted the puppy, King, while his neighbor extricated himself.

"Oh. Charlie."

"Alan."

Sasha slathered kisses on Alan's face, jumped on his thighs.

"Hey, Charlie, what's going to happen to these dogs? In the long run?"

Good question. A musher had died and left behind forty-three distance dogs, including twenty or so veterans of the Iditarod and the Yukon Quest. Francesca had never called the executors. "You got me. Are you charging her by the meal or the minute?"

"We'll work it out, brah." Alan stooped to examine one of Mia's dogs' feet. "So, she's old man Walcott's daughter?" The question was casual.

What's it to you, Alan?

Charlie rarely acknowledged the existence of people named Walcott to anyone but Francesca, who regrettably had reverted to her maiden name upon divorcing him. But this was a new tack for Alan. "You know the family?"

"Tony." Alan didn't seem to want to look at him, just at the dogs.

Charlie heard footsteps on the snow-packed street.

Tony Walcott was walking down B Street, and as Charlie watched, the climber crossed into the deep snow in Mia's yard. "Hey, man," he said to one or both of them, and he and Alan exchanged tepid high fives. Tony lowered his hand. "Hey, bummer about Mia. You guys were pals."

Alan didn't answer, as good a testament to grief as Charlie knew. Alan and Mia had been pals, running their dogs together every chance they got.

Tony glanced through the spruce and poplars toward Charlie's house. The windows were dark. Charlie waited.

His nephew—was an ex-nephew possible?—asked, "Francesca around?"

She was popular with the thirty-and-under crowd in Talkeetna—so popular that Tony was speaking to the enemy. "She's at a birth." Charlie had raised the Macleans on the radio; a baby girl had been born, but Francesca was staying a few days.

At the mention of a birth, Alan walked away to collect an empty dog bowl. *Mia.* Sorry, buddy.

Tony threw his black hair out of his eyes and peered at Charlie, and it was as if Mel Walcott was looking at him, but Mel would be spoiling for a fight, just like Roy Jr. Charlie remembered how badly he wanted to beat the shit out of Tony's father. But he said, "Can I help you?"

"Probably not. You're as bad as my dad and my grandfather. You don't want to get along with people."

Charlie had never been as young as Tony Walcott, even before he'd first shot a child from a gunship.

"I don't even want to talk to you," concluded Tony.

"That's all right. Your family's congeniality is well known."

"Hey, man." Tony pointed at himself. "I've made peace with my aunt. And now I'm kicked out of the house. Don't talk to me about congeniality."

It was easy for Charlie to keep a straight face. As basketball slipped to second priority, he pursed his lips at the trees, pretending to consider Tony's situation. Too good. Too good. Francesca and privacy concerns were gone in the blink of an eye. "Well, I hope you weren't planning to beg Francesca for a night in my house."

"Hey, I want to go home sometime."

Charlie knew he should take that into account. But Pammie Sue had a soft heart for her kids. She'd take him back. He kicked the snow. "Yeah."

Joining them, Alan's gaze stole toward the shack.

"Hey, you think anyone would mind if I used some of Mia's firewood?"

"Yes." Shaking his head, Charlie spun away. He started across the yard, then stopped. Faced them again.

His nephew's hair blended with the night. Alan, crouching near him to pet a dog, suddenly rose to go fill another dish.

Charlie strode back to Tony. Met young eyes. It was going to hurt to say even this much. "You're right. You're a kid, and you're right. I should be able to get along with your family and they with me."

Beside a doghouse, Alan straightened, like he was hearing a foreign language. *Don't blow this for me, Alan.*

"I appreciate your—making peace with Francesca." *Make my peace with her when you get a chance.* "I know she appreciates it. And if you're looking for a place to stay, I've got a couch. But, like you said—you want to go home sometime. Take care." Charlie nodded once, waved to Alan and headed for his house.

He made it as far as the break in the trees.

"Hey, Charlie."

This was a gift from heaven.

He stopped. Turned.

Tony asked, "Are you serious? About a place to stay?"

FRANCESCA RETURNED to Talkeetna Tuesday morning in Charlie's Cessna. As her feet found a grip on the snowy tarmac, she made out the figure of Alaska State Trooper Peter Sheppard at the window of the flight station. He lifted a hand in a wave. Waiting for her.

Charlie noticed, too, and she felt him watching as she pulled open the door and went inside.

"Ms. Walcott."

"Francesca." She ignored the tall spare figure behind the glass of the pilot's lounge. He certainly didn't seem to notice her. *I'm going to talk to him whether he likes it or not. But not now.*

"And I'm Peter. Can I buy you lunch?"

She hesitated at the thought of Charlie's fist connecting with the trooper's face. But surely her ex-husband wouldn't be so impetuous. He had collected her without extending a single touch, not a glance of intimacy, though he'd walked up to the cabin to admire the baby. On the way home, he'd been quiet except to tell her that Mia's attorneys had returned her call. "Thank you," she finally said. "Let me tell Charlie. My pack's on the plane."

"If you need a hand…"

Francesca smiled again. "Thank you." Otherwise, she'd be carrying it herself.

SHE MET CHARLIE beside the Cessna, on the far side from the flight station windows. He was squinting at a pocket notebook and writing something. Seeing her, he tucked the notebook away. "Miss me?"

"Charlie, has it never occurred to you to say that you missed *me?*"

He gave her one long-lashed blink. "But I did miss you, Francesca. That's a foregone conclusion. Nonetheless, I'll prove it to you at—" he checked his watch "—thirteen hundred hours." Their new housemate had gone to Fairbanks to ice climb, possibly succumbing to family pressure. No point in mentioning Tony yet. "I'll drive your pack over to the house if you say, 'Please, Charlie. Please.' And close your eyes when you say it."

Please, Charlie. Please. That was one youthful moment she'd never live down. Charlie's ego would never forget. "I'm having lunch with Trooper Sheppard."

"Oh, so now I'm paying the State of Alaska to steal my wife?"

"I am not your wife." *And the whole Alaska state government is not on your payroll.* Especially since Charlie had freely admitted many times past that he had no qualms about stealing from any type of government, ever since the federal government had stolen his innocence.

As Francesca gritted her teeth, his eyes brimmed over with affection. "Cesca, you may have as many husbands as you like, but I have just one wife, and she's you."

She tore at her hair. "I can't stay with you anymore. I'll move today."

"At least take a shower first. Though Trooper Sheppard may like your delicate Essence of the Interior—no, don't look alarmed, Cesca. The male fragrance, Essence of Denali, is far more overpowering, particularly in the cabin of a Cessna on a warm June day. But you should heed your mother's advice before you set out alone in Talkeetna. Have a shower and wear clean underwear, in case of an accident."

"Shall I take my pack now?" The cold hampered her language skills.

"Cesca, when did I start making you carry your own bags?"

She tried to forget that he'd said he didn't care whether or not she left. *You went to bed with him. It doesn't mean he's in love with you. You're fifty-two, Francesca, not fifteen.*

"Thank you. And thank you for flying me out there and back."

"Hey, Hawk will get my bill. I hope they get one from you, too."

Francesca realized again that she didn't even know

Alaska's midwifery laws. In Colorado, she'd had a business, set up in private practice, but here—

To hide her ignorance from Charlie, she murmured, "That one was on me." At least he'd taken her lunch date in stride. She wanted to remain on good terms with him, if only so she could fly to Anchorage free of charge to see Mia's body. What were the hours at the morgue? She needed to ask Peter.

She was partway to the flight station when Charlie called, "Cesca."

He had stepped around the nose of the aircraft, and Francesca suddenly noticed other people outside the building. Becka and Art Turner and two mechanics debating the merits of Surge and Mountain Dew.

Charlie didn't bother to lower his voice. "Before you commit to anything, make sure you see him in his uniform and hat." He smiled and waved cleverly toward the window at the Alaska State Trooper.

He absolutely would not get the last word, and she didn't heed the flight station door opening for her as she called, "I love men in uniform!"

BY THE TIME SHE'D EATEN HALF of a Mount McKinley sandwich at the Mountain Grill, Francesca had nearly forgotten Charlie's obnoxiousness. Only Essence of the Interior and not bathing for two days reminded her that she wasn't at her best.

No matter. Mia's death was foremost now. Francesca wanted to know what Peter had learned in her absence, but first she told him about the gold mine. Having grown up in Talkeetna, she remembered miners being killed at their claims. Mia's mining operation seemed relevant. "I don't know if Charlie knew about the mine. He hasn't mentioned it to me."

"Charlie," repeated Peter. "He's a character, isn't he?"

Francesca tried to forget the incident of the trooper uniform. "Mm."

"Daring men," he added, his remark taking in all the Talkeetna air-taxi pilots. He hadn't told her the reason for their lunch, and he squinted at her curiously. Their corner of the diner was otherwise empty, but his voice seemed loud. "I couldn't help hearing about your falling-out with your father."

Francesca didn't discuss their falling-out with family members, let alone men she'd just met.

"I'm sorry to bring up an uncomfortable topic. But I like to take the measure of a place. It's all…related."

"Have you seen the autopsy report?" she asked.

"Yes. The injuries are consistent with her hitting a tree."

"Tell me more. When did she die? How long after hitting the tree?"

"Not long. But perhaps ten minutes. Given the circumstances—Talkeetna, winter—it would've been difficult to save her."

"I'm a nurse. Please tell me everything."

"I forgot that." He appraised her anew. "I'll do you one better. Come on up to the Fairview after lunch, and I'll let you read the report."

She hesitated. She needed to clear out of Charlie's, the sooner the better.

"Plans?" the trooper asked.

"Nothing important. Tell me. Why did you want to have lunch?"

He flushed, which she found attractive. "I've been slow getting to the point," he admitted. "I want your afternoon, if you can spare it. I'd like you to come with me to see Mia's plane and her house and just give me your impressions of what is and isn't there. And I want your impressions of some people in town.''

''I hardly know anyone.''

''Alan Smith.''

''Oh, Alan.'' She shrugged. ''I really don't know him. But I believe he misses Mia.'' She told him about the call from Alan concerning Mia's dogs.

''Honeydew Lane.''

Francesca frowned. That was a name? ''I don't know—her. Who is she?''

Peter's looked thoughtful. They'd both finished eating, and he paid the bill and collected the check, seeming quiet and intelligent and sure of himself and very interesting. ''You're free?''

She was free.

As he held the door of the diner for her and she stepped out, her parka touched that of an incoming patron. She smelled diesel and coffee and saw the dented tip of his chin, then the deep creases around his mouth and eyes and—finally, the bill of his cap.

Her father stepped back.

''Hi, Dad.''

He grunted, and Francesca paused beside him and the open door. ''What did you say?'' she asked.

His glance fell indifferently upon the state trooper. ''I didn't say anything.''

His voice hadn't changed at all.

Out on the snowy road, Peter cleared his throat. ''Let's go to the Fairview first.''

MIA HAD DIED OF MASSIVE brain hemorrhage. Even if the person on the second snowmobile had tried to save her and succeeded, Mia would have spent the rest of her days on life support. When Francesca finished reading the report, Peter said, "I have some other news for you, too. We've found Mia's parents. They've been out of the country, but a neighbor said that one of their daughters took off about ten years ago and didn't come back. We've contacted them, and they're headed home now."

Francesca touched her heart. *Mia. You didn't do that to your parents.* That Mia had lied to her was secondary. *Oh, you poor people.*

"Let's go look at that plane," said Peter.

Mia had kept her Beechcraft in a hangar by the village airstrip. Outside the hangar sat a snowmobile with a pair of pliers serving as one handgrip. "I thought her snowmobile..." Francesca let the sentence trail off.

"Different snowmobile. This one was Old Faithful."

Francesca didn't bother to ask if he'd photographed the tracks left by this machine. She was sure he had.

Mia's hangar had been built since Francesca left Talkeetna, and Mia might have been the first owner of the gleaming Beechcraft. Francesca listened and watched as Peter outlined where the plane had sat the night Mia disappeared—and where the dogs were found staked. He showed her around the hangar, then inside the plane. The cabin contained emergency supplies and mushing equipment.

When she jumped to the dirt floor of the hangar, Peter asked, "Well?"

Francesca hesitated. It was such a small thing. *Sure, I would've taken mine. Tara would have taken hers. Ivy would've brought hers.*

But Mia'd had dogs to look after.

"What is it?" Sheppard had noticed her expression.

"Oh." What to say? "It's nothing. Midwives are all

different. But if I was flying to Nome, even with sled dogs, I would've brought my birth bag.''

''Describe that.''

''Well, I can show you mine at—when we go to Mia's. I have a black leather bag.'' She outlined the contents.

''There was something like that at her home. Would other midwives have taken a birth bag to Nome?''

''If I owned a plane, I would have a separate bag for my plane. I almost think...anyone would.'' She remembered her spontaneous decision to attend the birth of the Macleans' baby. ''But I suppose it comes down to whether you see midwifery as a job or a vocation.''

''How do you think Mia saw midwifery?''

Francesca met the trooper's blue-gray eyes. ''As a vocation. But I think I may not have known Mia very well.''

''No.'' His eyes lingered on hers a before he glanced away. He didn't lock the plane, just studied the wheels. ''How do you like it up here?''

Suddenly, things were personal. Yet careful. Not inappropriate.

''Well,'' she admitted, ''I left.''

''And returned.''

''Yes.''

He nodded slowly. She sensed that he was thinking about Mia.

But when he looked up again, their eyes caught, and she realized she was wrong. He did lock the plane, then. ''Back to work.''

An admission that the last couple of minutes hadn't been.

PETER SQUINTED through falling darkness at the figure crouched in the snow between two doghouses. The shape moved, ruffling the fur on a small husky mix, receiving a kiss on the face.

"Alan," murmured Francesca. She'd been outside most of the afternoon, but she wasn't cold. In fact, she was a little too warm. *Is this a hot flash?* Yes, of some kind. Menopause was a long process and so individual. But the moisture near her hairline must be thanks to a hot flash.

Or apprehension at Peter's and Charlie's next meeting.

"Yes. Alan," Peter answered. "He has a genuine affection for dogs." His tone was unforgiving.

Alan stood and shook snow off himself. When he saw the trooper, his blue eyes hardened. Catching up his pile hat, fashioned like a jester's cap, he left Mia's dogs. "Hello, Francesca. Sir," he added.

"Visiting your friend's dogs?" asked Peter.

"I feed them. Excuse me." Alan ducked his head and strode past them, golden-haired and spectacular even wearing Essence of Denali.

Ignoring the dogs barking, growling and howling, Peter led Francesca to the door of Mia's little shack, removed the lock and stepped inside. He sighed. "Forgot about this. We should have come here first." There was no electricity, he meant. He lit a small lamp, then several candles in holders as Francesca smelled ashes and plywood and the clean scent of herbs. A door served as a table, and one chair sat beside a woodstove made from an oil drum. Like Charlie, Mia had a loft.

Outside, the day dimmed. He'd taken her afternoon, as he planned. Refreshments at the Fairview led to an extended discussion of midwifery, all under the pretense of his learning more about the victim.

They both knew he'd actually learned about Francesca. Some things.

"So. I'd just like any impressions you have. Look around and remember that you're trying to find out what happened to your friend. Tell me anything that occurs to you, no matter how trivial it seems."

Francesca scanned the shelf of midwifery texts, journals on the desk, mushing newsletters. "I don't think—"

The stereo went on next door. Stevie Wonder. "You Are the Sunshine of My Life."

Peter consulted Francesca's eyes. "Do you suppose that's in violation of a noise ordinance?" He had to raise his voice to be heard.

Francesca edged to the south window. Over the doghouses, through the trees, she saw the light from Charlie's downstairs window.

"Trooper—" she hated to speak over such fine music "—do you know what women say about finding relationships in Alaska?"

"Yes." His eyes crinkled at the corners as he laughed. "Yes, I do."

OH, COME ON, CESCA. Come home.

Since when did police investigations happen by candlelight?

Charlie flipped through albums, composing a rock-and-roll love letter that Trooper Sheppard could read over her shoulder. Ah. "The Letter." Francesca loved how Alex Chilton sang that word of their lives—*aeroplane.* Dalton used to play that song every day at Chu Lai.

Enough of the Box Tops.

Here. The Turtles. "Happy Together." They had been once, and he couldn't think too hard about the words. Just find another song.

CHAPTER SIX

Talkeetna
August 8, 1966

The radio is playing "Turn! Turn! Turn!" and Stormy and I are flirting with the climbers from Dartmouth while we wait for Dad to get back from Mount Foraker to pick them up. They're going to Denali, and Roy Jr.'s up in the Super Cub, flying a miner to his claim. The other radio crackles, and I turn down the Byrds. "...two-oh-one-four Foxtrot. Lost contact after—" Crackle.

Stormy says, "I've been up there before. Just to the glacier."

"Shh."

"...southwest of Kahiltna Glacier..." Crackle.

"...is November one-nine-four-three Foxtrot on final descent to Talkeetna Village Airstrip."

Dad.

"November one-nine-four three Foxtrot, this is—"

I listen, and it's true. The Zombies are singing "She's Not There," and Stormy's still talking. I'm going to throw up.

My dad's plane comes in, and I go outside without speaking to anyone, to help him refuel. One of the climbers follows, but my father takes no time to talk before stretching out on the wing. I hand him the nozzle, and while he's filtering the gas through a piece of chamois he tells the climber, "Well, you fellas are going in the right direction. I've got to look for a missing aircraft."

Shit. Shit.

I can't go back inside and face conversation, so I walk between the hangar and the office and behind the buildings until the back of Charlie's hangar, the back door, is visible. So is our garden, but with all the poplars it's hard to see anything. I can feel Charlie's body against me, hear him singing "God Only Knows" in a perfect imitation of Carl Wilson, see him smiling into my eyes. Mosquitoes buzz around me, and I hang onto the outside of Dad's hangar. I'm going to throw up.

Dad is going to spend time loading the climbers' gear. *How can you stop and do that?*

I cling to the side of the building. Feet rustle the grass. Stormy must have come to find me. I look up, and I don't know if I'm crying or just sick. It's Dad. He sees my face, but I can tell he doesn't want to believe it. He says, "When Roy Jr. touches down, tell him we're looking for Marcus."

I want to thank him, but I just nod.

When he's gone, Stormy sits with me inside and says, "At least he loves you."

I know what she means, but I'm glad when she leaves. At home, I make dinner for Mom. Though she's feeling pretty well, we hardly talk.

Finally, she says, "You're quiet tonight."

"Oh." I smile and say something about the tomatoes. If only I could tell her, I'm in love with him, Mom, and I think he's dead. But I don't say that any more than I would tell her about Charlie's bed with the rough army blanket, in the room back of his office. Any more than I would reveal that I've been up in his plane six times this summer, that I've spent time with him in a tent in Denali, or the things he does to me, all the beautiful things. He's just twenty. He turned twenty in May.

Another plane overhead. I look out the window, and it's Art Turner. My mother and I wait while he taxis. We watch, and Art gets out to refuel. Two minutes later, I put the teakettle in the refrigerator.

Charlie's house

"FRANCESCA! YOU'VE BEEN GONE so long I forgot you were in town. What have you been doing with yourself since—" Charlie checked his watch "—eleven a.m.?"

She shut the door. Assorted plastic grocery-store bags, an unfamiliar sweater, a climbing magazine, a couple of spring-water bottles and a headlamp spilled off the couch and onto the floor. Charlie was compulsively neat. "What happened to the music, Charlie? That was quite a trip down memory lane." She shook her head. "The Strawberry Alarm Clock. Things a person forgets."

"What were you doing, reading the phone book to each other? Or do I need to check on Trooper Sheppard's professional ethics?"

Francesca made her smile gentle.

"Cesca, you're wearing the unsavory expression of a woman seeking greener pastures."

"Just a shower, Charlie."

"Want company?"

This was touchy. She didn't know what she wanted.

Before she'd gone to the Macleans' it was him. This morning it was him. And then—

It's so odd to have men interested in me. It was odd to see men her own age who weren't escorting thirty-year-old women. It was odd to have time for men of any age.

The silence lasted too long—two seconds—and he turned to the kitchen, restlessly searching the counter the way he used to before cracking open a beer or pouring a drink.

Francesca wanted to say, *I wish feelings weren't so complicated, Charlie. I wish your feelings weren't so complicated.* She wished her own weren't; after all this time, she was still afraid he'd raise an alcoholic beverage to his lips. Or maybe that was just her excuse, an external point of reference, simpler than looking inside Charlie for her resistance. Or inside herself. But even if she said something, he wouldn't give her a serious answer, wouldn't admit to having emotional needs or an ego that couldn't tolerate a woman spending two seconds deciding whether or not to share the shower with him.

I have to try. Sometime. The conversation could wait. Like her talk with her father? So far, that had gone no-where.

"Charlie, will you take me to Anchorage tomorrow? I want to see Mia's body." Oh, her parents. They would be up to see Mia's body, too—to claim it. She had to tell Charlie, but her suggestion about Anchorage had met with a faint flaring of his nostrils. He didn't feel as she did about viewing the remains of the deceased.

"I'll check my schedule."

She knew this Charlie, too. Distant. Her dentist said grinding her teeth would make her gums recede. Okay, so her molars wouldn't touch. Words leaped out. "Charlie, I'm not getting involved with you again if it's going to be like it was last time.''

"Cesca, you *are* involved, and it definitely won't be like last time.'' He opened a can of something carbonated, then set it on the counter, untouched. "This morning you missed me. Come on, I know you. What charm does Trooper Sheppard possess? Get me on the program. I'll take the formula.''

"It's n-nothing.'' She squeezed her eyes shut. Did she have to stammer? "There's nothing.''

Charlie rubbed his jaw. "It's his height, isn't it?''

"You know, it's taken me four whole days to remember what an incredibly insecure man you are.''

The phone rang.

Charlie checked the line and pushed a button. "Marcus Aviation, Charlie speaking. Hey, Joe. No... He did. The asshole. Well, write it down. We'll just tack it onto his other moving violations. I'll call in our report tomorrow.''

Francesca suppressed a sigh. Talkeetna's air-taxi operators spent an unwholesome amount of energy noting mistakes their competitors made, rules they allegedly broke. She studied the sweater on the couch until Charlie hung up.

He faced her. "You were saying?''

"That I need a shower, as you so gently suggested six hours ago.''

He didn't propose again that he accompany her, but when she emerged from the tiny bathroom, dressed in a pair of jeans that hung more loosely than they had in Colorado and a large woolen shirt and wearing fresh makeup, Neil Young was singing, and dinner was cooking.

He lightly caught the lapel of the shirt. "You do things to me, Cesca."

Blood churned through her. The worries of her life— even the puzzle of Mia's death, and everything about the time she'd just spent with Peter—diminished, faded beside— Really, how could she still find him fascinating? "Charlie, you make me feel about fifteen."

"The last fifteen-year-old girl who touched my emotions was Tara, and I can't say she charmed me at that age."

"We have emotions now?"

He perused her lips. "We've always had emotions. Some people say them just right. And some of us fly glaciers."

"You are the vainest man I've ever known."

"The most interesting, too." He was angling for her lips, and her heart raced, but he veered off, like a skillful pilot in One-Shot Pass.

She wanted the kiss and didn't want it; she'd returned to Talkeetna in spite of him. Now his mouth was touching hers. Neil Young sang that there comes a time. The words were folk poetry, and it was summer in Talkeetna again, and she turned her head slightly, escaping his lips yet preserving closeness. "Charlie."

His lips on her cheek. "What, Cesca?"

"I don't want to make any mistakes with you."

His backing off was infinitesimal but sharp as a downdraft. "That's easy. We chop wood and carry water, and you tell Trooper Sheppard, next time he calls, that you can't come out to play."

Sometimes you know you're going to say something regrettable before the words come out, and it was like that when she said, "I need to play."

He drew in his breath, then backed against the counter,

and he was the thing she wanted more than any freedom she could imagine. Even more than the freedom she'd just tasted, just now, today.

"I recall you play kind of rough, Cesca."

"It was the end of our marriage, Charlie."

"It was that."

Francesca stiffened. "I've never held up to you what you did in—" She stopped.

"Till now." He looked a little white. "So you need to play with Trooper Sheppard."

"Why do you have to bring him into it?"

"Convince me he isn't in it, Cesca. Let me guess. He's asked you to call him Jack or Steve, and he gives you sidelong glances and shares insignificant clues from his investigation, and before he flies off, with our young friend's death explained or not, he will kiss and caress you and ask to see you again, which he may or may not do." Before she could even feel deflated by this likely scenario, Charlie moved away with the advice, "Don't get involved with a cop, Francesca. If they're dirty cops, they're bad guys, and if they're good guys, they've got it tough. If you're even beginning to fall in love with a cop, you've read too many novels and too few statistics. Fall in love with a glacier pilot, Cesca. They're in it for the long haul. I'd recommend one to you if I knew any who fly as well as me."

"There's nothing you can tell me about Alaskan bush pilots that I don't already know. And there's plenty *you* don't know," she muttered almost under her breath.

"What's that?"

She fired a shot carelessly. "I mean that my father did more in his career than just fly people to and from a mountain that most of them wouldn't be climbing without the assistance of glacier pilots. He wasn't an air-taxi pilot. He was a bush pilot."

Charlie's brown eyes, clear eyes, had ceased all blinking. His complexion changed.

Why did I say that? Why did I say it? She flailed for words to make it right. "How can you risk your life for that, Charlie?"

It was too late. She'd hurt him. It was hell hurting Charlie. She'd rather be hurt herself.

He murmured, "We can't all be heroes, Cesca."

He'd never attach the word heroism to himself. She rubbed her brow. "Oh, Charlie."

"Hey. You're right. The earth won't change its orbit if I don't fly tomorrow. Or next May when the climbers come."

Yes, it will. Everything would be wrong if he didn't fly. But she kept the words to herself or she'd be saying out loud that returning to Talkeetna and this job had pulled him out of a death spiral.

She wasn't going to lose sleep over what she had told him. "I also meant that because of your appalling lack of imagination, you can't guess what it's like being married to a bush pilot. And I can."

"This is interesting, Cesca." He snapped a carrot stick with his teeth, chewed and swallowed. "Now, there's a book on a shelf over there that talks of a certain Talkeetna pilot setting out at forty-six below in a Fairchild 24 to collect a severely dog-bit child from Gold Creek. You were probably too young to remember that, but I'm sure you remember the team of scientists who got into trouble on—"

"I do remember, and I remember my mother sitting up *all night,* Charlie!"

"Cesca, if you're—let's keep it at 'involved with'—a

pilot, you just accept that someday he may not come home, or else you agree that he's the best pilot who ever landed on Kahiltna Glacier. Not to mention that your accursed sire has turned out to be the survivor of the pair.'' He twisted his mouth, finally sipped from the root beer he'd opened. "Pity about the Gold Creek mail. Those folks just refuse to acknowledge that the wind can blow an apple a million miles from the tree.''

He was talking about the mail run to Gold Creek, the sweetest year-round contract in Talkeetna. Her brother flew it now, and Charlie's insult to Roy Jr. was a backhanded compliment to her father. Francesca said, "I'm going to pay him a visit tonight. Dad.''

Charlie choked on the root beer, spit it into the sink.

"I saw him today at the Mountain Grill, and—''

"Cesca, when I take you out for a meal, it will be in style, to Anchorage, or a picnic on a breathtaking, eye-watering glacier or the remote reaches of our neighboring national park. At least to one of the better restaurants in town. It's nice, though, that he fed you something before running—''

"I'm trying to tell you something. I saw him at the grill, and I said, 'Hi, Dad.'''

Charlie watched her as though waiting for the end of a story he'd heard before.

"Then he made this sound, and I asked him what he said, and he said he didn't say anything.''

Charlie rested his elbows on the counter. "You know, here's another reason you're smart to stay at my place. You care about what happened to Mia, and so do I, and her house is right next door, and so are her dogs.'' He straightened suddenly. "That reminds me—''

Francesca gave an exasperated sigh and spun away, knocking down the bulletin board hanging on the edge of an overhead cabinet. It was no-nonsense, like Charlie's other interior decorations, and adorned by two photos. One was of his current plane. The other was Tara, beaming at the camera with her exuberant clear-skinned smile and a devilishness maybe deeper than her father's.

Seeing the photo, Francesca felt a longing for Colorado and her daughter's stubborn spirit and that little baby.... She closed her eyes. Charlie was saying something about Mia's executors.

"Guy left his home phone. Real eager to talk with you. My unfailing instinct says you've come into money. And, if you're lucky, someone else came into dogs."

SHE WAS MIA'S HEIR.

Mia's sole heir.

"Can you come to Anchorage?" asked Ivan Krakauer, Mia's attorney, when Francesca reached him at home. "She asked me to schedule the cremation, and it'll be done tomorrow."

"No, you mustn't do that!" Francesca explained about Mia's parents. Charlie had been dicing vegetables in the kitchen, but he stopped.

The attorney agreed, then said, "Besides some business here, there's a letter for you, from Mia."

"Could you please open the letter and read it to me?"

"Well, not as easily as that. I'd have to fax you a release, which you'd then sign before a witness, and fax back. Then you'd need to mail me the original."

Francesca glanced about the room. "Excuse me," she told Ivan. "Charlie, do you have a fax at the office? Will you take me down there? He has a letter from Mia."

"After dinner?"

She asked the attorney if he would mind exchanging the faxes in an hour, and he agreed, while she found a pen and piece of paper for Charlie to write down his fax number. He wrote out the number, and she dictated it to the attorney. After she faxed him the signed release, he would fax a copy of the letter.

When she hung up the phone, Charlie said, "A lot of money."

But he looked pale.

A FACSIMILE OF A LETTER was in her hands an hour and fifteen minutes later. Charlie was too polite to read over her shoulder, but he paced behind the counter of Marcus Aviation, making her nervous while she read it.

Dear Francesca—

Well, I never thought it would come to this, and you're probably wondering why. Why you. True confessions. Charlie's been like a dad to me up here. You were like a mom, giving me a chance, in Colorado.

I'm not much on family, but I guess you're mine.

I don't know what you'll do with property in Talkeetna, except that you're a local, and maybe you need to come back. Please be good to the dogs.

I could have named a musher to take them, but people go in and out of dogs.

If you don't decide to run the Iditarod yourself— ha ha—please make sure they have good homes, especially Sasha. She's saved my life more than once. On my desk, there's a list of current mushers you can contact with any questions. If Alan Smith's around, there's no one I'd rather see run my dogs. Speaking of Alan, if you're doing the Talkeetna hang, look after him for me, too, will you?

There's a lot I would have done for Charlie, but

I know he's set for life, and you're not. Well, now you are, I guess. Anyhow, he's been more than good to me up here. He was even somewhat right about Chris, my ex. I've always envied Tara having such sane parents.

I can't think of anything else to tell you. It's all yours.

Midwifery gave me back something people spent the whole first part of my life taking from me. *You* gave it back to me.

Live it up, Francesca. And don't die before you know what it's like to ride on a sled behind pulling dogs.

Love you much,
Mia

So late. So late, you decide to share these parts of yourself with me.

Phrases came back to her, and she reread the whole and cried.

Charlie cleared his throat, and she remembered his presence. He didn't offer his arms. She handed him the fax and wiped her eyes. When she looked up, he shoved the paper at her and walked away.

Once, long ago, he'd said that when someone died all the other people died all over again.

Her mother was dying again now.

And Mel. Oh, Mel.

And, for Charlie, many, many friends whose names were etched on a black Wall in Washington, D.C.

But Charlie wouldn't think about the fact that as you got older, more and more people died until finally, perhaps, you were alone, you knew no one, because everyone you loved had died.... Oh fear, oh fear.

He laughed, a bitter sound. "Sane."

The two who'd screwed up so badly with one kid and one marriage and each other.

She was foolish to expect his arms, to expect tenderness. But in his grief he seemed to find a detached sympathy for her. He hugged her stiffly.

Francesca's body and feelings disobeyed this signal for a distant and separate grief, one that would not acknowledge their errors—or her folly. The stacking deaths, the growing deaths, the specter of loss formed a mountain just beyond him.

She did not want him to die, didn't want to be left to live without him.

Warm. Charlie.

His scent, his body, had awakened her after a sleep of decades. He made her fifteen and fifty-two at once, and she was the old woman she would be and the girl he'd swept off her feet and into the high, thin air of Denali, and the woman he'd married and the mother of his child. He'd taken her with him to war and kept her safe at home, and how her heart pounded, *I left. I left.*

And his answered, *I failed. I failed.*

THEY RODE HOME on the snowmobile, her face carefully separated from the back of Charlie's parka hood, her mind chasing off the guilt she'd felt in his office, a nagging that had eaten at her from time to time over the years. That maybe she'd done wrong.

How could she think about that clearly when death was with them, and life was hot and urgent, and she wanted Charlie, wanted him so?

No tomorrow. Just Charlie and Mia's words, Mia's death, Mia's legacy.

...set for life... Well, now you are, I guess....

...such sane parents...

Mia had owned a plane and fed forty-two sled dogs and run the Iditarod and the Yukon Quest. None of it was cheap. Where had the money come from? When Mia had apprenticed with her, Francesca had seen no outward sign of wealth.

Who were you, Mia?

Charlie passed Mia's house and drove the snow machine beside his cabin. The lights were on, an incongruity. But the heat of their bodies dismissed it, dismissed the faxed letter, the crime, everything. Everything except the set of Charlie's head as she climbed off the snowmobile. His shadowed eyes and soft lips beneath his mustache. He reached forward to switch off the engine, and a moment passed before he stood.

She knew she could hurt him and that he knew it, too.

I can't! I can't!

I left.

I left.

"Charlie, my plans are—"

A quick look from him.

"—up in the air," she finished lamely.

"You're lucky." No humor in his eyes, just knowledge. Of her and her cruelty. "That's my favorite place."

She opened her mouth, closed it. Mia's dogs howled, singing, missing her. Yes, they must. "I—I'm going to move into Mia's as soon as I can get the key from Peter."

"Oh, good. You and Alan can walk to the Laundromat together. Encourage him to go more often, Francesca."

To shower. Alan, whom Mia had asked her to look out for, as though he were as helpless as one of her dogs.

"Cesca, don't develop scruples now. It'll look like hypocrisy."

"It's not for your benefit!"

The words snapped against trees and cold and the subtle hum of electricity and the distant whine of a snowmobile and dogs, dogs, dogs, Mia's and Alan's.

Naked eyes. Charlie's eyes could turn so naked. Then shutter up without blinking.

"That was a lie," she said. "It is for your benefit."

A half-second.

He flashed a grotesque smile and began to leave, then tossed words over his shoulder. "Your nephew's been sleeping on the couch, but you can probably talk him out of it."

Her nephew? She lunged and grabbed Charlie's sleeve. "Tony's here?"

"He had a falling out with his folks. Sound familiar?"

Francesca found her breath. "I'll go to the Fairview."

"Fine." He shrugged. "If you don't mind the gossip, I don't."

"What's to gossip about?"

His stance, hands in his pockets, was truly indifferent. "Oh, your leaving my house at night. People will imagine a little tiff, and Tony will blame himself, and your friend Trooper Sheppard will look askance at you, but what's that to me?"

She spent several seconds remembering how to speak. "I'm going to visit my new dogs." *Maybe there's room in one of their houses.*

"I'll talk to Tony about the couch. He thinks people over fifty only exchange tepid kisses, anyway."

Francesca's face warmed. Charlie's kisses were not tepid. "What are you going to tell him?"

"That he can't sleep on the couch, after all."

She couldn't quite breathe, and Charlie's eyes were all over her with a gaze that never moved, but it wasn't stalemate. It was checkmate. Without shifting, his eyes stroked her. "See you upstairs."

She stalked away, into the yard full of barking and growling dogs.

FOR HIS BENEFIT. What Francesca didn't understand about men would fill a book, but when the choice was a reluctant Cesca in his bed or Tony Walcott's knowing how weak-headed his aunt could be, Charlie had to choose the former. From the loft, he heard Tony snapping his sleeping bag, fluffing it. The light went out.

Charlie tried not to imagine Francesca walking to the Fairview by starlight. She wouldn't.

But he wished he had Mia's letter in the loft with him, to take his mind off it.

Mia. He winced.

Like a father to me.

Like a father to me.

He was learning to let it go, day by day, the not knowing. At first, hearing that Mia had parents somewhere, he'd been persuaded that he was wrong, that it was all his imagination. But, no. Mia had been much too interested in the old days in Talkeetna, too interested in how he and Cesca had fallen in love and if he'd ever loved another woman. He'd sweated in the office, thinking this letter held the clue, until he read it. This was the hardest letting go yet.

Sure, he could look into it more, maybe get an answer. But maybe the answer Mia had given in her letter was best for everyone.

Like a father.

When he closed his eyes, a helicopter burst apart, bright and broken, and he knew his friends were dead. There were more things to relive. Instead he played tricks on himself, dribbling a basketball in his mind, shooting baskets. The Alaskan night returned.

From habit, he lifted the cordless phone he'd taken to bed with him and dialed the number for the weather.

Anchorage.

He didn't want to see Mia. But Francesca would go, with or without him.

Francesca. Where was she?

What if she didn't come back?

He reached for the lamp, but her footsteps outside stilled his hand. The latch on the side door clicked, and Tony said, "Hi, Francesca."

Tony Walcott

My aunt's hair is long and curly, and the silhouette turns to lace in the darkness. One look at her, and I know she was a hippie and still is, just as I know my mother never was.

I sit up, and Francesca comes over and sits on the edge of the rocker. Like my mom, she is never relaxed. She looks worried as hell now. "Tony, you mustn't let things that happened before you were born come between you and your parents."

She and Charlie. Charlie told me, *Kid, there's a heap of things in this world that don't make sense, and you can't fix 'em all.* They're both full of it, and Tara would agree with me. "Nothing will come between me and my parents," I tell Francesca.

She's seeing something out the window that probably isn't there. "Good. Sleep well, Tony."

The water runs in the bathroom.

My father's lips are always dry and cracked. They shake when he's angry. He said, *You can choose between drinking beer with her and a place in this house. I hope you don't trade your family in as lightly as she did.*

What kind of family asks someone to make that kind of choice?

Mine. That's what kind.

CHAPTER SEVEN

Marcus Aviation hangar
August 11, 1966

We can't stop hugging. His whiskers and Denali sunburn are against my neck, his lips warm, and I feel each breath he takes and hold him harder, smelling his sweat. Warm means alive, and I don't care about anything but that he's here and warm.

On his bed, I try to touch him, but he says, "Easy, Cesca," and holds my hand.

"Please, Charlie. I love you. Please."

His eyes are on my whole face at once. The second lasts forever. He's never looked at me that way before.

"You need to finish school."

I'm eighteen, but I have one more year. I just nod and can't take my eyes off him. Because he's alive. God bless Art Turner forever. I touch a thread on Charlie's collar, and we're hugging again, and his leg's between mine and mine between his. My eyes are closed, and I am going to win, and he is going to lose.

But he keeps catching my hands and holding them.

"Listen. This is important."

He says he grew up in pool halls and on the road.

In a second, I learn what a mark is and in the next second what he and his father looked for in a mark. In the elderly, it was loneliness; in the young, pride. "It's so easy, Cesca. It makes you sick when you know how easy it is. People want to trust other people."

From Charlie, I hear how to set up a phony insurance scam—but that it's risky. The easiest is to win someone's trust over a long time, until they're letting you be their business partner or handle all their financial matters. "Never let anyone do that to you, Cesca. Look after your own investments, as long as you live."

One man, after they took his money, hanged himself. Charlie can barely say this, and he makes me look at him. "Did you hear me?"

I heard.

The man looking at me walked away from his father when he was fifteen and has never defrauded a soul.

He meant to scare me off, but he's made me love him more, want him more. The only thing that matters is being with him. "Please, Charlie." Make love with me.

Kisses. His eyes are sexy slits. "This what you want?"

He knows it isn't. I wish I'd let Stormy iron my hair last night.

But I didn't care about my hair. I thought he was dead.

Charlie's bed

SHE KEPT HER BACK TO HIM and listened for his breathing to grow even. He wasn't sleeping, and instead of chalking it up to their last words outside, she remembered Mia and what had happened at Charlie's office. He must be thinking about her, too.

I can't sleep on my side. I never could.

Not without his arm around her, his body fitted behind hers.

She rolled onto her back, and his hand clasped hers under the sheets.

The unexpressed cry in her throat had nothing to do with Mia and everything to do with the confident feel of his hand. The world had become these smooth sheets and his hands on her, his lips kissing her, his leg between hers. Her breath turned ragged, and he murmured, "Try to keep it down, Cesca."

When she laughed silently, her eyes teared, and they kissed, truly kissed, and she remembered what it was to have someone who was completely hers. But they were one person before it hit her again, everything that meant.

Everything it meant with Charlie.

IN THE MORNING, Charlie tucked her nightgown down in the sheets beside her. "You'll need this. Want some clothes instead?"

When his lashes lifted for a second, his eyes were unguarded. Almost feverish in their intensity and vulnerability and carelessness.

I didn't mean to do this. I didn't mean for him to look at me like that again.

But the expression was gone.

She nodded. "Thanks." Listening to him climb down the ladder, she touched the flannel nightgown Ivy had given her. Ivy. With Tara and the abandoned baby and Mia's death, she kept forgetting that her daughter in West

Virginia was pregnant. Due December first. *I must call her.*

Another memory hit her, like a second barrage. Not last night—she'd assimilated that.

No.

How could I have forgotten?

Easy. Charlie. And the attorney, Mia's estate.

Only now did she recall what she and Peter had discovered in Mia's cabin. Francesca had spotted it, where it had slid down behind the futon.

A store-bought friendship card.

I'll take that, Peter had said, producing an evidence bag.

Oh, my prints.

Handling the card by the edges, he'd opened it. The inside read, in barely legible script, ''Enjoy. C.''

Knowing what Peter was thinking, Francesca said, *That's not Charlie's writing, and he hates greeting cards. Her ex-husband was named Chris.*

Unconvinced, Peter had asked her to keep it to herself.

She had, so much that she'd forgotten about it between Charlie's accusations about Peter, her plans to visit her father, Mia's will, Mia's letter and—

This. Charlie's bed.

I did it. I did it again.

It was October, the morning sky still starlit, but ''Good Vibrations'' reached upstairs like an endless summer. He brought her clothes, and his stomach still rippled with muscle above his jeans as he climbed over her, playfully biting the covers off her, his breath already tasting like coffee.

And she could not kiss him back.

He only missed a beat. ''Where's that letter?'' As though the fax from Mia's lawyers was the only reason for his kneeling over her, nipping at her. You could take the wolf out of the woods, but...

The letter was in the pocket of the wool shirt he'd brought. She gave it to him and got dressed as though he wasn't there.

In the faint blue light from the window, he scanned the words once more, then handed her the letter. "Cesca, look at this. Read it, and tell me if anything strikes you."

She needed the bedside lamp. But she read Mia's letter without rush, without the excitement of just having learned there was a letter. "There's no date."

"Alan has lived here only a year and a half."

"She sounds almost as if—" Leaving the fax on the bed, Francesca buttoned her shirt.

"You may as well say it. I've already thought it."

"She sounds almost as if she knows she's going to die."

"It's probably a recent will. When you have assets, you revise them more often."

Francesca lifted her eyebrows.

"Surely you're not curious about my assets, Goddess of Earthly Delights."

Downstairs, the water in the bathroom went on. The shower.

"As a matter of fact, I'm not. But I am curious about how much you'd charge to fly me to Anchorage on a moment's notice."

The nakedness in his eyes had turned to keenness. It didn't matter which was there; under either gaze, she felt like prey.

"Once again, she pretends she didn't spend the night in my bed. It's all those years we spent sneaking around like Romeo and Juliet, Francesca. Didn't I predict you'd never be the same?"

"Or perhaps I should inquire at Roy Walcott Air Service."

"Cesca, you wound me."

"I understand their accident rate is very low."

"As is mine. No passenger has ever received so much as a bruise with me, which can't be said for your brother, because I happen to know that on one occasion a rock stolen from Denali flew out of a passenger's pocket and hit another passenger on the head."

"High crimes in high places." Recalling suddenly their conversation the night before, including what she'd said about flying climbers to the mountains, she looked away. She was dressed, and it was time to be gone.

But Charlie knew her thoughts, and his look was bitter. "Well, Cesca, a man could fly supplies to Anuktuvuk Pass—" in the Brooks Range, the middle of nowhere and often sixty below "—and a woman could be faithful to her husband. This heroism stuff is all a matter of perspective."

Downstairs, Carl Wilson was saying God only knew what he'd be...without her.

She flushed, wanting to be anywhere but under his eyes. "I'm not proud of what I did, Charlie. I told you a long time ago that I was sorry."

"I'll bet you were sorry. The first time I saw that longhaired coffee grower I knew you were going to be sorry."

"Let's drop this."

"What was it, Francesca? What did you see in him?"

"Sobriety. The ability to stay at home."

The shower was still running, and Charlie moved toward her on the bed. He pointed to his own face. "And did you ever look at me and think, 'This is the father of my child and he—'"

"I did."

"'—loves me?'"

She got the words out. "No, I never did think that." But it was a lie.

She'd known. Charlie Marcus would never cry over any woman's departure, just make jokes all the way to the courthouse.

Hugging her nightgown to her, she backed against his closet. She had to defend this withering thing, her justification. "Charlie, if you wanted me to stay, you should have asked."

"After you'd admitted there was someone else?"

"I'd like to drop this."

"Gladly."

He stepped past her to get a shirt, and a moment later, he was gone.

CHARLIE FLIPPED ON the coffeemaker and lifted his eyes at sounds from overhead. She was making the bed. Tony wouldn't deal with his sleeping bag all day.

He should tell her to fly to Anchorage with someone else.

But Roy Jr. had a grudge against her; you couldn't trust a man who wouldn't speak to his own sister. And Art—well, face it—the man didn't like it when the weather got a little rough. As for the other outfits...

If he didn't take her to Anchorage, would Peter Sheppard drive her?

When Tony came to the kitchen, Charlie set a coffee cup in front of him.

Tony said, "Hey, I'm not crowding you guys, am I?"

"No." For what this must be doing to Roy Jr., Charlie would've paid him to stay. Not to mention last night. *I'm in your debt, kid.*

But, oh, Francesca. They couldn't get through twenty-four hours before he heard the words she'd said to him in Hawaii one morning, one morning he'd come home to her arms.

"Can I ask you something?"

Charlie poured himself a cup of coffee, thinking that people should never ask that.

"You two are divorced, right?"

Eyeing him, Charlie drank from the mug.

"But you still get along."

"Are you going somewhere with this train of thought?"

His nephew hopped on the counter. Sitting there, long Walcott legs dangling, he stirred three teaspoons of brown sugar into his coffee. "It's like—" Tony gazed at the ceiling "—it's never too late for peace."

"Son." Charlie kept his cup clear of the sugar-happy spoon.

"What?"

He meant to tell him he needed some college. What came out was, "Men always remember their first. Women never do."

"No shit," agreed Tony.

HIS NAME HAD BEEN JAY HENRY, and his father owned a coffee plantation. Jay was third-generation Hawaiian, blond and blue-eyed, in all ways different from Charlie. He hadn't been to Vietnam, and he could stop at two beers. He and Francesca had met at the market, when her grocery bag broke and some papaya juice spilled all over Tara's Barbie doll, and Tara had cried. Jay had washed off the Barbie and introduced himself.

What Francesca recalled most bitterly was his surprise when he learned she was married. They'd noticed each other around the island for two years. But he'd never seen her with anyone but Tara.

Because Charlie was always absent—or home drunk.

Jay Henry had done one thing right or it would have gone no further.

When he learned she was married, he'd said, "Oh." And withdrawn.

Francesca straightened the wool blanket on Charlie's bed.

If I hadn't left, you'd still be drinking, Charlie.

Instead, he'd returned to Alaska and grown strong again, existing each day with those things she knew he still saw. It was better that she'd left.

And she mustn't stay now.

She mustn't, because the closer she came to Charlie— Yes, she could predict what he'd say to her every thought. Somehow, now she possessed the missing owner's manual. If she asked, it would say that strength is illusion and candor worthy of respect.

It would say this ain't no dress rehearsal.

He'd scared her from the first.

Charlie was listening to the weather on the phone and Tony was taking the Doors album from its sleeve when she came downstairs. Charlie wanted to shake his head, no, at the kid. That album wasn't music; it was something he did when no one was around, maybe once a year.

"Good morning, Tony." On the way to her pack, Francesca suggested, "Hey, Tony, put on some Beatles, will you?"

Mouth dry, Charlie hung up the phone, pretending it wasn't happening, ignoring that she remembered and was protecting him or all of them. "We've got some wind and precipitation. I'll fly you to Anchorage."

Francesca turned from the album with Jim Morrison's

young face and the outline chartreuse letters and "Marcus" scrawled across the front. He still had the very same record. *I have to get out of here. I have to get out while I can.*

But he'd offered to fly her to Anchorage. "Thank you, Charlie. I'm sure that will be best."

Charlie studied her, then winked at Tony, who still gazed longingly at the Doors. "Yeah, yeah, you say that to all the flyboys. Let's get out of here."

But she kept packing. "Just let me get my things together."

HER FATHER WAS AHEAD of the truck on his snowmobile.

"What does he do all day?" Francesca murmured.

Following Roy Walcott onto the Spur Road, Charlie ignored the question. Pilots lived at the airport, and retired pilots watched planes and talked planes and read planes and listened to the weather, and good men trusted their kids to make business decisions, and cruel men did not.

Francesca had taken Charlie away from his planes and the airport more frequently than anything in—well, a long time. Even when Tara had come to Alaska, she'd spent much of her time in the air with him and at the airport. Francesca needed more watching.

"He must be lonely," she said.

"Not hardly. Old man's never lost a plane. Always some starry-eyed worshipers gathering round." Her pack and duffel bag were in the back of the pickup. *Don't leave, Cesca.*

They passed the cemetery, and Francesca pictured her mother's grave. *He's lonely, Charlie.*

The heater was on, but she zipped her parka higher and pulled on her gloves.

FRANCESCA STARED THROUGH the glass at her friend's gray skin. Mia had been dead more than two weeks, and her limbs were still frozen the way they'd been when she hit the ground.

Fists jammed in his pockets, Charlie studied the lines between the floor tiles.

"We can go." Francesca told the officer who had brought them into the morgue, "Thank you."

CHARLIE DREW THE PORSCHE to the curb in front of the attorney's clapboard office building and let the engine idle.

"Aren't you coming in?"

His eyebrows shot up. "I'm invited?"

No. No, he shouldn't be, just as she shouldn't have gone to his bed last night. She unbuckled her shoulder harness and turned in the seat. "Charlie, can you and I just be friends?"

Two seconds of silence.

"Francesca, I'm the best friend you ever had."

"You heard me."

"Deny having a powerful and sustained orgasm last night."

"That's going to stop. I mean—" She hid her face with her hand.

"Maybe for a time, and who knows better how to—"

"This isn't about sex."

"I was going to mention your moods. What is it about?"

Her stomach was warm. She closed her eyes. "Okay, pretend it's about sex. Last night was…fine, but it won't always be like that."

"Cesca. You don't think I'm that fragile."

I think you're the most fragile person I've ever known. "Please just answer my original question, Charlie."

For a blink in time, he was all too-bright eyes that loved too hard and cared too much, and then the instant was gone and he looked as he had when he'd met Tara's first husband. Only husband. "We were in love for fifteen years, during which time you walked away from your family for me and married me to keep me safe and had my baby. No, Francesca. We can't 'just be friends.'"

That look again. She'd slept with him once, and she'd slept with him twice, and she loved him and didn't know why she was afraid of him except that he made everything a little too real.

And hurting him was the worst thing she'd ever done.

She bit her bottom lip, studying him as though he was a stray she shouldn't really take home. Charlie watched the road.

A Range Rover drove past, making him think of Tara and her stolen baby and Isaac, with children.

Which made him remember Mia and two or three things Francesca didn't know.

He switched off the ignition.

Funny. Francesca might walk away because she liked Trooper Sheppard better or because she wanted to make up with her family or just because she was past fifty and set in her ways.

But she'd never listened to her dad.

She's always trusted me.

She reached for the door and proved it all over again. "Are you coming?"

IVAN KRAKAUER WORE a three-piece suit and smelled of pipe smoke. With a thick head of brown hair going gray, he seemed chronologically younger and physically older than Charlie. Charlie would have his same lithe body at eighty. And Francesca doubted he'd ever need reading glasses, either, the same way she was sure her father didn't. She introduced him as, "My friend, Charlie Marcus."

"Ah, yes. The pilot," murmured Krakauer.

"The same."

The lawyer nodded. He seemed to have heard of Charlie through means other than Mia, and Francesca noticed the faint awe certain people demonstrated around Charlie, just as they always had around her father. It irked her and made her proud.

They settled on leather chairs in the lawyer's office while he arranged himself behind his walnut desk and drew out wire-rimmed glasses and began to read Mia's will. Nothing complicated; everything she owned had become Francesca's. The state troopers had her keys and would turn them over to Francesca.

For the first time, she held Mia's original letter in her hands.

Charlie eyed Francesca.

She took the cue. "Ivan, Mia's letter isn't dated. When is her will dated?"

Charlie examined the front of Ivan's desk, apparently ignoring their conversation.

Krakauer's face closed. "Her will is dated December seventh of last year." He changed the topic. "How are the troopers coming with their investigation?"

Francesca admitted, "I don't know. I'm not even sure that there was a crime. I don't believe they really know what happened. Ivan, did you know that Mia's parents are alive?"

Charlie shifted.

Francesca explained, "She didn't have much money when I knew her."

The attorney remained blank.

Charlie had gone still.

THEY DROVE FIRST to the state troopers' station, to retrieve Mia's keys, then saw the Realtor about the unsold house. The Realtor promised to call Francesca if there were any offers and asked if he should drop the asking price. She said not for the moment.

"Where to?" asked Charlie in the car.

"The bank." She fingered the key to Mia's safe-deposit box.

Beside her, Charlie said nothing and never switched on the radio or tape deck.

Francesca ignored the knot in her gut and his silence.

SHE SAID, "Well, here's her birth certificate," and from the oak chair in the corner of the bank cubicle Charlie watched a strand of hair tumble down the side of her face. She read, her lips parting slightly.

He held the armrests so he wouldn't get up.

She put her hand to her face and breathed in and out. "Charlie."

Then he rose, though he already knew.

CHAPTER EIGHT

Denali
July 8, 1967

We're eating blueberries and not saying much. I don't feel like talking or even hitting mosquitoes. But from time to time, I look at him. He is the rest of my life.

Charlie gazes past my shoulder, with his twenty-two across his knees, where it wasn't a moment before.

The sow and cubs are in the water. The bear looks at me, and I look at her and feel my mother knowing, knowing that I'm here with Charlie, knowing that Dad broke every one of my forty-five's last fall, knowing a lot of things we all kept from her. Now she can see these things, see everything.

There's a plane in the sky, and the sow stands up. One of her half-grown cubs runs at the noise, then all three head away, across the creek and up the vast sloping taiga, merging with the reds and golds. The shadow of the plane crosses us, and Charlie's eyes lift from the bears to the sky. He stands.

I eat several more blueberries fast, as though I won't have the chance again.

"Come on, Cesca."

The Cessna returns as he's breaking down the tent, and I read the tail numbers. It is Dad's newest plane, and I've never seen Roy Jr. fly that low, but Mel is with him. Instinctively, I sit, then lie down, a long way from Charlie. My hair lifts up, and the ground shakes under me. I'm nearly deaf at this familiar sound, and as I lie on my side and back like a Vargas girl, I see Roy Jr.'s profile. His wheel-skis nearly skim the wing of Charlie's plane.

Charlie is still standing. He just keeps breaking apart the tent and watching the bears become distant humps of gold.

Lake Hood

FRANCESCA HUDDLED in her parka as gray clouds sucked away the last daylight. As Charlie finished his walk-around, and her gaze followed his body and his hair that used to be the color of twigs, except when the sun hit it.

He'd driven back to the plane without asking if there was anything else she needed to do in Anchorage.

What did you feel seeing that birth certificate, Charlie? Do you feel what I do?

Mia was born at St. Joseph's Hospital in Honolulu, Hawaii. August 15, 1968. The next day, Francesca had told her physician that she had new plans for her own child's birth. Because she did not want to have a baby in a place where people did what had just been done to Stormy. No one should ever have babies that way. No one should ever give up her babies without seeing their faces or holding them in her arms. Through Stormy's anguish and a hippie midwife on the big island, Francesca's life had been changed forever. During her labor, she'd seen dolphins in the lagoon outside her home and walked into the water with them, holding Charlie's hand, while contractions traced her spine. That was Tara's story and theirs.

Not dear Mia. Mia had been born in Hawaii and taken from her mother and fraternal twin. Mia was adopted, and Mia had come to Talkeetna.

"You ready?"

Lines bracketed Charlie's mouth and eyes where she'd never noticed lines before. He zipped his parka higher. A Piper Cub landed, touching down on the ice with no grace and no calamity.

"What are you thinking, Charlie?"

His eyes scraped over his plane, and he had been so silent for an hour that she knew he would lie.

"In Chu Lai, we drank at night and flew in the morning."

Her chest tightened. She wanted to touch him, but he was already striding toward the plane as though fleeing. She was inside the Cessna before it occurred to her that he had no reason to run away.

Charlie Marcus never lost sleep over anyone else's mistakes.

JOE BURKE WAITED FOR THEM at the airport to help wrap the plane against the elements. It was twenty-five degrees. In the dark, Francesca noticed the unlit windows of Roy Walcott Air Service. Everyone had gone home, and her gloved fingers hurt from the cold. But with Tony at the house, her only chance to talk to Charlie would be when they climbed in his truck to leave the airport. Wishing he'd hurry, she stamped her feet on the tarmac as Joe said, "The climb's on again."

"Figured. Hey, look at this blade. You got a file?"

While they worked on the propeller, her feet grew numb. Stopping at one point, Charlie said, "Go get warm, Cesca. You want the keys to the truck?"

"I'm fine."

He finished sooner rather than later, and they walked to the truck. Francesca's woven carryall sagged under the weight of paperwork she'd brought from Anchorage—photocopies of documents from the safe-deposit box, paperwork from the attorney. Her fingers and toes had grown wooden, and she felt teary.

No, Francesca. It's not the cold.

In the cab of the pickup, Charlie spread his parka over her legs.

"Charlie."

He started the truck and looked over his shoulder. "Mm?"

"Don't go yet." Her hand on his sleeve, she tried to catch his eye. "Charlie, is Mia— Did you...?"

Wouldn't he stop her, shake his head, tell her no?

Instead, he waited.

Must she say every word? "Did you sleep with Martha Storm?"

His brown eyes didn't blink. "Yes."

It seemed he was going to back the truck out of its space, but he stopped and turned from her, his hand over his mouth and chin, his arm resting against the steering wheel.

Stormy's part in it stung worse than Charlie's, and Francesca wondered why—and what she'd done to make her friend do that.

"It was after you went to Anchorage. I was angry."

Francesca replayed later history—meeting Stormy in Honolulu the day Bobby Kennedy was assassinated. The letter Charlie sent her from flight school: the answer is NO.

He released a long breath. "And..."

And what?

Charlie never sounded like this. Except when he talked about Vietnam. You had to be pretty stable to be trusted with millions of dollars worth of aircraft. Charlie had gone back for a second and third tour, and when he'd come home she should have told him he could do anything he liked, but he'd wanted to return to Talkeetna. Glaciers. She'd refused to go.

Was drinking yourself into a stupor every night the same as cracking?

"In November of nineteen sixty-seven, I sold your father the mineral rights to..."

The mine. The papers on the mineral rights had been in Mia's safety-deposit box. But there was a rich vein in Mia's mine, and any mineral rights Charlie had sold her father in 1967 would surely have been—

"...for fifty thousand dollars. The vein I'd explored trickled out—"

"Charlie. You knew that would happen, didn't you?"

"It seemed likely."

She saw his eyes and his mouth, and he threw his arm behind the seat to check behind him, through the light dusting of snow on the rear windshield. He backed out of the space.

He'd known, known the vein would trickle out. He didn't have to say so, because she knew Charlie perfectly.

They'd nearly reached the cemetery.

"Stop. Stop this truck."

He drew to gentle halt.

I want you to say something. I want you to say you didn't do it, that you acted in good faith.

With her father? After...

Never.

"Mel was in medical school," she said. Her family had never had fifty thousand dollars to spare.

The windshield wipers swept away the snow.

Charlie's silence made it all true.

Francesca opened the passenger door, grabbed her belongings and got out. He had lied to her for thirty years. He had caused her brother's death. And there was absolutely nothing to say.

CHARLIE WAITED FOR HER LIPS to move, for her voice. A long curly lock of hair whipped across her white face. Snow caught on her head, on her clothes, as she shut the door. And when she grabbed her pack from the bed of the pickup, it was something he had only pictured in his mind till then.

Because he'd been flying the day she left Talkeetna.

This time, she headed up the Spur Road, not south toward Anchorage.

She wasn't leaving, just leaving him, and he was sure she would go to them. She strode into the snow with her head up, a fifty-year-old woman with a heavy pack on her hips, carrying a duffel bag with one of her strong midwife's arms. Now that she knew, thoughts he'd lived with for decades shifted, replaced by something more real and more clear.

Charlie sat in the truck in the middle of the silent airport road and tried to force everything back down inside him, to rearrange things as they'd been. He could not.

DRY-EYED, Francesca checked into the Fairview. Noises and faces were as nothing around her. She carried her bags to her room and adjusted the heat and lay on the bed.

TONY WAS AWAY from the house, and Charlie wasn't sorry.

He didn't even turn on a light, just felt his way toward the glowing light on his answering machine to check his messages lit the woodstove the same way. He sat in the rocker. There were scarier things than being shot at and worse things than being a second too late ordering your gunners not to fire. One of the worse things was learning your beautiful brown-eyed daughter had been raped and tortured, as Tara had in '88 as a *matrona* in Chile, and one of the scarier things...

He clung to each sizzle and crack from the stove, each sound of wood giving under heat. He sat and chose not to go to the trading post. *Just sit, Marcus. Hang out.*

Heat tingled through his limbs, and his feet steamed in his wool socks.

A log fell apart in the stove.

Music would drag at him now, making his brain heavy.

Standing, he grabbed the phone and dialed, holding his breath. He hung up before it could ring, but it was already ringing.

Too late.

He should put some more water in the kettle on the woodstove.

His phone rang. Home phone. He lifted the receiver. "Hi."

"Hi." Long silence. Some people could hear without words. "See you in a few. The kid still there?"

"Not at the moment." His stomach writhed. "Hey, what's the schedule tomorrow?"

"Nada."

"I'm going to the store. The door's open."

HIS EYES ROAMED the pop cases, and he opened the door of the refrigerated case and reached for a six-pack of Surge. The door closed on his arm, and his hand released the plastic binding the cold, wet cans. He withdrew his arm.

The woman running the register was about twenty-two, had skin like china and drove a car with Vermont plates. He didn't know her name, and she probably didn't know who he was. Except that everyone in Talkeetna knew him.

He moved three feet to his right.

He opened the door of the next case, and here the cardboard holding the bottles glittered silver and gold, and he reached.

THE LIGHTS WERE ON, and the Mamas and the Papas were California dreamin', and the house smelled like cigarettes. Charlie helped himself to one, letting it dangle from his lips as he grabbed a bottle opener from a drawer.

Joe's legs swung against the kitchen counter as he tapped ashes into a coffee can lid. "She find out?"

He drew on his cigarette. When he'd left the service, he'd quit smoking. So had Joe. Charlie tipped back his head, and beer ran down his throat.

His friend changed the subject. "So, Hayley—" the woman climber from New Zealand "—says she'd like to live nearer some big mountains. She likes canoes, too." Joe had one and could handle it better with one arm than Charlie could with two.

If anyone would let him fly again, he could probably figure that out, too.

Cracking a smile, Charlie opened another beer and walked into the living room to turn up the music.

His friend followed and crouched beside the crates holding the albums. "She still looks a lot like that picture you had in the hootch." At Chu Lai.

She. But now Joe was talking about Francesca. For maybe a minute, Charlie had forgotten. Another picture, of Francesca holding Tara, he'd kept with him, against his body. He'd sewed it inside his T-shirt every time he changed. It got sweaty and wet and stained and warped and bent and ruined, but it wasn't to look at; he had others to look at. His voice felt unused and unnatural. "You know, I used to tell her, 'Don't risk anything you can't afford to lose.'"

Joe threw back his head and laughed. "And then he went to Vietnam."

WHEN FRANCESCA AWOKE, she didn't know where she was. Then it came back, and she was as lost and homeless as she'd been in the summer of 1967 when her father had told her to choose between her family and Charlie Marcus.

She had chosen neither, and last night the other half of neither had dispossessed her.

With the calm of morning, she knew that it had all happened a very long time ago and that a month after Mel was drafted, Johnson had ended graduate student deferrals. If death back then hadn't been a matter of place and time and chance, what Charlie had done could be washed away.

If.

She saw Mel as he'd looked the day she'd left Talkeetna, and it was how she would probably always see him. He had never believed in the war. Her family's dispossession of her had grown through the years to a familiar bitterness, like a mild physical complaint she had to live with. But Mel's death... Always, always it stabbed her, the sadness eternally fresh.

Charlie had seen someone hit a booby trap, and so she knew. It wasn't Mel he'd seen. But Charlie's standing there, so close to his friend, close enough to later find a piece of bone that wasn't his embedded in his arm—was that a price paid, an exchange made? Did people get what they deserved?

She salivated too much, nauseous. Breakfast was unthinkable.

What about Stormy? What about Charlie's letter that said ''...the answer is NO.''

He was going to war.

She blinked, her stomach churning and, yes, aching. Without checking, she knew she was bleeding, and she wondered how long she would bleed this time.

She must get up. Get dressed. See Peter Sheppard.

Call Stormy.

Oh, dear God, she did not want to call Stormy. The betrayal—just now, that was nothing, because Stormy had lost a child. Francesca didn't want to tell her. And just as she knew that Tara could not make up for the loss of Ivy or Ivy for the loss of Tara, she knew that the existence of Mia's twin brother, somewhere, would never make up for the loss of Mia.

I have to call her. She has to get here before that body is cremated, before Mia's other parents come. Oh, God, Mia's parents...

Charlie.

One thing at a time.

Breathe.

Why must she speak to Peter? Did he have to know

any of this? So someone was with Mia when she died and didn't report it. That person wasn't Charlie.

Her mind stalled on the thought.

That person was not Charlie.

But she wanted to see the greeting card again, the greeting card they'd found at Mia's place.

Mia, you knew who I was, didn't you, when you asked to apprentice with me? Somehow, you knew I'd been your birth mother's friend.

But why hadn't Mia said so?

TROOPER SHEPPARD WAS OUT. Using the phone in her room, Francesca forced herself to dial information. She tried Honolulu listings, first Martha Storm—then, remembering, the single word "Stormy." A hit. Hand shaking, she punched the number, and when the phone rang and rang and no machine picked up, she was relieved.

She called Ivan Krakauer. It took her just minutes to get across that Mia had been adopted and the identity of her birth mother was known beyond a doubt and Mia's body must not be cremated until that woman was contacted. The attorney offered to call Stormy, and Francesca nearly sagged with relief, the easiness and wrongdoing like a decadent food she wanted and could just eat and forget about.

Her voice shook when she told him no.

Next. What to do next.

I should go see Mia's midwifery partner. The troopers had said that Mia had belongings at the clinic. They'd given Francesca the number of the clinic, and when she phoned a woman answered. Rainbow Clinic.

For no reason except that her friend had worked at a place whose name was a promise, or maybe because she could picture Mia with pregnant women, helping them,

Francesca's eyes watered. "I'm Francesca Walcott. I'm a friend of Mia Kammerlander's and I want to come by to retrieve her possessions." *Shouldn't her parents be doing it?*

But she named me. And there must be a reason.

"I'd also like to meet with her partner, if that's possible."

"Let me see if Honeydew's busy."

Honeydew. *Where had she heard that name?*

The receptionist came on again. "She can't come to the phone. Would you like to make an appointment?"

I just want to talk about Mia. Moments later, she hung up and made a note in her day planner. Day after next, she'd visit the clinic and see Honeydew Lane.

I've got to talk to Stormy. What was the name of her dive shop?

Francesca tried information again, and the operators couldn't give her Yellow Pages listings.

She phoned Tara. Her daughter was out, and Francesca left no message, instead tried Ivy.

"Oh, Mom. I'm so glad to hear from you. How's Alaska? Have you seen your family?"

The West Virginia had crept back into Ivy's voice.

"Well, I've seen some of their faces. We haven't spoken much." And now—after what Charlie had confessed, she couldn't go to her father. She wasn't ready to put words to why.

"That's so hard for me to imagine."

Ivy's husband's family had made her life miserable when she first returned to West Virginia. Francesca decided to tell neither Ivy nor Tara about Mia's parentage. That was Charlie's job. "How's the baby, honey, and how are you?"

"Really good." Tension stole through that faint Appalachian drawl. "Everything's just fine here."

"With Cullen?"

"He's wonderful. Gabby's wonderful. She's such a help. She was just with me at a prenatal." Ivy's thirteen-year-old daughter was her midwifery assistant.

Francesca asked if Ivy had heard from Tara, and Ivy hesitated. "Yes."

Perhaps Tara was more frank with Ivy than with her mother. Well, at least Tara was talking to someone—and Ivy was a good confidante, warmhearted and wise.

Ivy asked, "Have you seen Dad?"

"It's a very small town. Look, sweetie, I'd better go."

HER BODY HOLLOW AND ACHING, Francesca walked down B Street on the new snow, the bright, cold air stinging her skin. Charlie would be at the airport. No worry about running into him, and she could see Alan.

The musher stood outside his cabin with his dogs, weight on one leg, glaring at Peter Sheppard. Francesca wanted to offer Alan his pick of Mia's dogs, and maybe he could help her place the others. And she needed Peter to unlock Mia's house.

What am I going to tell him?

He should be told that Mia was adopted—and whose daughter she was.

Stormy's. Stormy's and...

Those children weren't necessarily Charlie's.

But he thinks they are.

In Alan's yard, she tensed at the barking of his dogs. A compact husky mix strained at his chain, trying to taste Peter Sheppard. The trooper wore a fisherman knit sweater and wool pants over his Sorel boots. His eyebrows lifted. "Hello."

"Hi, Peter."

The expression in his eyes would have been flattering if not for the things Charlie had said. Well, it was flattering anyhow.

He faced Alan. "You won't be going anywhere." A question.

"Can I run my dogs?"

"Where?"

"You want a map?"

"Yes."

Alan's fine nostrils flared. He wheeled and strode to his plywood-sided house.

Peter turned to Francesca. His seriousness stirred her as his intelligence had in the past. *But I can't tell him about Charlie. I'll tell him everything else.* With Alan inside, they were alone. Why not begin? "Peter, I learned the other night that I'm Mia's heir, and I saw her attorney and the troopers in Anchorage yesterday."

"I heard. The last, anyway. I'll take the lock off the house for you. Though you may want to install one of your own."

"Thank you."

He must have seen her parted lips.

Why must she say this out in the cold, beside Alan Smith's barking dogs, with Mia's setting up an equal racket across the street? Like giving a report to a commanding officer. But she wasn't going to suggest another meeting or a different place to talk, not after Charlie's obnoxious predictions. "Mia was adopted. I saw her birth certificate. She was born in the same hospital on the same day, delivered by the same doctor, as my friend Stormy's twins that she gave up for adoption."

The trooper's face took time to move—to speak. "I

want to hear more about this. Let's go across the street after I get—'' one breath ''—Alan's map.''

FRANCESCA SURVEYED Mia's one-room cabin. *I need to clean, to take care of her things.* Twenty-four hours ago, she'd planned to live here. With Mia's money, why not put in a water line and a septic system or line to the city sewer?

Because. She couldn't live next door to Charlie.

I can't stay in this town.

How could he have done it?

On top of everything, the lies. He'd married her with these secrets and kept them.

He must have been frightened of losing her.

She placed logs in the stove, arranging newspaper and kindling. The fire caught, and Francesca shut the door.

''What were you just thinking about?''

She didn't tremble. It was like discovering cord loops or shoulder dystocia; she had to act with confidence. ''My ex-husband.'' With a smile, Francesca hurled water on the trooper's curiosity. Crossing the tiny room, she settled on the futon, removed her boots and sat cross-legged in the cold.

Peter straddled the single chair.

Francesca told him, ''Martha Storm was my best friend in Talkeetna. I left in late nineteen sixty-seven. Charlie and I went to Hawaii, and in May of sixty-eight I ran into Stormy in Honolulu. She was looking for me, looking for a friend, I guess.'' Boy, was she leaving gaps left and right. ''Stormy was pregnant with twins, and I was pregnant with my daughter, Tara, and I kind of held Stormy's hand through the birth and the babies being taken from her.''

''Slow down. Who's Stormy? Give me a name.''

"Martha Storm. She's the younger sister of my sister-in-law Pammie Sue, and she was my best friend...."

I'm the best friend you ever had.

"She was my best friend." Francesca pressed her lips together. "I assume it's not usual to notify birth parents of a child's death."

"No." He released a breath. "Except that—"

"Let me tell her first."

"I'd like to see that birth certificate. And any other papers you might have regarding Mia."

"They're at the Fairview."

His eyes were gently keen.

While the stove crackled, she became afraid.

"Who was the father?"

Francesca's face felt flushed. She dragged a hand through her hair. No sweat at her temples, but she said, "Oh, gosh. I'm sorry. This happens." She made a deal of unzipping her coat. "Stormy never told me."

Peter bit his lip, and Francesca knew his thoughts as surely as if he'd spoken them. *Stormy will tell me.* "Why does your family blame your ex-husband for your brother's death?"

Her heart pounded. "You should ask them that."

"You don't know."

She hesitated, and in one second it was too late to lie. So she kept silent.

"Did they know each other in Nam?"

Really, she needn't even show him Mia's letter.

"Why didn't you come home for your brother's funeral?"

Who in hell have you been talking to? It could have been anyone. Her nerves were singed by that body too close, those intense blue eyes and square jaw. He cast his eyes down once, in compassion for her, then rose in a gesture of self-disgust and went to the window.

Francesca studied his body and his expression and his act with a rueful smile. *You're good, Trooper. But you're nowhere as good as Charlie.*

She eased up from the futon. "If you have no more questions relating to Mia's death?"

They were almost nose to nose. He didn't look at her body, but she knew he wanted to, just as she knew her jeans were hanging loose and her gray-wired hair was wild and beautiful as unforgotten summers and she was bleeding and bleeding and her skin slowly wearing the years. And she belonged to someone else.

"Yes," he said. "The twins. What was the sex of the other child?"

"Male."

The other child. The other child. *There's another child, and it may be Charlie's.*

Peter tapped his fingers on the doorjamb, and it was as though he was touching her, giving one of those quick squeezes that meant, *Stay alive.* Then he let himself out, leaving her alone in Mia's house with just a simple hook latch to lock out the world. Francesca left it undone. She would have to go to the Fairview and get her things. *I can call Stormy from here.*

No electricity or water, but Mia had a phone.

She gave Peter enough time to make it to Main Street, then laced on her boots and stepped outside. No trooper. No lights next door. She left Mia's and crossed the street, beckoned by the light in Alan's window. Shawn Colvin played from inside, under the clamor of dogs.

Alan answered the door in his wool socks and sloppy, oversize, Andean sweater. He hadn't shaved since the day they'd met, but his skin was still smooth, golden, young, unmarred by wind or cold, even with his healing cuts and bruises. His eyes were a bright turquoise. "Oh, hi." Dogs pushed against his legs and hers. "Come in."

He offered her a tattered couch in a cabin even more primitive than Mia's. Clothing on particle-board shelves, no rug, dog hair. The music came from a smallish CD player and twin minispeakers that seemed loud for their size. He didn't turn down the music. One of the dogs jumped onto the couch beside him and put its paws in his lap. Another laid a fluffy head on his knee.

"Couldn't wait to get rid of that guy." He widened his eyes in an expression meant to seem maniacal. "Oh, well. I'm glad you're here. Mia talked a lot about you." Alan rubbed his hair. "Yeah, I was thinking of running her dogs tonight, but Trooper Sheppard has a way of putting a damper on life."

"I've come about her dogs, actually."

But that wasn't all. Mia had told her to look after him, and something here needed looking after. His woodstove was an oil drum like Mia's but without a regular door, with a door made from a piece of sheet metal instead, and the door glowed hot. His long fingers combed one of the dogs' ruffs. Another dog gnawed a pair of jeans on the floor, and Alan ignored it. Francesca thought he could ignore a lot, maybe miss a lot.

But he hadn't missed what she said.

"Mia made me her heir, and I need to find homes for her dogs."

His face was immobile, now wounded deeper than his cuts and bruises, but she went on. "I wondered if you might take some of them."

One second. Two. Three. "I'll take them all. Can I keep them over there and have her food?"

I'm going to live over there.

No matter. Mia had said to look after him. "Sure."

Outside, a dog growled, and others joined in. Those inside stood, ears alert. One walked to the door and whined.

"It better not be that trooper. Hey, do me a favor and get the door, Francesca. I'm going outside."

As Alan slipped out the back door into his yard, Francesca rose. Unlike Mia, he had a doorknob with a lock. She twisted it and opened the door.

The cold came in.

Charlie's eyes with their arched and sloping brows met hers, seeming to watch her from a distance, in a sexy way that made her see him as he'd looked once peering at a camera lens in Vietnam, his head back, caught by surprise and yet allowing the photographer his moment. She'd taken that picture to bed with her. "Cesca."

She rushed past him to the snowy street. Who needed touch to feel warm, to tremble? Things shifted inside her. His betrayal erased hers; two wrongs, three wrongs, made another. But justice laughed, and the twilight, the trees, the smell of her hometown, banished lies. *It hurts, Charlie! Why has it always hurt so much to love you?*

Because it hurt to look upon his lacks.

And it hurt even more, what his nearness demanded. That she look on her own.

A PHONE RANG, across the Pacific, and a receiver clattered up from its cradle. "Hello?"

Oh. She was home. This was it. "Stormy? It's Francesca."

"Franny!"

On the bed in her room, Francesca tried to imagine how it would be if she was about to hear that Tara was dead, and she could not.

"I was just thinking about you, girl! Are you coming out?"

"I'm in Talkeetna. Stormy, is anyone there with you?"

"My bud Shelly. In fact, can I call you back? What's your number there? We're just going out for pizza and beer."

Francesca was going to ruin that date. The words trickled out, clumsy, even though she began with the fact that Mia, her apprentice, was dead.

Stormy cut in. "Why are you telling me? I could have gone my whole life without knowing this."

Francesca's heart pounded. God. *What have I done?* Her mouth opened. Fifty-two years old, and how could she still be so thoughtless, so hampered by her own view of existence? But maybe with age came a reflex to speak the truth even before you knew it was true. "It's what·I would've wanted you to do for me."

The other receiver fell back into its cradle with a click.

And silence.

Dread pooled inside her. Doing the right thing had been so important, and she, a midwife, had screwed up by second-guessing the feelings of a birth mother, of any mother. She ought to think about that, ought to examine her actions.

She didn't.

She had only one thought.

How could you sleep with the man I loved?

CHAPTER NINE

Hilo, Hawaii
February 15, 1968

He lies on his stomach under a palm tree, sand all over his bare shoulders. He doesn't see me, and I drop down on my knees beside him and slide my finger under the waistband of his cutoffs, against his smooth, sun-tanned back. There's a folded piece of paper in his pocket.

He rolls over.

"You're not at work." He flies tourists and assists with rescues for Big Island Helicopters, and I've been waitressing at a restaurant in Hilo.

Charlie pulls me down on the beach beside him and kisses me, then hugs me close.

"You're not at Honolii, either," I say. Surfing. He surfed in California when he was a kid, and he's taught me to surf here. I love Hawaii. I love him, but he's not working and he's not surfing. He's just lying beside the lagoon near our house.

And he never answers.

Is he hurt because I wouldn't marry him? Last night was Valentine's Day, and I shouldn't have put him off again. But we *are* married. I like this, this feeling of being more married without rings. Even though I have a ring, carved from a seashell, that he gave me.

He is completely mine, and I'm completely his.

Desperation can grab you in the middle of a sunny day, with your lover's arms around you. As though something is chasing me, I cling to him. "I want to marry you."

The way he laughs—

Look at me, Charlie.

He's pulling a thread on my cotton bikini top. "That…should…wait."

Something's wrong. Charlie never says so little, never says things so quietly. And after a second of hugging like this, after I first touched him, he should have been looking around to see if we were alone or just telling me, *Let's go home*. But he's not thinking about sex, and he's not letting go of me, either.

Terror isn't heart-pounding or heart-stopping or a feeling in your stomach. It's all over your body and your mind. Now the fear that has gripped us both after making love or when either of us awakens in the night, the fear that looms over us, has a permanent home and soil in which to grow; now it won't go away with a prayer or an embrace. It has bloomed, huge, and it envelops everything. "Let's go get married. Right now."

He shakes his head, and he pulls away from me and gets up.

"Charlie. Please."

He takes the piece of paper out of his back pocket, looks at it without unfolding it. He drops it in the sand.

I don't have to look at the letter—not right this minute—but the way the sun is hitting his shoulders will never happen again. "Charlie!"

He walks away in the sand, and I leave my cut-offs on the beach on top of the draft notice and run after him.

In the water, I wrap my legs around him and kiss his wet skin. "I want to marry you. I want to marry you, no matter what."

He kisses me back, trying to do everything normally, but he doesn't get excited.

"We're getting married." I hug him harder, closer. "And it's because I love you. You can't back out. I said I'd think about it, and I've thought, and…"

His kiss is deeper, but it's not about sex. We are suddenly in a very different place, and it's the place where we're both afraid he will die.

Charlie's house

CANDLELIGHT GLOWED in Mia's window. From his own, Charlie waited, for a glimpse of Francesca.

His phone rang.

I could call her.

Absently, he answered. "Charlie Marcus."

"Hi. Are you flying tomorrow?"

He swished the ice cubes in his glass. "I guess not."

"You gonna pull back on the stick, or should I bail out now?"

Charlie smiled. "Who are you going to work for? Walcotts?"

"Want to find out?"

What is this? "Sure. Work for whoever you want."

There was a click, and Joe was gone, and in the same minute his front door opened. He felt the wind.

Tony saw him and took a long time closing the door.

Charlie searched his albums for Creedence, looked for the spine. There it was.

The kid stayed quiet.

With the album in his hands, Charlie straightened. "Sorry about last night." He'd called Roy Jr. a coward, which he was. He'd told Tony what his father had said in the pilot's lounge. And a few other things. *Oh, come on. If people can't take the truth...*

"I just came to get my stuff. Thanks for letting me stay."

"Where're you going?"

"Alan's."

"You'll be sharing the floor with Fido and Rover."

"I don't want to wear out my welcome here."

"You're not doing that. Don't go to Alan's."

Tony swung his pack to his shoulders and fastened the hip buckle. He was the second person Charlie had seen do that in forty-eight hours. Charlie walked away, to the kitchen, and the front door shut.

The last drops of amber spilled into his glass.

His eyes watered, and he heard an explosion and Joe Burke screaming and sobbing, and he saw other things that were uniquely his. He had to force himself to picture Joe fixing a wheelski on Kahiltna Glacier in fifty knot winds.

He went to the phone and dialed.

"Marcus Aviation, Joe speaking."

"I'll be in tomorrow."

"It's your life."

Charlie probed his cheek with his tongue. "See ya."

In the bathroom, he brushed his teeth and shaved and gargled half a bottle of Scope. Then he went to the door and put on his boots.

FRANCESCA BURNED SOME of Mia's sandalwood incense while she sorted her friend's clothes and tried to forget her conversation with Stormy the night before. At least she'd escaped seeing Peter Sheppard today. Would Tara want this sweater? It was the right size.

The dogs began barking, and the snow squeaked outside. Alan? No, it would be the trooper.

The knock was three rhythmic raps.

Oh.

She opened the door and let him in, and Charlie closed it.

Francesca drank from her bottle of water and resumed shaking out sweaters and turtlenecks, examining them.

He eyed the furniture as though wondering who had sat on it last. Some things never changed.

At her shoulder, he said, "Your eyes are that color."

Whoa.

She swung her head away.

Some things never changed, but this thing broke her heart a little bit. "I guess—" her voice shook "—you're not planning on flying tomorrow."

The futon passed his inspection, and he stretched out and lifted the stick of incense from its holder and watched the smoke curl, then put it back.

Francesca folded the aquamarine Shetland sweater and set it aside. "Do you get away with this often?"

"Let up."

She knew that tone. "You want to get out of my house?"

He sprang to his feet and left, and Francesca put her hand over her face, wishing she just didn't care.

A WOMAN WITH A NEWBORN sat beside her in the waiting room of the Rainbow Clinic. Francesca smiled at the baby with its thatch of blond hair. The mother tucked a blanket around the baby and cast a shy glance at Francesca.

"Pretty baby," said Francesca. "All kinds of hair."

"My mom says it's going to turn carrot red. Mine was like that, too."

Francesca glanced at the mother's hair. It was Titian.

"I guess it's a family trait," murmured the woman.

Francesca glanced toward the office blinds, then the reception counter, seeing neither. Family trait. New grandchild. Yes, carrottops were a Walcott family trait. *Was this the baby Mia caught before she died? The last baby…?* She shifted in the chair. "I'm Francesca Walcott."

The round O of the woman's pink mouth reminded Francesca of Pammie Sue.

"I'm Debbie." She flushed. "Your niece."

Yes. Yes, it was that baby. Mia's last baby. Too soon. *You were too young, Mia.* She spoke through the grief as though it wasn't there. "It's nice to meet you, Debbie. Your mother says you own the deli. What's the baby's name?"

"Kate Elin."

A nurse appeared in the doorway to the clinic. "Francesca?"

"I'll see you, Debbie. It's nice to meet you."

The nurse showed Francesca to an office rather than an examining room. She barely had time to study the familiar midwifery titles on the wall and try to make out a few snapshots taped above one of the two desks before a small brunette came in. Her long hair was drawn back in a ponytail, her cheeks stained pink with rosacea, yet the whites surrounding her hazel eyes were startlingly clear. Even her blue long-sleeved T-shirt and burgundy jeans said "midwife" to Francesca.

Francesca stood up, immediately comfortable. "Hi."

"Hi, I'm Honeydew. Have a seat. That's Mia's desk. I haven't done anything with it. I can have Ellen get you a box, if you want to pack things up."

Francesca sank back into the upholstered swivel chair. "Could I do that and pick the things up later? I don't have a car." A situation that would have to change. Still, there was a simplicity about walking to the Laundromat in the mornings to shower. Funny. After Charlie's sarcastic suggestion, she'd ended up walking to town with Alan and Tony that morning, sharing bagels with them while Tony ran a load of clothes and talked to a girl from New England who worked at the trading post and Alan corralled Mia's new puppy, King. The name had stuck. Alan had borrowed quarters from Francesca for a shower, and Tony had bought the bagels.

"Sure." Honeydew left some judgment unspoken. She regarded Francesca patiently, in the way busy people are patient.

Why the tension? Uneasy, Francesca went forth. "Mia apprenticed with me in Colorado."

"I know." Honeydew's bright look was a nonsmile.

Francesca put away her disappointment. She wasn't sure what she'd wanted—except to feel some connection with Talkeetna's midwife, Mia's partner. It was silly—presumptuous—to think.... Did Honeydew feel that Francesca had stolen business from her by attending the Macleans' birth? She must have heard about it. Francesca had radioed the family twice since the birth, from the trading post, and learned that Susie and the baby were well.

It would be intrusive to ask about the birth Mia had attended the night she'd died. That was client information and confidential. *What did I hope to get from this woman?*

In her heart, she knew. If she'd hit it off with Honeydew, there might have been the possibility of developing a midwifery practice together. With physician backup...

Francesca, you're over fifty years old. What makes you think...

She stopped the thought. "Well, I wanted to meet you. I think I'm going to stay in Talkeetna, and—" *I'm not really saying this* "—naturally, I'm looking toward practicing midwifery."

Honeydew sat back a bit, her steady eyes assessing Francesca, the whole picture before her. "Oh." Then she leaned forward, forearms on her knees, and cupped her chin in her hand. "Let's talk."

TWENTY MINUTES LATER, Honeydew left to see patients, and Francesca approached Mia's desk. Honeydew had suggested she stay till lunch and visit with Dr. Bob. Without Mia, she'd admitted, they were swamped at the clinic. Though Honeydew remained aloof, she was open to the idea of working with Francesca.

But Francesca wondered how good a fit it would be.

Give it a chance. Working with another midwife often fostered a unique mutual respect which turned into a deeper friendship. Like the one Francesca had shared with Ivy when they worked together.

The snapshots over Mia's desk were of dogs—and one of another musher whose white grin Francesca recognized. Though she'd never seen Alan laugh like that, never seen him so happy.

Carefully, she collected every slip of paper and note on the desk, skimming each until a name stopped her.

Joy Morrow. Why was that familiar? Just a name and a number. *I can call.*

Later.

Oh, so much to pack up. Books and birth records. Honeydew might want these. They'd shared clients.

A baby cried in another room, then quieted. She liked the smells and sounds of the clinic, liked the floral wallpaper in the waiting room, the posters on the wall in this office. On Honeydew's side was a beautiful poster about surviving breast cancer, a Chagall print of women dancing in a circle and a poster of a very sexy young man holding a naked newborn.

It would be nice to be in partnership with another midwife.

She released the thought, killed her anticipation. Too recent was her certainty that Stormy would jump on a plane and come to Talkeetna, that she would be with her childhood friend again.

Really, men were so much less complicated.

Some men.

SHE WAS IN THE LOFT of Mia's house—her house now—opening files on Mia's laptop, the one thing she'd brought home from the clinic, when the dogs went crazy. Someone knocked on her door, and low voices and laughter drifted up to her.

"Coming!" She dropped down the ladder and opened the door.

Alan had painted rainbows on his cheeks, and love beads showed through the opening in his parka. Tony wore rouge, lipstick and a skirt that must have come out of someone's ragbag—over climbing tights. He said, "Trick or treat. Just kidding. Want to come to the party with us?"

She thought. Oh. Next Monday was Halloween, and this was Friday. "What party?"

Alan shivered. Were those pajama bottoms? Last-minute costumes. "Can we come in?"

She smiled. "Yes."

Alan tried to see out the dark windows—looking for something? "I forgot to ask. I guess…can I have Mia's mushing gear?"

"Oh. Sure."

"*Shaka!*" His hand formed a symbol she knew well, and she blinked. Then dismissed it.

"Can you come?" asked Tony.

"No costume."

"Throw something together. We did."

Francesca thought through the entire contents of the shack. Funny. In Precipice, she would never have considered going to a Halloween party, even if she'd had a chance to prepare. But with these kids Tara's age knocking on her door and inviting her to come out and… What could she wear? "Give me a few minutes. Go over to Alan's, and I'll meet you there."

Alan gave Tony a thumbs-up, and they shambled out.

IT FELT COMFORTABLE to be alone, alone among all these Alaskans in their costumes, some elaborate, others as hastily assembled as her own. Well, she wasn't exactly alone. Beside her, Alan sipped punch and occasionally raised his voice over the music to ask her questions. Did she know lots of people? Who were her old friends in Talkeetna?

Francesca yelled her answers over the music of the local band, the Moose Nuggets. But she found herself edging away, dancing alone and staring in wonder at her surroundings.

She'd almost left Tony and Alan at the edge of the Village Airstrip when she learned their destination. The building where her father used to keep his planes had been renamed the Hangar and converted into a recreation center or dance hall. This was the site of the party. She'd asked Tony, *Is this building still in the family?*

He'd said, *Live a little.*

As the band finished a song Tara used to play on the car stereo—Nirvana, Francesca thought—her nephew wandered over with the pretty girl from the trading post. He met Alan's eyes. "At least Orville Wright's sober tonight, the asshole."

Almost reflexively, Francesca scanned the crowd.

Two men in turn-of-the-century suits with narrow ties and derby hats at twelve o'clock. Francesca didn't recognize the other Wright brother until she saw the metal protruding from his left sleeve. Joe had shaved his beard. Beside them, a blondish Pippi Longstocking resembled Becka from the airport.

Charlie saw her and strode toward her.

Francesca searched for the exit and fled.

"Francesca?"

She started at the voice.

The scarecrow was more than adequate—in a few ways.

"Peter!" Francesca forgot she had anything to hide from him. In her long black skirt and T-shirt, draped with burlap sacks from Mia's cabinet and a length of black patterned cotton her friend had used to cover the futon, she tapped the ski pole she was using as a cane and cackled. "Ah, my pretty. The young, what do they know?"

Peter threw back his head and laughed. Eyes shining, he said, "You are the most attractive hag I've ever seen." The band had started up, and he turned an ear toward them, then leaned near Francesca. "I think I know this one. Would you like to—"

"Dance with me, Francesca."

It was not a good thing when Alaskan men growled.

Francesca made herself look at him. His name badge, complete with a computer-generated Smithsonian logo, read "Orville." She spoke lower than the first verse of "Magic Carpet Ride." "Go away."

"Right away, you said? Of course." Relieving her of the ski pole, which he tossed under a nearby table, Charlie tucked her hand under his elbow. "Just take my arm, dear, and I'll help you across the street."

The scarecrow had grown tense. Abruptly, he stepped forward. "I believe this dance is mine."

Alaska was part of his job description.

Charlie glanced at her.

Her blood raced. Not from attraction. No. Nothing so simple.

Communication could fix anything. Anything, however dreadful. *False, Francesca. Totally false.* "Will you excuse us, Peter?" She felt like every woman who knows she's being stupid about a man.

Peter drew back inches, a cop again. "Of course."

As she and Charlie reached the dance floor, the band launched into "Freebird," and Francesca noticed Wilbur Wright and Becka and some people she couldn't identify drinking punch and watching her and Charlie. Becka leaned close to Wilbur, saying something, and he nodded thoughtfully.

Charlie's hands found her waist.

"Please don't touch me."

He obliged immediately. "I understand." His expression said they shouldn't risk her having an orgasm in front of all of Talkeetna.

The song was interminable, her costume too warm.

She gazed at the old windows. *I used to look through that window for his plane.*

Charlie slid her shawl from her hair, releasing a cloud of baby powder. "You're hot. Want to go outside?"

She needed to go outside.

She needed to talk to Charlie. No, to hear him. He would fix it, repair her misery.

Alan was where she'd left him, shrugging at a comment from the scarecrow. Francesca saw only a hint of the other day's tension. Peter raised his eyes, and she met them briefly and kept walking, accepting the ski pole Charlie thrust into her hand.

They passed the money table, and cool air rushed over her skin. A man in street clothes had just opened the door, and Francesca waited for him to come through, but he stopped, staring past her, then at her, then past her again. It was Roy Jr.

She stiffened, replaying Tony's coming over earlier that night to ask her to the party.

In the next instant, she saw Mel's grave.

And I'm leaving this building with Charlie.

Young lady, you can decide right this minute if you're going to be part of our family—or run around with him.

Faint, she held the ski pole close to her.

A hand on the small of her back guided her toward the door.

Her brother straightened, and the door swung shut behind him. He didn't move.

Not this. He and Charlie could stand here till Christmas before one of them said, "Excuse me," or the other stepped aside. Like the North-Going Zax and the South-Going Zax.

Francesca stared up, into Roy Jr.'s eyes. "Hello."

He glanced her way, and his arm pushed open the door and held it.

Her gaze on his face, she walked through. Icy air swept over her, and her head rushed with blackness, then cleared.

Behind her, feet scraped on snow. She spun, and a blur of bodies whirled past, a derby hat sailing through the cold and to the snow. Wood splintered and cracked as Charlie hit the building, Roy Jr.'s fist twisting his shirt.

She sagged over Mia's ski pole.

Charlie murmured something, and her brother slammed a fist into his face, and his head hit the hangar, breaking more wood.

Blood gushed on the snow.

Francesca cried out, "Roy Jr.!" and her voice sounded stern, like her father's or her mother's. "That's enough."

Her brother punched Charlie in the stomach, and she turned away because she didn't want to see Charlie hit back and she knew he would and heard it as she left.

The ice was slick, and she used the ski pole. She should tell Alan and Tony she was going. Francesca tuned out the voices, the shouting. She didn't look back.

Mia is dead.

Mia could be Charlie's daughter, and when Francesca had written to tell him that Stormy wanted them to adopt her children, he had written back, "Re: Stormy. The answer is NO."

And Mel.

Her sweet brother had finally answered one of her letters to him in Vietnam, letters sent to the address Stormy had given her. Mel's reply was Francesca's only communication from a family member. He must have known what Charlie had done to the family, to Roy Sr., selling him that mine. And maybe he'd known that Charlie was on his way to Vietnam, too.

But my brother is dead. And only because...

How can I forgive you, Charlie?

Steam from her breath. Wet air.

She stopped, reading the white letters on a gray building. Marcus Aviation. Walking on, she took the first side street and idly reviewed her talk with Dr. Bob and Honeydew earlier that day. Honeydew, had ended the meeting joking with Francesca and Dr. Bob. Smiling when she said, Welcome aboard!

Three days a week, Francesca would work at the Rainbow Clinic.

Tires crushed the snow behind her. The pickup billowed steam as it drew past, Charlie's profile a shadow behind the driver's window. A hundred feet beyond her, it stopped.

She stopped, too.

Then, with the ski pole as a walking staff, she wandered up the snowy road to the passenger side.

Before she reached the truck, the door opened, and Joe Burke stepped out to hold it for her. "Thanks, Joe." He had been Charlie's copilot when a rocket from a ship behind them, ignited by lightning, had blown off his arm. On other days, before and after, Charlie had sat in that seat.

Joe's badge read "Wilbur."

She climbed into the truck. Charlie had collected his hat, but his tie hung askew. He and Joe helped her find the ends of her seat belt, and Joe said, "We haven't been formally introduced."

She gave him her hand. "Francesca Walcott."

He had dimples and the same kind of sometimes-naked eyes as Charlie.

The truck eased forward, and Charlie turned south, then west, and pulled up in front of a small cabin. Joe climbed out, and with his prosthesis tipped his hat to them.

HE DIDN'T EVEN MAKE JOKES about her being a nurse. While she swabbed his face, Charlie stretched out his legs, one between hers, and held the seat of the wooden kitchen chair, one of three chairs for his table. "I'm sorry, Cesca."

"Did you start it?"

His eyes closed, and she wiped around them. Such long, long eyelashes.

"You tell me," he said.

"Roy Jr. is foolish and ignorant." If Charlie could be sorry for fighting— Her own emotions lay heavy and thick as wet sand.

His dark brown irises stared at her. *Is it really okay, Cesca?* He wasn't asking if it was okay about Mel but about certain seconds of time in Vietnam, like a moment's play he believed had killed a friend, like sitting on the right or the left in the aircraft on a given day or flying at a particular altitude when Joe was hit. Like being in the air instead of on the ground, as though his chances were better up there when every single pilot in his company had sooner or later been injured or killed, Charlie included. There had never been a mother in the throes of childbirth whose eyes were like Charlie's. *How often I used to see that look.*

And the next look, too, which was worse, grim and accepting that this was all there was, and which had come more and more often, no matter how many times she'd said, *I understand,* and he'd said, *You don't get it.*

There was nothing she could ever say to Charlie and no mercy he expected, ever. Mercy was each moment of life as it came but never the expectation of another breath in the future, and he lived, in shifting degrees of awareness, with everything he'd done, every mistake he'd ever made.

Every mistake.

She held his head against her, right against her legs, and before he moved away she thought of saying, *You didn't know, you couldn't have known.* Instead, there was Mel, with his mischief.... Mel. Oh, Mel. Charlie should have looked down the road and seen that her father wouldn't be able to keep Mel in school.

She thought of saying, *It can't be undone.* But how useless. Unless to say it of his choices or hers, the choices she'd made knowing everything she knew about Charlie, and his burdens.

She stroked his head. "I'm sorry."

But he was already pulling back and staring, staring away.

They had played this out, too. It was hard to reach him in this place, and she always tried, because she couldn't bear to see him in pain. When they were married...

Come on, Charlie. Snap out of it.

Sometimes he wanted to go back, needed to rethink all kinds of things that she could only imagine, like why wasn't he flying the lead helicopter on the day Dalton went up in flames, and why wasn't...?

She couldn't play games. She couldn't pretend she'd be here for him in any permanent way.

Why not, Francesca? Why do you keep running away? He still loves you.

Because I value my freedom.

You know perfectly well that's a lie. You've been free for thirty years.

No.

That was the lie, the biggest lie of all. She'd never learned to be free. In some ways, she'd been most free since returning to Talkeetna. For hours of each day, she'd forgotten about the mess Tara had gotten herself into. She'd let it go—it was Tara's problem, after all.

And she'd been free, yes, free, in Charlie's arms.

No, you weren't free. Because you won't love him back.

I can't love him back.

He'd gotten up and was examining an album. The Doors.

Okay, he might take that out and listen to it and cry once in a while for the rest of their lives. She knew who cried at war. Everyone. And there'd never been time to grieve and never time to swallow the enormity of people dying, sometimes screaming and screaming, once just gathered up in a burst of light and then sprayed all over, sometimes present one day and gone thereafter, sometimes your fault and no one's fault and someone else's fault.

"Charlie."

"Mm." He set the record on the turntable.

She went to him. "I'd like to take a shower."

He tilted his head back as though considering—or because he didn't want her to see his face. He shoved his hands in the pockets of his trousers; he'd shed the jacket. When he glanced at her, she almost believed the teasing smile.

"You and Alan." His voice scratched. "I should put

a coffee can outside the door to collect your quarters. What are they charging at the Laundromat?''

"With you."

His eyes settled on hers. "Cesca, some nights, not even your devoted ex-husband is in the mood for sex that you will pretend to forget in the morning." His eyelids fell, lashes obscuring his feelings.

Charlie abandoned the stereo and the Doors and stretched out on the couch, wishing she'd leave and wishing she wouldn't. His ribs hurt when he moved. Cesca thought one of them was broken, but he was sure it was only bruised. She wanted to take care of him. Big time. She was pulling over the rocker.

"Charlie. Why are you still...interested in me?"

"It's Alaska, Cesca. The odds are good. You should know that."

"So, I'm just the only available woman in Talkeetna at the moment."

"Not the only one. What are you after, Cesca?"

Nothing she could say to him after the things she'd done. She could only ask, "Where do you expect this to go? What we've been doing? What do you want from me?"

"Just kneel beside this couch, and I'll show you."

She bent over him, to help him up. "Come on, man of my heart. I'll share the shower with you. And then I'll make you an ice pack."

In the shower, he drew her close, hugging her, then kissing her, kissing her although he shook for reasons that probably had nothing to do with her. And everything to do with her.

She touched his face and said, "I won't leave."

He spread shampoo in her hair and didn't answer.

A CRY WOKE HER out of a dead sleep, and she had to wake him. "Charlie. Charlie."

He blinked. "Sorry."

She curled closer to him until he lay on his side and she was at his back, holding him.

How could I leave you, she wondered, *so many nights? So many nights to be alone?*

Answers came easily, as real as the too-alert sleep of a man who'd been to war. Though some of them failed to address her guilt, they quieted it. She could say the reasons she was absolved, pray them, chant them. They were many. Mel, Stormy, twins he'd refused to adopt, alcoholism, abandonment. The failure of their life together.

She was almost asleep, with her head between his shoulder blades, when he said, "Have you spoken with your family?"

"No."

He didn't ask why not, but she wanted to say it, to try to make up for things she could not make up for.

"I made my choice a long time ago." Yet even as she said it she knew, knew, that she would try to make peace with them somehow. But she couldn't have gone to them when she was angry at Charlie. They would've said, *I told you so,* but that wasn't the problem.

They hadn't been to Vietnam, and they would never sit down and listen to what Charlie had to say. They would never hear his stories or care, and she wondered, sometimes, if they would ever have listened to Mel.

A short time later, he rolled onto his back, and the kisses felt as deep and important as those the week Tara was born, the week he left for Vietnam. Kisses became words against her mouth. Even now, he knew things about her changing body that she never had to say, and he was sweet and tender. When she lay over him, he said,

"Cesca, you don't have to be so careful. I swear, nothing's broken."

But minutes later, when his lips were pressed to her shoulder and she couldn't see his face, she suddenly felt everything inside him, as though they'd become one person. She had to be very careful—of his body and his emotions—and she remembered something Tara had said about broken hearts, that a broken heart was one that couldn't love.

When more time had passed, and she still felt the emotion of release and he was still thanking her, still telling her she was a wonderful lover, Francesca said, "We love and fear and hurt and think we're going to die of it, and then we love all over again, and we keep doing it until we do die."

Charlie said nothing.

He was blinking, and his cheeks shone in the faint moonlight. She asked him if he wanted to talk about his dream. Instead, he told her again about messing around on the perimeter, playing Ping-Pong with no table and no rules except not to let the ball touch the ground, and finding the dead VC, and arguing over who would get the AK-47, and wondering if it might be booby-trapped, because it looked almost set up. The guy looked really dead—too dead. He talked about walking away, goading each other to take the weapon and hitting the Ping-Pong ball deliberately to the perimeter, and then that light, so bright, a supernova....

That was what he said, and Francesca knew what he didn't say was that there were defects in him, he wasn't alert enough or thoughtful enough or brave enough. Like the time he could've gotten Miller out, but he was afraid of the fire, how he tried, and Miller was pinned, and finally he ran away, rolling to get the flames off his clothes, and later Joe Burke told him he was never on fire.

"You don't understand."

She said, "I know."

His hands were in her hair and all over her, not for sex but for comfort, not from lust but from soul hunger, when she added, "I can keep living next door. I don't mean to make decisions for you. This only has to be as...serious as you want it. That was presumptuous of me to say what I did, that I won't leave."

He stilled his touch, then resumed. He said nothing.

"You should tell me what you want, Charlie."

But he was still eating her up with his hands and his mouth.

"You used to tell me, Charlie."

"I'm telling you."

She heard. Her picture had been on his body every day. That was what his hands and lips were saying.

There was no one else for him.

And as unforgiving as Charlie saw himself, she saw her own evil and cowardice and human illness, as she had known them when she walked away from his love.

Roy Jr.'s house

"YOU ARE TOO OLD," Pammie Sue Walcott told her husband, "to be getting a black eye once a week."

"I hate his face. I've never hated a man in my life as I hate him. I loved my brother. Loved him. He was my best friend and a good man, and he would've been a doctor. He wanted to be a doctor because of what happened to Mother. He wanted to keep people from suffering."

Pammie Sue thought of Mia. Lately, she seemed to think of her every few minutes. She longed to tell someone. She longed for it every minute—every minute until bill-paying time or tax time. Until she had to tangle with her father-in-law and his fifty-one percent.

Things always looked harsher at night. And tonight, Roy Jr.'s face took the prize.

"How dare he bring my son into his home?" he asked.

"I imagine he knew it would provoke you."

"Tony should've had more sense."

"Tony doesn't know what Charlie Marcus did. He doesn't know anything. And if your father weren't so consumed with pride, we could tell him. Your dad should've gone to the law when it happened, but, no, he didn't want anyone to know that Roy Walcott had been a fool. Well, he's the biggest fool in Talkeetna."

"I won't hear it."

Pammie Sue disliked being yelled at, and she would be yelled at if she said more. But— "Don't hear it, then. That doesn't make it less true."

"I could say some true things about you, Pammie Sue. I could say you're eager for him to die and hoping you'll get your hands on his money."

She walked away, wanting to walk out of the house and never come back. Roy Jr. wasn't completely blind about his parents. But he was the only one allowed to say a word about them. Things like, *My father is a great man. He's got his problems, but he's taught me everything I know about integrity and honor.* Integrity? Was lying to yourself integrity? That was what Roy Walcott had taught his son. Self-deception. And Roy Jr. had learned well.

"My father is a great man, Pammie Sue, maybe too great for you to understand. He taught me everything I know about integrity and honor."

Enough. I've had enough. If she walked out of the house and wandered away in the snow, would he care enough to come looking, or would he just let her go? Often, it would be such a relief to speak the truth, to let the words go where they might. When had she begun to realize that it was a wife's portion to remain silent? When had she begun to die a little under this reality—that whenever she rose up, he shoved her down?

"Maybe there's not a lot of that in your family," said Roy Jr. "But my father taught us the important things in life."

"Let's see. That would be—risk money with people you've never trusted, alienate your children and grand-children and, most of all, attack combat veterans of the Vietnam War at Halloween parties." There was enormous relief in saying this, but she'd have to do some fast talking to make Roy Jr. feel once again that she believed him wonderful. "Oh, honey, I'm sorry. But please don't fight anymore. Look what he did to you."

His reply was profane, and he said it two or three times. "Do you have sympathy for that thief? Are you thinking he's suffered? I'll tell you one thing, Pammie Sue. He doesn't feel an ounce of remorse over the death of my brother. Not even a little bit. He's not what you think."

Pammie Sue considered. It could be true. She didn't know the man. "I'm sorry, Roy Jr. I was way out of line. Your father is a great man. I don't know what got into me. I just can't stand it when you fight."

He opened the refrigerator to pour a glass of milk, which was what he always drank before going to bed.

Tired, Pammie Sue wandered away to the empty living room. Her tears came suddenly, and she went to the bathroom to hide them. She wanted no comfort from Roy Jr. but only to cry. For Mia and for her own marriage and for men, for the whole male sex, because the truth was just too painful for them.

CHAPTER TEN

Hilo, Hawaii
November 21, 1968

"Are you sure this is okay, Cesca?" He's close behind me, so close, holding my hips and leaning over me to kiss my shoulder blades.

"It's okay. Until my water breaks, Sofi says the worst it'll do is start labor."

"And outwit the Army. I heard what Sofi said. I think your midwife is running on three cylinders. Maybe you should go to the hospital." But his voice is rough and half-slurred, and soon we're together, and my eyes water. Why can't he have a deferral now? He has a child and it's inside me.

"This all right? Am I hurting you?"

"No." They take young men. They want men when they're young and strong, and they give them back crippled or dead.

"Shh, Cesca. Shh… Oh, honey, don't."

This is the bed where our baby was made. *Hold me, Charlie.* The baby thumps inside me, and Charlie is very quiet behind me.

Outside, the palm fronds talk to us, whispering. A wet breeze comes in the window. We spent weeks talking about these smells, inhaling them from this bed. But I've smelled them much longer alone. We should never have left Anchorage. "I wonder why Mel didn't go to Canada."

It starts to rain. It clatters on the roof and on the big leaves in the yard. Charlie tucks the sheet around me, around both of us, all three of us. He hugs us, and he doesn't answer.

When I told him yesterday what Stormy said in June, that Mel was drafted, that he's in Vietnam, Charlie went outside and stared at the rain. I brought him Mel's postcard, and he read it and just stood there on the porch.

He feels so good. His body is precious to me, but it belongs to the Army now. "Stormy says the thing about chopper pilots is they get shot down and captured."

Stormy has gone to Honolulu. She wanted to give us time by ourselves before he leaves. She hasn't even seen Charlie. But I'm glad we're alone.

"The thing about chopper pilots is—" he says.

Waiting for him to finish the sentence, I feel his face in my hair and his hand on my skin, over the baby.

More of him presses against me, and his face is warm on the back of my neck, warm in my hair, and he is shaking. "I love you." And he is crying.

It makes me sob. Hurts my stomach like cramps. Will my grief kill the baby? I turn around and hug him. On my back, I take the weight of his head and shoulders on my chest. His hair is so short. I touch his ears and his cheeks and his eyebrows and eyes, his eyelashes all wet. This is what his nose feels like. Oh, your lips, Charlie.

His lips move beneath my fingers, and there is another tear on his cheek. "I'm sorry."

We agreed that he'd get in and get out. Instead, he's promised six years, and everyone knows the Army's promises mean nothing. But they trained him as a military pilot.

"It's okay, Charlie."

We try again to make love, and this time I press my mouth to his forearm, press my cheek to the skin and muscle, and he doesn't stop even when his arm is wet from my eyes. For a moment, my lower spine is tingling, hot and painful. The feeling goes away.

His fingers are gentle. "I love you."

My spine tingles again, the heat creeping up my lower back. I have been practicing yoga. The kundalini energy, the serpent, lies coiled at the base of the spine. The serpent is rising.

My midwife is not running on three cylinders. Charlie wants to see our child before he leaves, and she told him he could get the baby out the same way he got it in.

He's inside me, his hand on me, too. I twist my head to kiss him, and he helps, and he says it again. "I love you."

The sensation in my spine returns. Please, God. "Don't stop. Just keep doing that, Charlie."

Charlie's house
The next morning

"I WANT TO TALK TO HER."

Francesca replaced the phone in the cradle without dialing. "What are you going to say?" Tara didn't need her father growling at her over the phone.

"I'm going to find out about Isaac."

"Charlie, I really think he's okay. His patients love him. He's mature. And Tara never listens to you, anyway."

"This isn't for her. It's for me."

"Oh." Francesca dialed, and Tara answered. She sounded cheerful, the baby was fine, where was Dad? "He's right here."

Francesca made some coffee and tried not to listen. But Charlie's style was hard to ignore.

"Your mother is fine. Tell me about Isaac."

Go easy, Charlie. Honestly.

She watched him hang up a few minutes later and stare at the phone, as though by doing so he could visualize his daughter's boyfriend. It was ironic, in light of that summer, that summer when Tara was thirteen and he'd handed her over to his father on what was supposed to be his own visitation. And Tara hadn't called Francesca. She'd protected Charlie and lied for him and made excuses for him the way Francesca herself sometimes had, often had. And Francesca had said, *I was right. I was right to leave.*

When she'd called him, she'd asked, "Do you really know when you've done wrong, Charlie? Do you really know when you've let people down? Do you know that he used her to help con some people out of fifty thousand dollars?"

"Did he, now? I hope Tara got her share."

I was right. I was right to leave.

But now she was in his house, and Tara was thirty, and Charlie was behaving as a father ought to, and Francesca knew that sometimes he said things out of pride, that he knew he'd messed up but wouldn't admit it. Tara must have forgiven him; she'd never turned down plane tickets, trips to see him, trips to the Bahamas or Rwanda or wherever they felt like g⟨...⟩ about what was happening no⟨...⟩

Abruptly, Francesca let it go. ⟨...⟩ coffee, Charlie?''

He joined her and poured his own.

She had been envious of Tara, flying a⟨...⟩ ⟨...⟩tic places.

He took me to Hawaii. The most exotic place she'd ever known. She'd loved Hawaii, and she'd loved him, and the Army had stolen him from her and given him back, the worse for wear. Or maybe… She set down her cup. ''Do you think things would have been different if I'd agreed to come back to Alaska with you? When you came home?''

He drank his coffee and rubbed his jaw, as though he wasn't sure whether or not he'd shaved. She wasn't going to get an answer.

Well, they had other things to discuss. ''I guess maybe I should leave my things at Mia's.''

''Cesca.'' He shut his eyes momentarily. ''Go to Mia's, have her phone disconnected, get your things and come back here. Move the furniture, hang things on the wall, put your clothes in my closet, dry your underwear in the bathroom. And when you feel moody, you can walk over to Mia's, fire up her stove and lie around on her bed until you get cold and lonely.''

Francesca hugged him, an impulse hug, her head against his.

He returned the embrace. ''Just don't get sentimental. And by the way, you still haven't done what she told you to.''

''What's that?'' It was no surprise she'd forgotten something.

''Mushing. You should ask Alan to take you.''

a sled behind pulling dogs. "Have you ever
__ that?"

"For one year. Someone told me dogs were the best
cure for—" he looked rueful "—disappointment in
love."

"Are they?"

He snorted. "Are you kidding?" And he picked up his
keys and went to get his coat.

FRANCESCA SAW HER at the trading post two days later,
after her own first morning's work at the Rainbow Clinic.
It wasn't so long since they'd seen each other, and
Stormy had kept her graying blond ponytail. Beside the
produce, the cold bins of cabbages and carrots and lettuce, they stopped, and Stormy's shoulders sagged, the
lines in her face deep, her eyes red and watery.

"I owe you an apology, Francesca. I'm sorry, yeah?"

That very Hawaiian habit, ending sentences with the
word "yeah," like a question. A thought stunned Francesca, a thought far more shocking than Stormy's presence in Talkeetna.

"Stormy—" Francesca grasped her arm. *But what if
I'm wrong? It has to be a coincidence.* She scrutinized
her friend's turquoise eyes. *I just can't tell. I want it to
be, but I just don't know.* Stupidly, she said, "I'm sorry,
too."

Stormy nodded. She had tofu and soy milk and rice in
her basket, and Francesca asked, "Where are you staying?"

"At Pammie Sue's." Shaking her head, she picked
over the broccoli without intent. "Roy Jr. doesn't look
so good. Boy, they never got over you and Charlie, did
they?"

Francesca was glad Stormy didn't know there was more to it.

You and Charlie.

What about you and Charlie, Stormy? Did you have his babies?

She trembled. Tony's friend, the girl he liked, wiped down the checkout counter, and some people she didn't know picked over yogurt in the dairy case. She told Stormy, "I'd like to talk," and she was ashamed that she wasn't pouring out her sorrow, saying she'd loved Mia. Had she lost her capacity for empathy, for compassion?

Stormy asked, "Where are you staying?"

Her throat tightened. "I'm with Charlie." Somehow, "living" was left out. "At his place. It's next door to your…daughter's."

"I haven't been there. I got in last night on the red-eye and talked to the trooper and a little to Pammie Sue. I was going to find you. I feel bad about—the phone."

"So do I. Let's forget it." She didn't want to ask Stormy to Charlie's, but that was the obvious place to talk. Or— "Did Peter tell you…?"

"That you're the heir? I heard." Stormy's eyes fastened on something past Francesca, near the floor. "I'm not sure yet that I want to know about her. Or maybe I'm sure, but I'm not ready. It's such a waste, and my sister is being kind, saying she knows how she'd feel if she lost one of hers, but it's not the same and she *doesn't* know. Yeah?"

And she told you that you'd be a lousy mother. How can you stay in her house, Stormy?

"I'm going to shop later," Francesca decided.

Stormy put her things back, leaving tofu among the cabbage heads, and they left together. The sky hung in oppressive gray, and Stormy asked, ''Have you seen the lights yet?''

''No. It's been snowing a lot.''

They didn't move from the street. Stormy had been back to visit from time to time; Talkeetna probably wasn't such a shock to her. But Francesca didn't want to talk about any of these things. No one else was near. *I have a right to know.* But she couldn't quite say it. Not even, *It would be decent of you to tell me.*

All she could do was ask, ''Were the twins Charlie's?''

No change of expression.

Francesca's heart seemed to implode. *It's true, and she's just realizing that I know, or maybe she's believed it all along.*

Stormy hesitated—first in some kind of refusal and then, perhaps, in uncertainty. ''No.'' She drew out the word. Her gaze was square. ''Franny, that happened a hell of a long time ago. It was a one-night stand, and he was on the rebound, and you should forget it. I had, until you mentioned it.''

How can I forget it? You knew I loved him!

But there was the rub. Stormy *hadn't* known. Charlie hadn't known. Francesca hadn't known. She'd known only that her mother was dead and her father no longer wanted her. Not unconditionally, as parents should love their children, and even at nineteen she'd known that it was no way to treat your child, your own flesh and blood. The wound had been so painful, to hear the father she needed, suddenly her only parent, tell her that she could be part of his family—her family—only if she renounced Charlie Marcus.

For Francesca, Charlie was never the point. How could her father behave that way over any man? And what had

Charlie done but compete with him in business? It was only later that—

Another realization. Clarity. *He did that for me.* The gold mine, the con. Because he'd been standing there when her father said those things. Charlie had heard.

Roy Walcott had done wrong, and the world became less right for Francesca that day, and when he'd returned her letters and hung up the phone when he heard her voice, all kinds of compromises became possible, because he had compromised what a parent should be.

Stormy stuffed her hands in the pockets of a teal coat Francesca had seen on Pammie Sue and peered across the street at a house where they used to play before the family moved.

"I'm so sorry," Francesca said, "about Mia." She had to blink, and she had no right to cry, to feel as she did, when Stormy was so stoic. "I want to tell you about her when you want to hear. If you like—it might be too much—but you could stay at her place. Her dogs are still there. Alan—" *Slow down, Francesca.* "Her friend Alan—they're his now, and he comes over to feed them."

Stormy nodded. "Let's…. Can I call you?"

"Sure. We're in the book." Where did that "we" come from? It felt inserted, unnatural, but had sounded as cool as her lies to Peter Sheppard.

"Her parents took her ashes," said Stormy. "I guess I'm glad. She was theirs."

But why had she left them? Francesca, too, knew about the parents. She hadn't wanted to meet them. She returned to the moment.

Tentatively, Stormy reached out.

They embraced, and Francesca thought that meaningless one-night stand had been a long time ago and wished it would never nick her like a pin and knew it would, knew that from time to time it would.

She needed to tell Charlie, to tell him Mia wasn't his. Instead of finishing her shopping, she headed for the airport to find him.

Why not walk along the Village Airstrip? It was the same distance, and...

He won't be home.

But what if he was?

She hurried, her boots firm on the snow. Passing Charlie's unused frame hangar, full of memories of love, she buttoned up her feelings about the Halloween party. She avoided looking toward the Hangar. What had happened there was some desecration of her past, of things she'd still managed to hold dear. Helping her father refuel and talking to his passengers and always, always, looking for Charlie. She wished the party had never happened, wished she'd never gone but wished even more that... She supposed she wished her father's old hangar was simply sitting empty.

There was the cabin. She crossed the strip, thinking how she'd avoided the place when she'd gone to see Mia's plane, how she'd avoided it all along. A green Jeep sat in the drive. The garden fence was maintained. She saw his snowmobile. He must be there.

Yes, that old lamp with the curved white glass shade burned within the window, beyond the curtains gathered like a girl's ponytails.

I'm scared.

What if he shut the door, just as he'd returned her letters and hung up the phone? He'd pretty much ignored her at the Mountain Deli.

Well, she wasn't nineteen anymore. She wasn't nineteen with her mother dead only a day.

He'd shoveled his walk, and she refused to tread quietly or any way but directly, and she didn't use the knocker but her fist. Then it was too late, and she knew an almost unbearable sadness because of the grain of the wood and the sight of the door handle and the old square knocker that was functional and nothing special. Her mother was not inside.

How could you tell me to leave?

The door clicked, and he opened it. And drew back.

She'd planned nothing. "Hello, Dad."

Was he choosing, considering whether or not to admit her after thirty years? In the end, he just stood there.

"I'd like to talk." Just what she'd told Stormy. So much pain—a past full of it.

He stepped aside, and she came in, and the house didn't smell quite the same, and he had bought other furniture, but the couch had been reupholstered, and the wooden things were unchanged. Her mother was not there.

Her mother would never be there again.

Francesca escaped into practicality. Did he clean the place himself or have someone else come in? *I used to do it all.*

She mustn't be angry now. She mustn't feel rage, and she did. He had shut the door, but he didn't invite her to sit and didn't offer her anything to eat or drink.

"I've come back to Talkeetna to live."

Her father was a very old man, but he walked with grace, unstooped, as he crossed to a recliner and sat down and gestured that she could sit where she liked. She chose the far end of the sofa. Maybe the way was to make small talk, to mention the new great-grandchild and not mention Roy Jr.'s and Charlie's fistfight.

"I don't know why," he remarked, "you think I would have anything to say to you."

"Well, you must at least have some criticism up your sleeve, Dad." Francesca bit her tongue. Anger and sadness had frayed her nerves. *Loss—that's over.* She'd lost him the day after she lost her mother.

His eyebrows rose slightly, and he looked the old gentleman but kept silent.

"You know—" words were coming, and not the words she wanted "—at first I thought it might make a difference to you whether Charlie and I were on speaking terms or not. But it wouldn't matter."

"It would not."

She couldn't bear the silence. "I want a relationship with my family, Dad. I've done nothing to deserve this…exile."

He peered out the window, although there wasn't anything to see. "I assume you lived on the money he took with him from Alaska."

"Dad, I just found out about that, and you know what?"

He waited for her to speak.

"My husband went to war, and he went back for a second tour and a third—" *And I resented it.* But he'd gone because he couldn't stay home when other men were dying—or maybe just couldn't stay home, though she'd only discovered that later. She'd resented it, even knowing that Charlie was trying to pay, to pay for Mel, for others. How to say what she knew, what Charlie hadn't had the right words to explain but she'd understood, that he'd just killed and killed and killed and— *I wasn't myself, Francesca. Or maybe I've become that. It's evil.* "He was angry, and he conned you, and he never intended for Mel to go to Vietnam and die."

Her father's face could still change color. "If that's the case, he's never had the nerve to say so. The best that coward could do was offer to buy back the mine—and then it paid out for him, wouldn't you know? You know what courage is? It's the ability to look someone in the eye and say that you did wrong, and Charlie Marcus walked and talked like a coward from when we first caught the smell of him. Sneaking around with a high school girl. He never knocked on this door, did he?"

Francesca's body grew overwarm, and she blushed, for herself and for Charlie. *He's not being fair. I don't have to defend myself or Charlie.*

We were teenagers.

He had a rotten father.

"Just what would you have done if he *had* knocked on the door?"

"Ha!" He barked. Then his face stilled. "I like to think that if he'd come to this door and said, 'Mr. Walcott, I care for your daughter but realize she is too young for me. However, I want you to know my feelings,' I like to think if he'd said something like that, I would have answered him civilly with as little prejudice as possible toward the fact that he had stolen business from me—and lied to do it."

Business. "I apologize for my own lapse of faith in your finer qualities." She had not meant to sound sarcastic. "Charlie was appropriate with me."

"We will never agree on this subject."

"I—" How childish. She was about to burst out with the same cry she would've cried if she'd ever had the courage when she was eighteen, when her father broke all her forty-fives. But she'd never said it then, and she didn't want to say it now, couldn't bring herself to say it out loud. But as she realized she was stopping herself from saying it, as she had before, it became important to say. "I love Charlie very much. We have a daughter—" *Whom you ignored. How could you be unkind to Tara? It's like kicking a puppy.* "How could you return her baby pictures?"

"He killed your brother."

"Mel stepped on a booby trap set by the Vietcong. He wouldn't have blamed Charlie. He wrote to me, Dad. He said to kiss the baby. He wasn't holding grudges." The cruelty came casually. "Surely you acknowledge that you invested money you couldn't afford to lose."

Immediately, she was appalled yet relieved to have said it. It was like fighting with Charlie, this saying of things that shouldn't be said, and yet she *had* said one of those things, and to an eighty-year-old man.

But her father was remote and self-contained. Her words didn't hurt him, and she knew that what she'd said was nothing he hadn't lived with for thirty years.

"I have reviewed my part in it." He sounded tired. "I was a fool. Yours—was malicious."

Everything around her seemed still, suspended.

"He's sorry."

Her father cocked his eyebrows again, as though at an interesting fact he'd never heard before.

She fell silent.

"Now, I see the man every day, and I've seen no sign of remorse."

"Well, I sleep with him at night, and I have." Oh, heavens. She shut her eyes, then opened them.

He sat back with a heavy breath.

"Dad, I want to be on speaking terms with you. And with Roy Jr. and Pammie Sue and Tony and Debbie and Kate Elin and Gilbert and Anne—yes, I know their children's names, but not because anyone in this family told me. I want you to know my daughter. How could you be cruel to her? What did you do when she came here? Tara hasn't got a mean bone in her body! How could you turn your back on my child and pretend she didn't exist?" Picturing Tara, Francesca half whispered, "She's beautiful." Inside and out. "What is wrong that you couldn't take pride in this vibrant young woman who is your grandchild?"

He lifted his chin slightly.

Why was she wasting her breath? *Have I just forgotten?* She sighed. "I didn't come here hoping we could be close. Just civil. You always loved Mel best and me least, and I've always told myself that Mom loved me best. Other girls hated their mothers. I never felt that way, never wanted to be different from her." Francesca rose and wished she'd stayed seated, because there would be no reason to come back.

"You left some things in your room."

Her breath felt odd. He meant that she'd left things and they were still there. Francesca looked toward the hall and remembered how very small her room was—but it had been her own, and the boys had shared. "I'd like to see them."

"Take it all." He lifted an aviation magazine from the coffee table, dismissing her.

CHARLIE PLUCKED *Meet the Beatles!* from the box on the kitchen table. He turned it over, then glanced in the box. "I thought he broke these."

"Only the forty-fives." She had brought a box of things, just a few things, from her old room. She'd carried them down a side street, not Main, to Charlie's house. *Our house.* Everything else she'd neatly packed into boxes or garbage sacks to be given away or thrown out, and her father really had scarcely looked up from his magazine.

Clasping the edge of the dusty box, she wondered if Tara would want these few old clothes, just for fun. Some were in style again with Tara's generation. Tara's, Tony's, *Mia's*... Suddenly she remembered how she'd arrived at the Village Airstrip, what had happened earlier. She told Charlie about Stormy.

He walked to the refrigerator and opened it. "I used a condom. I guess I thought it could have..."

Was he sorry Mia wasn't his child? Mia and—

"Charlie. Charlie, do you know where Alan's from?"

He straightened up, a pop in his hand. After a moment, he shook his head.

"He's from Hawaii. I'm sure of it. The other night, before the Halloween party..." It was going to sound stupid to Charlie.

"Could be. I'm getting your drift." From the front window he could see Alan's house. "He's not home. Do you think Trooper Sheppard's hit on this notion?"

Francesca refolded a peasant blouse she'd loved. "Probably. He's pretty sharp. Not as smart as you, Charlie. Don't look that way. But Alan wouldn't have been with her when she died. And if he was—maybe that's best. He loved her."

Charlie lifted a Rolling Stones album from the box. Francesca had borrowed it from Mel and never returned it. "Stormy say who the father is?"

She shrugged, deliberately not caring, not wanting to know. "She might call. She's staying with them. Charlie, I think Dad wants an apology."

His head shot up. "For what?"

She missed the clue, a certain intensity in his eyes.

"Well, to start with, he was offended by our… 'Sneaking around' was the way he put it."

His look softened, and he studied the record albums. He set them down and walked away, to stoke the fire in the woodstove.

"And—the mine."

He stiffened. "Well, that's not going to happen."

"Would it kill you, Charlie?"

"Yes." His eyes snapped at her.

She understood. And would never understand.

SHE WAS EXHAUSTED, too exhausted to worry about whether or not he made love to her or if living with him was permanent or if it even mattered. She loved down pillows and the scent of cedar and the fact that he hugged her and kissed her, and she could fall asleep beside him while he listened to the weather.

The world drifted heavy.

"I never liked sneaking around. That was wrong."

Francesca rolled over and hugged his waist, careful of his bruised ribs. "I love you." The easy words seemed to strangle her. Would they always sound false?

Now he'll hate me for having said that. I don't think he wanted me to say it ever again.

He didn't answer or move, and she wished he would respond to her touch, look for a kiss.

After humiliating seconds, she withdrew and lay still, awkward with tension, no longer sleepy.

She would not apologize or try to say something else to make it right.

I refuse to beg.

The night was quiet. He got up suddenly, but it was to check his alarm. Then he lay against her, kissing her throat. "Tell me how much you want me, Francesca. Say, 'Please, Charlie. Please.'"

She could hardly laugh, just hang on, touch him. It was okay.

Roy Walcott

She has left things orderly. She was always like that, her mother's daughter.

She is right, in her way, that I should accept her and Tara. But I could never see her daughter without remembering that she is also his. I despise that cheap swindler, despise the weakness of him. How can I pretend to respect him or have anything to say to him? He was never decent.

And there is Mel.

He killed Mel. That it was unintentional, born of other evil, does not matter. And the fact of the matter is, he was in the air and Mel was infantry, Mel never had a chance. If he'd come home, he might have been sick; so many of them were sick, not right again, like Hugh Griffin after being in the South Pacific in the Second World War. Or like that Joe Burke, who lost his arm.

Mel could have stayed in medical school, and he could've become a doctor.

I will never stop missing my son.

And I will never have anything to say to Charlie Marcus.

CHAPTER ELEVEN

Honolulu, Hawaii R & R
March 6, 1969

I didn't know. I just didn't know. I had to tell him about Mel, and I never knew this would happen. Charlie seemed so happy to see me and Tara. He has a list of sundries he's promised to take back to friends. I keep from him the things people say about the war. The stupid things they say to me. Oh, you poor thing. Did he get drafted? At least he's a pilot.

Charlie would just lose it if he knew.

But I didn't expect this.

I should never have brought up Mel, but how could I not? My brother is dead.

And what Charlie is saying now has nothing to do with Mel. In a few days, I've heard Charlie confident, angry, swaggering, offhand—and sometimes just a little edgy and impatient. I don't think he really meant to tell me that the gunships deal with friendly fire by returning it, but after he told me, he just looked at me, as though daring him to say anything was wrong with that. Now, he's saying…

These confessions are private, the most private. I don't want him to have to live with his mistakes. They aren't his. They're just things that happened. I hold him, but suddenly he gets up to stand at the window and goes out on the hotel balcony to light a cigarette. Tara's asleep beside me on the bed. On the beach, we always sit in the shade now. She's so little, and I can tell she'll have Charlie's olive skin.

When he comes back inside, he says, "What do you want to do?" But his eyes dismiss everything in the room, including me and Tara. He is no longer with us.

"Tara's sleeping," I point out. *Make love to me.*

He comes over, and I kiss his stomach.

Finally returning to me—with his mind, I mean—he touches my hair, and I open his fly.

B Street

"ALAN!"

He was harnessing several of Mia's dogs, and Francesca hurried toward him in the cold, thinking about ice and broken bones and osteoporosis. She walked, the years weighing on her in a sack.

He looked up, and she searched for Stormy in his face and found someone else.

Oh.

My imagination.

But what if it was true? How could he do that?

She must be imagining it.

Poor Pammie Sue.

Francesca was wild with thoughts of how it might have happened and how strange for Stormy to be staying there. How could she? How could he?

Charlie had. Stormy had.

"I need to talk to you. And—and I want to go for a

ride. On the sled. Please. If you'll take me. Mia said I should find out what it's like.''

The dogs barked, tearing each other up. One became a little excited and two more excited and three ecstatic and four chaotic, and they all wanted so badly to leave that the line and hook holding the sled to a metal post seemed much too frail. What if they broke loose?

Alan bent to rearrange a pack and some canvas bags on the sled, and he smiled at the dogs. ''They're fast, yeah?''

She remembered the phone call with Stormy and tried to be calm, tried not to leap to conclusions. ''Alan, did you know Mia has a twin?''

He straightened.

''Will you please talk to me?'' she asked.

''Does everyone know?''

''Alan, your birth mother is here. In Talkeetna.''

He blanched, and she saw him swallow. Snowflakes came. ''They're bending the pole,'' he said. ''The dogs. ''Climb on if you want to go.''

She did, settling on the lumpy food bags and all the load of the sled.

''Hold on. Watch your hands. All set?''

''They won't crash?''

''The sled's heavier now. We're gone.'' He released the hook, and did not have to speak to the dogs.

Her breath left her with the lurch forward, and she was thrown back while the wind cut into her and the dogs' tails waved. Their bliss was bodies moving up and down, running, running. The feel of ice under the runners, of a bump in the road, of needing to hang on at the corners, of fear and excitement—these were not the source of pleasure. It was the dogs and their breath and the sound of them and their fur blowing, their complete sincerity.

Francesca's eyes teared, and she saw nothing but dogs and only noticed buildings passing and the school and then a track into the woods.

The joy of the dogs was everything, until it occurred to her that Mia had not been alone when she died.

JOE BURKE HANDED CHARLIE an e-mail he'd printed. "They want someone who knows the West Rib."

Charlie read the e-mail. "It sounds like *she* wants someone."

"We should find them a guide."

"They need to find their own guide." Charlie helped mountaineers any way he could with his plane, but he would not contribute to their choices—except the choice to fly with him. Flying with Marcus Aviation was in everyone's best interest.

The door of the office opened.

Peter Sheppard came in.

"Well, Trooper Sheppard. Where can we fly you today?"

"Mr. Marcus, I'd hoped to visit with you some. Is there a private area where we can talk?"

Joe leaped out of his chair. "I've got work to do." The door swung shut behind him.

Charlie invited the trooper behind the counter and gestured to a chair.

Sheppard surveyed the office, examining the glacier photos on the wall. "Mr. Marcus—"

"Charlie."

"Thank you. And I'm Peter. Charlie, when I'm somewhere on a murder investigation and a fistfight breaks out involving two pilots, and it was another pilot who died... You see my feelings. There are no coincidences in police work. What can you tell me?"

Charlie stuffed his hands in the pockets of his flight jacket. Did Cesca like blue-eyed men? The guy was tall. *No, Marcus, she likes you.*

He told Sheppard about the gold mine and Mel Walcott's leaving medical school and being drafted. "But the gold was there. I bought the mineral rights back, and the gold was there. Nonetheless, the family holds me responsible for everything that happened."

"But you gave the mineral rights to Mia Kammerlander."

Charlie blinked. Not even Cesca had really figured that out, though it was true. When he'd struck that other vein, the rich vein—Mia could use the money, he figured. Guilt or duty hadn't played into it.

Well, Sheppard spoke as though he knew. Charlie decided Sheppard knew a lot. "I thought she might be my daughter."

"And you felt guilt over Mel Walcott's death."

Charlie went to the coffeepot, wondering if Joe had reused the grounds again. It was an ongoing debate: thrift vs. potability. "Coffee, Trooper?"

"No, thank you."

Charlie poured himself a cup.

"We were discussing your feelings of guilt over Mel Walcott's death."

"We were?"

"It would have been natural after you tried to swindle Roy Walcott."

Carefully phrased, Charlie thought, to get a rise out of him. "Tony Walcott was staying at my house recently. Apparently, he'd been talking to my wife, and it was too much for his family. I think that may have been why Roy Jr. threw the first punch. And the second. And the third."

Charlie still felt bad about fighting in front of Francesca, but Roy Jr. would have killed him.

"The incident that occurred between your ex-wife and her family in 1967 was the reason you tried to sell Roy Walcott the rights to a mine you believed was worthless."

Charlie changed the subject. "Back to the fistfight—there are all kinds of tensions between air-taxi pilots. You've been around Talkeetna. Now, I flew choppers on three tours in Nam, flew planes and choppers in Alaska before that. The competition around here doesn't have much to offer in comparison."

Sheppard tipped his head. "I can imagine the feelings on both sides. The Walcotts' over losing a son in a war we inevitably lost—in their view, he was killed because you'd conned them into buying a worthless mine. And I can imagine your feelings…trying to live down your guilt by fighting in that same war."

Charlie stared at him. Drank coffee. *He's a state trooper, Charlie.*

What did Cesca see in the guy?

"We didn't lose a war. We lost men." *We lost limbs. We lost minds.*

Sheppard stilled. Suddenly, he leaned forward with his elbows on his knees. "I'm sorry. This case is getting to me. I wasn't thinking."

Some act. Humoring a crazy veteran. Sorry didn't cut it. And "wasn't thinking" was a lie.

A second later, the trooper clasped his hands behind his head and leaned back in Joe's chair. Outside, snow fell. "Who do you think was with Mia when she died?"

Charlie considered. Alan. Alan was obviously with her when she died. But that didn't make it murder, and it didn't mean shit. Alan was harmless, and Peter Sheppard was the kind of guy he hated. "That's your job, Trooper. Mine's flying planes. And I have some passengers coming in at—" He checked the clock. "They'll be here any minute."

"So, you didn't try to con Roy Walcott into buying the mineral rights to a mine you believed was worthless?"

"Trooper, am I under arrest for something?"

"No."

Charlie rested his elbows on the counter and perused a schedule he'd already memorized, then focused on the coming flight to Gold Creek.

Sheppard asked, "Why did you go to the Village Airstrip the night Mia disappeared?"

Charlie knew something else about Sheppard. He guessed and stated his guesses as facts. "I didn't. I was playing basketball."

"After the game."

"I stopped here and then I went home. You know, Trooper, I'm not stupid enough to lie to you. You're barking up the wrong tree."

"Tell me, Charlie. What's the right tree?"

"Can't help you." But maybe Sheppard could help him, satisfy his curiosity. "I don't suppose you know who Mia's father is."

"I don't."

"But Stormy told you it's not me."

"That question didn't come up."

Thanks, Stormy.

Charlie forgot for a fraction of an instant what Sheppard had said about the war. He imagined people who could have slept with Stormy. It probably wasn't even anyone from Talkeetna—but, if not, why had Alan and Mia come here? Stormy didn't live here anymore. His favorite choice was Francesca's father, but he couldn't really see it. What about Roy Jr.? Or Mel? The perfect son fathering a child out of wedlock. In which case... "You know, Roy Jr. would have plenty of reasons for not wanting any of Mel's heirs around."

Alan.

What if someone had, say, forced Mia's snowmobile into the tree?

Alan could take care of himself.

No, Charlie. Alan cannot take care of himself. The kid is helpless. Strange how he liked Alan better thinking of him as Mia's twin.

Oh, come on, this was Sheppard's job.

Sheppard seemed to be pondering what he'd said.

"What are you doing here, anyway? Talking to me?"

"You and Mia were good friends. Your ex-wife is Mia's heir. And you brought her back to Talkeetna."

"Trooper, I'm not hurting for money. But you know what? I bet Roy Jr. wants control of Roy Walcott Air Service worse than anything in the world."

"I have spoken at length with Roy Jr."

Through the plate glass window, Charlie recognized the car of his passenger, an author who divided his time between Gold Creek and Seattle. "Would you mind scooting along—or else booking a flight? This looks bad for business."

"ALAN! How long are we going for?"

"I'll take you home when you're cold, unless you want to run behind the sled!" He had to bend toward her to say this.

"Could we go home and talk? About Mia?"

"Let me finish the loop, yeah? It's better for the dogs."

Two hours later, Francesca sipped hot chocolate in Alan's shack. Sweat stained the underarms of his long-sleeved T-shirt.

"You're Mia's twin," she repeated. "Aren't you?"

"The trooper already guessed. I told him not to tell anyone."

"Why didn't you or Mia tell anyone?"

"We were searching for our birth parents. You must have given your name when we were adopted or something, because you were a contact person in the records, Mia said, as our mom's friend. Mia was working with a lady named Joy Morrow, who helped her find me, yeah?"

"Why did Mia leave her adoptive parents?"

Alan studied the ceiling. "She's my best friend." Tears ran from the corners of his eyes. "She's dead, and she's still my best friend. She told me secrets. She doesn't want everyone to know."

"It's okay." The mug warmed Francesca's fingers. "That's fine."

"She thought Charlie was our father because he left Talkeetna suddenly.... The timing, yeah? But she wasn't sure. It's like—if people don't want you, why bother?"

"Charlie is not your father." Francesca said this because she heard the resentment in Alan's voice. In the same moment, she saw Charlie's letter. *The answer is NO.*

But she had chosen, chosen him again. And choosing meant ceasing to keep score, ceasing to decide that he wasn't a good enough man.

"What are your parents like, Alan?"

"Missionaries, same as Mia's. But better than hers. I like Hawaii, but dogs... Dogs are the best. I talk to my parents."

"Did you tell them you found your sister?"

"No. Because Mia's secretive. She didn't want anyone to tell her parents where she was."

Time to move forward. "Alan, do you want to meet your birth mother, if she's agreeable?"

He nodded, looking young and scared.

"Why don't I go home and call her?" Alan didn't have a phone, and it would be better to talk to Stormy without him listening, anyway.

"THIS IS FRANCESCA CALLING. Is Stormy there?"

"No. Actually, she's not," said Pammie Sue. "Shall I have her call you?"

"Thank you. Please tell her it's important." Francesca gave Charlie's number, and Pammie Sue hung up without saying goodbye.

Francesca worked at the clinic that afternoon, seeing pregnant clients along with Honeydew. The money would be minimal, but with Mia's assets it was no concern. What troubled her was how Alan must feel at not being Mia's heir—and the fact that she hadn't chosen Alan. Why?

At five-thirty, Francesca found Charlie in the waiting room.

"Hey, baby, want to go grocery shopping?"

He was so handsome. It was so good to hug him there where she hadn't expected him, to be kissed. He held the door for her, and his truck was outside with the John Lennon bumper sticker on the back, with a quote from "Imagine."

Charlie drove to Wasilla, and it took ten minutes for her to fill him in on the day's events.

"I was riding along on the sled, and I thought, 'What

if he was with Mia when she died?' And, Charlie, why didn't Mia just make him her heir?''

"Because he's a moocher and a spendthrift, and she was a tightwad. She had a lot of ideas about guiding Alan into someone he'll never be. He gets some money from his folks. She didn't approve of that.''

"But she never talked to you about *her* folks?''

Charlie shook his head.

"They were in Anchorage, and we missed the chance to meet them. I think they abused her. Alan knows, whatever it was. Who do you think was with her when she died?''

"Alan. But I don't think for a minute he killed her, and you saw the autopsy report, and we both saw her.''

Mia could not have been saved.

In Wasilla, he took her to dinner at a fine restaurant that served natural foods and wild game. Their server wore a long white gown, and Charlie explained, "They're some religious order. The menu's arranged from the most pure—vegetarian—to the least, supposedly. But the food's good.'' Before they'd selected, he said, "I miss dancing with you.''

Their dance Halloween night, Francesca reflected, had been too brief—and too tense. "Is there somewhere to go? There's always your place,'' she added. "We can dance when we get home.'' Your place. Home. Which was it? *It doesn't matter. Home is where he is.*

After dinner, they worked their way up and down the supermarket aisles, filling a cart. People recognized Charlie and nodded or said hi or asked how things were going.

In the parking lot, Francesca slipped. One second, she was upright, the next she'd gone down, hard, on the ice. Tears of anger, anger at falling, sprang to her eyes, while her brain rocked inside her head. If he makes a joke now...

"You okay?"

"Yes." But she clung to him getting up, held his arm as he pushed the cart to the car. *I feel old, Charlie.*

But he was there.

How strange and wonderful that he was there.

THERE WAS NO MESSAGE from Stormy. "I wonder if Pammie Sue even told her that I called." Francesca thumbed through the directory to find her brother's number again. She dialed, and he answered. Francesca took a breath before speaking. "Roy Jr., this is Francesca calling. Is—"

The phone clattered down, disconnecting the call.

Searching through albums, Charlie didn't look up as she replaced the receiver.

"He didn't even wait to hear what I had to say. How am I supposed to get in touch with Stormy? This is important to Alan, and it's not ethical to reveal the identity of one to the other without permission." She realized she'd already said too much to Alan. "Charlie, I'm going over there to see him."

He stood to get his coat and boots. "So much for our date."

TONY AND ALAN AND THE GIRL from the trading post sat in the little shack by candlelight, surrounded by dogs.

Tony said, "I hear they need a guide for that expedition."

Charlie shrugged. "I'm just the pilot."

"What expedition?" asked Francesca.

"November ascent of the West Rib." Tony tossed hair

off his face. "I could do that. Wouldn't look too bad on my résumé."

"It would look like you're an idiot," Charlie answered.

If Tony wanted to go, Francesca decided, no one could dissuade him. "Alan, what we talked about earlier—" She didn't want Tony to get wind of whom she'd called. "I haven't been able to make contact."

"Oh." He nodded. "It's cool."

"It would be cold," Tony admitted, still on his own train of thought.

Francesca wished she could reassure Alan. This should be a time of hope, joy in reunion. But she couldn't predict what Stormy would do.

After the call to Hawaii—and after learning about her and Charlie—she felt about Stormy as she'd begun to feel about Mia after her death. *I really don't know her at all.*

"HERE, THERE AND EVERYWHERE," and she was in his arms, moving with him, shifting as he kissed her, when the phone rang.

With a quiet sigh, Charlie broke away. He punched a button on the phone. "Marcus Aviation. Charlie here.... Is he still in the pass?"

She switched off the music, thinking of her dad, alone in his house, not wanting anything to do with her.

I just have to accept it.

He hung up. "A guy running dogs north of Skwentna. His whole team went into a suck hole and died."

Francesca saw Mia, saw photos of Mia and her dogs, felt Mia's musher's heart, how it would have been broken by such a calamity. "You need to pick him up?"

He kissed her and reached for his parka.

"Can I come down to the office? Where the radio is?"

"It's not even snowing, Cesca."

She forced herself to relax. *It's going to be this way.*

The door shut behind him, and she hugged herself, choosing again to stay, to stay with him.

SHE MADE HERSELF GO TO BED, and sleep came. She trusted her gut. Even breaths, a warm feeling—she knew he was safe. At some point, the bed sagged beside her, and she snuggled near the heat, near him. They kissed, and he wanted to make love, and she took his body against hers, all the time suspended in a disinterest that might or might not come from menopause.

Afterward, her cheek still pressed to the hair on his chest, she said, "God, I feel old."

"Enjoy it. It only comes around once. Need me to rub that creaky neck of yours?"

She rolled over so he could. She couldn't help the fear. It was habit, comfortable and uncomfortable as a worn pair of slippers that should be replaced. "Honeydew said you went out together."

His warm fingers rubbed her spine, finding the knots and unraveling them, before kneading her neck. "A few times."

"She's younger."

He probed her scalp, rubbing, scratching, massaging. "You don't have time for this, Cesca."

Francesca knew this conversation, knew what came next. Time was a precious commodity; no one got a second turn. Why worry about anything? Anything.

She knew it for wisdom, impossible wisdom; her wild up-and-down emotions made it seem useless. Now, need ruled her, the need for security. *I'm so in love with him. I never want him to want anyone else.* Not another Honeydew. Or another Stormy.

Why was this happening? Hours before, marriage hadn't mattered. Now she wanted to know he was hers, permanently, in a world where nothing was permanent.

Charlie dropped off at once, and her voice shook him awake.

"Charlie, will you ever want to get married again?"

He hugged her sleepily. "I am married."

It should have made her happy and didn't, because she understood him so perfectly. Charlie wouldn't risk another divorce with her. And there was only one way to avoid that risk—and that was not to marry her again.

ONE WAY OR ANOTHER, she must speak to Stormy. In the morning, Francesca looked up Roy Jr.'s address in the phone directory. He and Pammie Sue lived a few blocks off Main Street, just four blocks from Charlie's. Just four blocks away, yet she might as well have remained in Colorado.

That murderous rage of Roy Jr.'s at the Halloween party... He behaved as though Charlie was to blame for Mel's death, yet he had no idea what Charlie had been through, even who Charlie really was. *My family hated him from the start.*

Charlie had shoveled the steps. No ice. In the crisp, blue-sky morning, Tony and Alan and Gelsey, the girl from the trading post, filled dog bowls next door. Francesca waved, but even at a distance, Alan's pallor showed. *Please love him, Stormy.* If only the three of them could have met—Stormy and both her children.

And the father, too.

Except... It can't be. I can't even think about it.

Francesca hurried past Joe Burke's little cabin and a blue four-square. Who used to live there? The girl had been in her class—

Roy Jr. had bought a frame house from the fifties, not the place he'd lived when she'd left Talkeetna. At least he'd be at the airport this time of day. She didn't want to see her brother after what he'd done to Charlie.

The house was pale yellow, the front door and shutters white. Empty flower planters edged the porch railing. Pammie Sue had always made things look nice. But Charlie said Francesca's father had a controlling share of the air-taxi business. It seemed cruel and unnecessary to Francesca, the sort of thing that could make people seethe. Roy Jr.—she calculated—was sixty years old.

The bell chimed, and footsteps answered. Pammie Sue, in creased navy slacks and fresh eye makeup. Francesca felt wild, ungroomed, in comparison.

"Hello, Pammie Sue. Is Stormy here?"

Stormy appeared from behind her sister, a smaller version, skin darkened and lined from the Hawaiian sun, her sweat pants loose and faded. She had never been like Pammie Sue.

We have to talk in private.

"Would you like to come in?" Stormy asked.

"Can you come for a walk?" Francesca asked in the same moment.

They walked, leaving Pammie Sue's suspicious gaze behind.

"Stormy, Mia's brother is in Talkeetna."

Stormy walked silently, her stride still athletic. Francesca imagined her friend surfing in Honolulu. Because Stormy wasn't answering and Francesca didn't want to press, she asked instead, "Did you bring your guitar?"

"Not this time."

Boots on snow, everything still.

"It's not so dead here in winter anymore, is it?" asked Stormy.

"No. So many restaurants open. I'm surprised." A pause. "Do you want to know about him? He wants to meet you."

"Let's…do that."

Francesca told her about Tony, too, that Tony had been staying with Alan. But last night, Tony had said something about moving to Gelsey's. "Alan doesn't have a phone. I think—I don't think he'd mind if we walked over. And the other kids will make themselves scarce. I'll deal with them if they don't."

"All right."

They continued toward B Street. "He lives across the street from Mia's. You haven't been there yet, either, have you? That's Charlie's—our—" oh, it felt like a lie "—Charlie's house. And Mia's…" She did not touch Stormy. No clasping of hands for courage or comfort. They were not forever friends; what Stormy and Charlie had done had erased that.

Alan's light was on, and Stormy never looked toward Mia's place, even the dogs in her yard. Francesca led the way up his snowy path, cut haphazardly by a shovel. She knocked, and Alan opened the door in his wool socks, smelling like he hadn't bathed.

His mouth opened when he saw Stormy.

He was alone.

"I'll leave you," Francesca said.

Alan Smith

Our birth mother reminds me of you, Mia. It's something in her eyes, like she's resigned to things.

"Roxy, off. Sorry, she jumps. They're sled dogs. They'd blow it on the obedience circuit. Sit down."

She crosses her legs on the couch. Young, like

Francesca.

Shit. Shit.

Hugging her for the first time. I hug her for you, too.

"I didn't know what else to do, Alan. I tried to find other solutions, but I was alone."

"Who is my father?"

She sighs like you, too. "You don't have one. Shall we leave it at that?"

Mia, what is this crap? She's pissing me off.

"Is it Marcus?" Suddenly I hate him.

"No. If you could know your father, I would tell you."

The dogs lick my face. My birth mother is here. I can't tell if she hates me or not, and I want my parents. I've got eighty sled dogs here in Talkeetna, and I want to go home.

"It's for you, Alan."

"I can take it."

She looks like you again, Mia. She gets up.

"Let's take a walk."

CHAPTER TWELVE

Hilo, Hawaii
June 30, 1969

Dear Cesca,

Sorry to learn our efforts failed. I have asked the CO to schedule my next R & R to coincide with your ovulation, and he said, "No problem," which is US Army for, "Very funny, Marcus." It may not be such a good idea, anyhow, for reasons you and I avoided discussing in Honolulu. Never fear. I'm known here for my exceptional cowardice and ability to flee unharmed at the first hint of danger.

Yesterday, a chopper exploded when enemy tracers hit the rockets. Joe and I were flying wing. The people who died were...

On our bed, I read names. Charlie has sent pictures, and Dalton is in many of them. Now this boy is dead. What's Charlie doing? What's he doing right now?

Is someone shooting at him?

The thoughts whirl, maddening. I have pictures of his hooch and of the gunships and of his friends, and he has described the heat and the sand and the smells. I only imagine the sounds. I believe, somehow, that the fact that one chopper exploded improves Charlie's odds. It wasn't his. It wasn't him. I'm glad, and there's guilt in this.

Tara stirs, waking from her nap, and I give her my breast while I look at Charlie's picture. He might be dead right now, and I wouldn't know yet. My heart pounds, and Tara's brown eyes watch me solemnly, acknowledging my terror.

Charlie's house
Evening

THE KNOCK BARELY CARRIED over the sizzling of the skillet on the stove and Emmylou Harris on the stereo. Francesca frowned at Charlie, and he left the stove to go to the door.

He cleared his throat. "Stormy."

"Hello, Charlie. Is Francesca here?"

She tensed, angry and jealous at seeing the two of them together. She wanted to hurt Stormy, to turn her out. What must Charlie have felt when she... *We were married. How could I have done that?*

Until she came to Talkeetna, she'd never confronted it. Now she knew why. His betrayal was easier to bear than her own. Hers seemed larger, bigger than her and Charlie. Symbolic. He'd slept with her best friend, stolen from her father, her brother had died, and yet—

Maybe it was natural to be harder on herself.

Or maybe, still, hers was the worst betrayal. She'd betrayed a veteran of that war that had defined her as it defined him, the war that had killed her brother. In hurting Charlie, she'd wounded them all, all those men. And herself, an idealistic self she'd then abandoned.

Was that what she really couldn't stand?

As Stormy came in, Francesca gestured to the couch,

taking the rocking chair while Charlie resumed cooking. Stormy had interrupted their evening routine. That routine would vary in the summer. Constant flights in and out, to Denali and back.

It will be fine. She was a pilot's daughter, and Charlie was the best pilot who ever landed on Kahiltna Glacier…

"Franny, I'm calling a family meeting, and I want you to come."

"I'm not sure I'm welcome."

"I'm asking you. It's at my sister's house. I've asked your dad to come."

Tension, wiring her up, aging her when she wanted every minute, every hour, every day. "I assume Charlie's welcome."

Silence from the kitchen.

"Sure." Stormy sounded breathless. "Look. Please don't be mad at me there. I won't be able to take it if everyone's mad. And neither will Alan."

Alan. Family meeting.

Heat flooded her face. *I thought it was Roy Jr. I thought you slept with your sister's husband.*

Maybe she'd wanted to think that.

But she'd guessed wrong. "It's Mel, isn't it? It was always Mel."

Stormy said, "Eight o'clock," and she got up.

"I COULD JUST LEAVE YOU THERE." Charlie ducked his head under his hood as they walked.

"I'm not going in unless you're welcome, too."

"Honey, this is Talkeetna. You're asking a lot."

"You and Roy Jr. can hate each other tomorrow. But tonight, you're my—" Her what? He wasn't her husband anymore. He wasn't her family. Her eyes were dry, half-frozen.

He was the man she'd loved when she was a teenager. He was the man she'd married, the father of her child. He was part of the reason she'd left Talkeetna. He had persuaded her to return. He was her lover and her best friend.

And it was impossible to say any of this.

He was her ex-husband. Ex. X.

"He might not let me in his house."

"Would you let him in yours?"

His footsteps fell in rhythm through the silence, the thought. "For you, Cesca, I would do almost anything."

"Except marry me again." She hadn't really said that. Was it a symptom of menopause, this blurting things out on snowy streets at night? Making things awkward when they didn't have to be. "Forget I said that."

They turned the corner, heading for Roy Jr.'s house.

She let it go, the fact that she'd said what she felt. But she said more. "It's really what I deserve. I hurt you."

"Cesca, please," he murmured. "Not in public."

"I'm not being maudlin. I'm being factual. I was unfaithful. I abandoned you when you—"

"Cesca."

She looked at him.

"Desist." Head near hers, he muttered, "I've got a reputation to uphold. It could actually cost me business if people believed you were dissatisfied with my intimate attentions." His voice rose gradually. "No one in Talkeetna knows how difficult it is for any one man to sate your constant appetite for oral sex."

As he spoke, the door to a house across the street opened, and someone went inside.

"Charlie!"

"And here we are." Roy Jr's.

She lingered in the street, not approaching the house.

"It's typical that when I express honest emotions, you try to embarrass me."

"I thought you were stating facts. Being factual. Emotions, let me refresh your memory, are feelings. Guilt, remorse, self-loathing—"

"Oh, shut up." She found the front path by the porch light's beam, then glanced back to see if he was following. He was, at his own pace.

She pushed the bell; it chimed, and her heart quivered as she listened for footsteps.

Stormy opened the door. "Come in."

Charlie wouldn't go in ahead of her. She forced herself forward. Pammie Sue waited in the kitchen with Roy Jr. He was a storm on the horizon, face dark, lips cracked, canyons in his skin as his wife eyed him uneasily. Alan sat on the couch. His hair was wet, and he seemed clean and handsome and young and afraid.

"Come in," Stormy repeated, and Charlie entered, hands in his pockets.

As Stormy closed the door, he nodded to Alan. Then— "Hello, Pammie Sue."

She answered with a nervous gesture.

"Want some coffee?" Stormy asked.

Roy Jr. stalked from the kitchen, through the living room and disappeared into the shadows of a hallway.

Charlie shook his head at Stormy.

Francesca caught his arm, steering him toward a seat. Keeping him close in her own frailty, unprotected by the right to say to her family, *This is my husband.* Just now, she hated him for that. "How are you, Alan?"

"Good. Okay."

No cousins present, not even Tony. Had they been invited?

The doorbell chimed again.

Stormy carried a glass of wine to the door. "Come in."

Cold air on their backs. From the silence, the length of time it took for the person at the door to move, Francesca knew who had arrived—and that he'd seen Charlie.

Then she heard his sigh.

"Roy Jr.," Pammie Sue called, rustling past. "Your dad's here!"

Roy Jr. emerged, taking his place in a recliner without reclining.

"Dad, sit down," urged Pammie Sue.

"I can stand."

Francesca's sigh was explosive and as spontaneous as the things she'd said to Charlie on the street.

"Suit yourself." Stormy collapsed on the couch beside Alan and briefly took his hand. "I wanted all of you present to tell you something I suppose I've kept silent too long."

"Oh, I don't think so." Francesca's father faced the door as he spoke. "Martha Ann, I don't imagine you have anything to say that this family needs to hear or that justifies inviting me to my son's house under false pretenses."

Stormy sat up straighter. Francesca remembered that her friend had been at the cabin on the Village Airstrip the night her father broke her forty-fives. Right before he did it, he'd asked Stormy to go home.

Stormy said, "What false pretenses?"

He sighed again and stepped toward the door.

She rose, in slow motion. "Your son Mel was the father of the twins I bore. Mia Kammerlander and Alan Smith. This is your grandson."

"That's a lie."

Francesca jumped at her brother's sudden explosion.

"Mel talked to me." Roy Jr. pointed his finger at Stormy. "He said you were doing everything you could to get in his pants."

Alan jerked to his feet.

"Roy Jr.!" Pammie Sue cried.

The door opened behind them, and Francesca glimpsed her father's back as he left. Alan followed, and Charlie was out the door before Francesca could speak.

"You animal!" Stormy screamed at Roy Jr. "How could you say that in front of him? How could you say it to me?" She gulped her wine, crying, and Pammie Sue tried to touch her, but Stormy tossed her hand away. "Don't touch me! You never wanted me to keep my children. You thought I'd be a bad mother, and you made me believe it, and now one of them is dead!"

Some instinct kicked through Francesca. Sometimes, at a birth, emotions got out of hand, and this was like that. "Stormy. Pammie Sue. Sit down."

They did, and she'd never doubted they would.

"Where did Alan go?" Stormy sobbed against the back of the sofa. "I knew this family could never take the truth. People who couldn't stand you and Charlie—"

"You did everything in pants in this town."

"Roy Jr.!"

Francesca said, "Roy Jr., I can't imagine that you think you're helping. Mel wasn't a saint. He was a wonderful—" Her eyes teared.

"Your boyfriend killed him! Get out of my house."

"My husband," whispered Francesca, "did not kill Mel."

Roy Jr. stood and practically ran to the door. "I'm going to find Dad. And you—" he pointed at Stormy "—are gone."

"I'M GOING TO RUN MY DOGS."

Charlie nodded. The kid had legs a mile long, and it was hard to walk beside him without running. He rubbed the back of his neck, then pulled his hood up. They both noticed the lights. Charlie stopped and moved around the trees to get a better view of the colors in the sky. "I don't think Cesca's seen them since she's been back." He bit his lips, but emotions came. Since Vietnam, he often couldn't help that. "I miss Mia. She used to come over and bring those ginger beers from the trading post."

"Yeah."

A man Alan's age who had never been to war and who ran dogs might cry shamelessly over a dead dog but not over a dead sister, not in front of anyone.

Charlie said, "She thought I was her—your father. I wanted it to be true."

"Well, the truth's different, yeah?"

"Your mom's not a slut."

"She's not my mom."

There were some tears now.

"You like those ginger beers? I'd kind of like one, but last time I went to the trading post, I picked the wrong case."

"I'm going to run my dogs." Alan glared.

Alan was smart, and Charlie felt many regrets. *But I couldn't let Cesca take all those babies. She had one, and—*

What if he'd died?

Mel Walcott's kids.

"You all right, brah?"

The things Alan didn't know. Things only Francesca knew, some Stormy knew. Alan probably didn't even know— He doesn't know!

It's not my fault. The existence of this kid does not make it my fault or my problem that Mel Walcott died.

"Hey, Charlie. Want me to hang out till Francesca comes back?"

Now Alan was worried about him.

Well, hey—if he had something to keep him busy, the kid wouldn't go hitting a tree. "Yeah. Thanks."

"STORMY, I'M SURE Mel didn't say that." Pammie Sue handed her sister a fresh glass of wine.

Francesca was into her second, Charlie be damned. He probably wanted a drink—Mel's kids—oh, yes, he probably wanted a drink, too.

"I'm sure he did say it." Stormy drank some more, and Pammie Sue worked on her second glass. They huddled around the coffee table like old friends commiserating, except it had always been Francesca and Stormy against Pammie Sue, and it wasn't like that anymore. "I just—we never felt the same about each other."

"I never heard either of my brothers talk that way about women. Girls." Francesca swallowed.

"Alan. Where's Alan?"

"Charlie's with him. I'm sure of it." Charlie could be so kind when he chose to be.

Alan was Mel's son.

"I should pack," murmured Stormy.

"You can stay at Mia's. With the stove going, it's quite warm. Or Alan would have you there, I know."

"And after that?"

Pammie Sue refilled her glass. "People think sex is such a sin. People think screwing everyone in Talkeetna is a sin, and I'm not saying you did that, Stormy. No one really knows, yet they—"

"What do *you* know about it?" Stormy stared. "Let's

just compare sins, Pammie Sue. Okay—my worst sin. Abandoning my children. That's what adoption is. Don't give me crap about how generous it is.''

"It's not abandonment." Francesca couldn't bear it that Stormy believed that. "It broke your heart, but you couldn't take care of twins alone. It wasn't abandonment. I know what abandonment is." Oh, she wasn't going to share her sins, no. She shut up, then blurted, "You're right, Pammie Sue. People make judgments, and they know nothing."

"Like you're one of the damned, Franny? 'Fess up." Stormy grabbed the wine bottle and emptied it into Francesca's glass. Pammie Sue rose suddenly. "What have you done?"

"There's no more in the house," Pammie Sue said. "We don't keep wine. Roy Jr. doesn't drink. I do when we go out, but that's not much." She sat and resumed drinking.

All the glasses were empty.

Francesca tried to drain the last drops from hers. "What is this, Truth or Dare? Look, we all have our problems and regrets."

"Oh, stuff it."

"I was with her," said Pammie Sue. "I was with her when she died."

Francesca watched, the room tilting, as Pammie Sue's carefully made-up face melted, changed, altered.

"It wasn't my fault. I can't tell myself it was my fault. But she knew, she knew Mel was her father, and she told me, and I just couldn't leave it at that. Because of the business…"

"What did you do to my child?"

Francesca clutched Stormy's hand.

"Nothing! I went to the airstrip after her, and I asked her to please keep it to herself—"

"This family! I can't believe this family! Pammie Sue, you used to be a Storm, but you're all Walcott! Did you hurt my daughter?"

"No! We were arguing, though, and her dog got loose. Oh, it was my fault, the same way it was Charlie's fault— I know how he must feel. I've felt this way for days. She just hit the tree. And I sat with her. There was nothing I could do for her but be with her. There was nothing!" Pammie Sue sobbed. "But yes, it is my fault, and there, it's said, and I'll go to jail."

Francesca rubbed her face.

Stormy didn't seem to breathe, just sat against the rose-patterned upholstery, stunned and silent.

Pammie Sue's sobbing rose and fell.

I suppose, Francesca thought, *someone should call the police. Call Peter.*

"I'm going to turn myself in. I've told you now. But I didn't hurt her. I didn't mean to hurt her. I didn't know the dog would get loose. I didn't know she would hit a tree. Just like Charlie couldn't have known.... Yes, I understand him now."

You don't understand him. Charlie wouldn't lie....

Pammie Sue picked up the phone and called the Fairview Inn and asked for Peter Sheppard's room. "Trooper Sheppard, this is Pammie Sue Walcott. I'd like to tell you about the night Mia died.... I'm at my house. Yes." She hung up. "He sounds uneasy. This must be a bad time for an officer. Oh, Stormy, will you ever forgive me?"

Stormy shook her head. "How?"

WHAT A THING. What a thing.

The trees made black skeletons against the northern

lights. Stormy walked beside Francesca. There was nothing to say.

Begging a woman not to reveal the identity of her birth father. For greed. An argument, a loose dog, an accident, a death.

They had stayed until Peter arrived and afterward, till Pammie Sue had phoned Roy Jr. Where was Tony? Francesca had offered to track him down—probably he was at Gelsey's. But Pammie Sue had said, *I think one of us should tell him.*

One of us.

The phrase remained with Francesca. How petty I am to care about this, about this endless division, us and them.

She must take care of Stormy, care for her as she had when Stormy had given up the babies. Stormy had stayed with her through the rest of Francesca's pregnancy when Francesca was so afraid, so afraid about Charlie, even though he was only in flight school. She must be a midwife again, be a midwife now.

She took Stormy's hand. "I became a midwife because of you. Because of what you went through. It was such an awful thing for you. You suffered so much, my poor friend, and you're so strong."

"Why did she become a midwife?"

Francesca thought. "She was never verbally angry, but… Oh, God, look at that!"

Stormy cried. "I always forget. The pinks."

"Anyhow, she was calm. Doctors would do something that made me furious, and she was like glass. But underneath—she said she wanted to be a midwife to help women, that women were held down. She was irreligious."

"Alan said they were very religious, her parents. They had ideas about girls, he said. They wanted her to marry, and she was very young, barely out of high school. They didn't want her to do this or do that."

Francesca listened to a rustling and realized it was the wind. The light from Charlie's windows cast long, angular patches of amber on the snow and on the shrubs. "You come stay with us, and we'll check on Alan. There's a couch. I don't want you to be alone."

"I'm not sure what I want. Your brother called me a whore in front of Alan, and Alan will always know that about me. Franny, was I such a slut?"

"Stormy, you were my best friend, and you were the sexiest girl in Talkeetna. What Pammie Sue said is true—those things don't matter." Except sleeping with Charlie.

No.

But neither of them knew. Neither knew I loved him. Isn't that what I decided?

"Those are exactly the things that matter to a son."

"Alan is very nice. And he—needs something, I think. Besides, he knows that just because Roy Jr. said a particular thing, that doesn't make it true." Francesca shut her eyes. She'd never been close to her oldest brother, but when she'd returned to Talkeetna she'd almost let herself believe that some day, some way, they could find a kind of friendship.

"Oh, shit, I can't stay here, Franny."

I really don't want to hear about what you did with Charlie. It stunned Francesca that she could still be having these thoughts, in spite of everything that had occurred that night. She did not respond.

Stormy gazed toward the barking dogs next door—and the dark, crooked shack.

Francesca said, "Come on. I'll show you." Was it

weakness not to beg Stormy to stay with her and Charlie? Through his front window, they could see Alan's rangy figure sitting on the kitchen counter. "Oh. We should go in."

Stormy saw him, too. "No. He left, Francesca. He doesn't want to see me."

"He didn't want to fight with Roy Jr. Come on. We'll see if it's all right."

"No. Take me over there." She pointed to Mia's house.

"Stormy, don't you want to be there when he learns about Mia—and Pammie Sue?"

"His parents should be here! He has a good relationship with them. He called them today and told them everything."

Not everything.

Francesca waited.

Stormy fluttered, a quick motion, then lowered her head and struck out for Charlie's porch.

TWO HOURS LATER, Stormy and Alan left together, to settle her in at Mia's.

Charlie closed the door behind them and held the handle briefly.

Francesca's head throbbed. She hunted in her things for her homeopathic headache remedy, wondering if it would work for a wine headache.

"You couldn't have taken care of three babies."

She lifted her head, pushed back her hair. *The answer is NO.*

Part of her mind heard his remorse, but the insight darted away with her next breath. "Charlie, they might have been yours."

"I used protection. And she wasn't— Look, you knew her, Cesca."

After what had happened at Roy Jr.'s... No. No, he wasn't saying this. "Go to hell. Just go to hell, Charlie. You screwed her. You used her. Go to hell. Go to hell. You're an asshole. You're still an asshole about it. You know, it hurts to be used."

"Are you telling me you know something about that?"

"I know something about women. You used her. You used her, and you weren't willing to take responsibility—"

"For someone else's kids. Let up, Cesca. You're doing a menopause thing."

She became profane, and it felt good, diamond-hard, intelligent and confident, to say hurtful things. "You're shallow, Charlie. You know that? It's shallow to use women that way, and then say, 'The answer is no.' In Talkeetna, you're the hotshot glacier pilot, and women bid on you at bachelor auctions, and you're Orville Wright every Halloween, but you're still just a man who can use a woman."

"I was twenty-one and on the rebound. Assume I've grown a little, Cesca."

"I did, until you just said that she was with everyone and that justified your ignoring your responsibility."

"My responsibility was to you and our daughter."

"Oh, you were always so responsible, Charlie."

He switched out the main light, leaving only the lamp over the stove burning. "I can do that, too, Cesca. Drop it." He came closer and said softly, "I hesitate to mention it, but you've been drinking."

She rolled her eyes. "Touché." Then she added, "It should give you a taste of what it was like, trying to live with you, to communicate with you."

"Francesca, could we just jettison some of our history? Let's say—I'll try not to mention the fact that you broke our wedding vows, and you can try not to keep track of my shortcomings. Deal?"

"Not mentioning something isn't the same as forgiving. Or forgetting."

"Cesca, I can't forget. There are certain things in my life I will never forget, and you did some of them. There it is."

She grabbed her face as tears came, again. Heat and sweat and Pammie Sue and Roy Jr.

And Hawaii and Jay Henry's bed.

"I'm sorry! I'm sorry! I would take it back if I could!" She fumbled with the vial of homeopathic pellets and popped some in her mouth and held them under her tongue while her eyes streamed. Trying to keep her mouth shut, she put the bottle away and raced to the bathroom for a piece of toilet paper to wipe her eyes.

When she came out, his head was against his arm on the ladder, and she'd seen him stand that way before and couldn't remember when. She waited for him to say something, to say he forgave her, to say it was all behind them.

Instead, he went into the bathroom, and she heard water running, heard him getting ready for bed.

CHAPTER THIRTEEN

Hilo, Hawaii
February 14, 1975

Maybe things will be better if I can just go through with this.

His breath is foul, and his gut sucks against me. I stroke his face, so that he won't accuse me of not being interested.

"Cesca."

I'm going to throw up if he breathes on me again. Is rape like this? Like sex with your own husband who's drunk every night? When he complains if it doesn't happen, complains that you're not interested, like he's the world's greatest lover, when he is in fact disgusting to you?

You're damaging our marriage, Charlie. Sex is never going to be the same.

Where he used to be hard, he has a beer belly. The word *flaccid* comes to mind.

Come. If you would just come, this would be over.

He can barely ejaculate when he's drunk. If it would only end. *Make it end. Please, make it end.*

His breath.

Tomorrow… Tomorrow, Miranda has a prenatal. I might have to turn that baby.

"Cesca, look at me."

Holding my breath. Stroking him. Touching him is how it usually works. He sucks my nipples, but he knows it's not worth it, why bother? I groan. Make him come. Make this be over.

I hate him. I hate him.

Please make it end.

Rainbow Clinic

"HI, FRANCESCA." Gelsey Northrop's smile was shy against her young white skin.

Francesca hid any surprise at seeing Tony's friend. She had known, coming into the room, that this was a prenatal. A very early prenatal.

Almost two weeks had passed since Pammie Sue's confession. With Stormy's and Alan's blessing, Francesca and Honeydew had held a community memorial service for Mia at the Village Airstrip. Alan and three other mushers had driven her dogs around Talkeetna, and the service had ended at the Fairview Inn. Since then, Stormy had returned to Hawaii and Peter Sheppard quietly to Anchorage, never speaking to Francesca again about anything other than the case. Pammie Sue faced minor charges, though Mia's parents had stormed Anchorage, demanding more. Stormy and Alan both said that neither Roy Jr. nor her father would accept that Mel was Alan and Mia's birth father. Francesca had seen neither of them, but she'd visited Mel's grave with Alan and given Alan a picture of her brother, one she'd taken from her old room.

And Charlie had flown her to Anchorage to shop for a birthday gift for Tara, which they'd mailed to her. Together. Francesca still hadn't told Tara or Ivy how things really were.

No, and she never would. How they really were involved things she never wanted Tara to know. But she saw the inequity, that Charlie weighed the grief he'd given her and Tara—all of it—against her infidelity. Did he think *she* had nothing to forgive? That he'd played no part in the failure of their marriage?

"Hello, Gelsey." Francesca perched on a wheeled stool and smiled at the tiny brunette. "How are you?"

"I'm…pregnant."

Her excited smile relieved Francesca somewhat. Gelsey's reaction must mean…

"Tony and I are," Gelsey clarified. "He knows. He's really happy. He wanted to come today, but he's meeting some people coming in for a Denali climb."

Francesca hid her feelings that the expedition was insane. No one belonged on the West Rib in November. And what about Charlie? His wings could ice up…. "Tony isn't going, is he?"

"Actually, he is. They wanted someone who knows the route."

How could she be so serene? Carrying Tony's baby… He's not even thirty. How could he take this risk, so unnecessary? "And—you feel all right about that?"

Gelsey shrugged. "It's really not my choice. This is what he does, and it's money."

However much money, it wasn't enough, just as it wasn't enough for Charlie. Charlie, who would drop fruit and other supplies to the climbers periodically; Charlie, who would rescue them if—when—they got into trouble.

The midwife in her took over. *Care for Gelsey and the baby.* Francesca left the stool for another chair, with a back, to take Gelsey's history.

"We, um, want a home birth," said Gelsey.

Though Francesca nodded, smiled, she was numb inside, because it seemed oddly like her own pregnancy—learning about it after Charlie was drafted, fearing.... But Gelsey showed only acceptance and pleasure. Francesca wanted to say, *Don't you know how dangerous it is? Don't you know that the weather up there is like the North Pole?*

Instead, she poised her pen over the chart. "How old are you, Gelsey?"

The airport

HAYLEY CUMMINGS, from New Zealand, and Günther Holzer, from the Tyrol, jumped out of the Cessna. As Charlie began unloading, Joe and Tony came to the side of the craft to help. Joe had grown back his beard; his dimples deepened as he smiled at the passengers.

Hayley's long, curly hair was red, and her skin showed the weather of many mountains. Her eyes flickered over the metal at the end of Joe's left coat sleeve before she met the mechanic's gaze. "Are you Joe? I'm Hayley Cummings."

She's blushing. Hiding a grin, Charlie grabbed another pack. Joe was a good-looking guy. He couldn't hear any more of the conversation, just the rise and fall of their voices and of Tony's and Günther's.

Another trip to Anchorage tomorrow, to pick up the other two members of the expedition.

As he secured the plane, Roy Jr. crossed the tarmac to enter the pilot's lounge. The man was going to wear out his face scowling.

You're taking his kid to Denali in winter.

Tony was a man and could make his own decisions.
And there was only one best pilot in Talkeetna.

"THEY'RE GOING TO HAVE A BABY!" Normally, Francesca wouldn't have discussed a client's status, but this was
Charlie. "He shouldn't be going there."

"Take it up with Tony."

You shouldn't be going, either.

But it was his job.

At four it was already dark. She'd walked home from
the clinic, and Charlie had arrived soon after. Now he
was doing sit-ups, his feet hooked under the couch, preparing to go for a run.

"I'm going to call Tara," she said. "She has to move
out of that house...." It was something she'd nearly forgotten, that the lease was up on the Victorian, that the
house was changing hands. But Tara planned to find a
place with her apprentice.

"Give her my love."

The sight of his body, his back, the way he moved—
even the sound of his voice—seemed fleeting, something
that might be taken from her. Francesca's eyes burned,
and spontaneously she rushed to the door. "Charlie."

He paused but was still in motion, in some way already
gone.

She kissed him anyway.

He said, "Hold that thought," and left.

She hurried to the phone and dialed Tara's number. It
rang twice, then clicked.

"The number you have reached has been disconnected...."

Disconnected. Well, of course—the house. Isaac would
know where she was. She phoned his home and got his
machine, and one of his boys, who hadn't quite lost his
Rwandan accent, saying, "This is the McCreas'. We

can't come to the phone, but please leave a message.''
Beep.

Francesca parted her lips to leave a message, then hung up. She would try again when he was home. Messages were so awkward, particularly if he and Tara weren't getting along.

I should try the Mountain Midwifery number.

She received the answering service and found herself not wanting to reveal that Tara had moved and not bothered to tell her where.

I've never told her where I'm staying, after all.

She changed into leggings and a sweatshirt to begin her thirty-minute yoga practice, and she was flushed and warmed and drinking red clover tea when Charlie came in.

"How is she?"

It surprised her that he'd asked about Tara first. But it shouldn't, she realized. He'd grown; he'd changed.

Francesca explained about the disconnected line, her efforts to reach Tara. "I'm sure she's found another place in Precipice." Her gut twinged. No. It was nothing. She couldn't respond to every little worry about Tara or she'd go nuts. Besides, during her yoga practice, she'd had an idea. "Charlie, I want to have a Thanksgiving dinner here. It's still a few days off."

"Who are you going to invite? Your family?"

"Yes, as a matter of fact."

He slid his hands beneath her sweatshirt. "How about a shower?"

"I thought we'd have everyone. And Alan and Joe—and your climbers."

"Oh, that would be a great mix. My passengers. Your brother."

"I guess that wouldn't work." She bit her lip. He drew

off her sweatshirt, and she followed him to the bathroom and the shower. "Well, just family, then."

"You may as well invite everyone, because no one in your family—barring Tony and Alan—will come." He kissed her, and Francesca drew up the layers of his shirts and grabbed him, hard.

Charlie, I don't want you to die. To die at all. To die without ever saying it was all right, that what she'd done hadn't damaged both their lives irreparably. And he would never say it because it would never be true. What was true was that it had damaged her more than it could ever hurt him. She'd been living with that a long time— and never noticing. "I love you."

He was cocky, eyes half-shut. "Prove it, Cesca. Show me. Show me how much I mean to you."

He wanted a smile and she couldn't give it.

"Not that way." Charlie twisted the knobs in the shower, feeling annoyed. Why did people bother with guilt?

Her eyes begged too hard, and he needed relief from that yearning gaze, the look that wanted something from him, that wanted the past she'd trashed, he'd trashed, they'd both torn up and burned.

Under the hot spray, through the steam, he sang "God Only Knows" to her, and knew it wasn't what she wanted and wasn't what he wanted, but there was no bridge to that place, none at all.

They'd burned that, too, and they could only make love on the ashes.

"YOU COULD JUST CALL THEM on the phone," Charlie suggested. "Since they're going to make their excuses anyway."

"I want them to have to look me in the face and say

no.'' Francesca zipped her parka. She'd blow-dried her hair, something she rarely did, but she didn't want to go outside with wet hair. ''Will you come with me?''

''I can't see the point.''

''My father mentioned the fact that you've never stepped foot in his house.''

''And now he probably feels we're living in sin.''

Francesca drew on her gloves. ''He said you should've come to him and told him you wanted to marry me someday. But that you realized I was too young.''

''Let's be realistic, Cesca. He wants me to knock on his door and take the blame for your brother's death.''

''Charlie, he's an old man.''

He gave her a look, and she understood why she put up with his lack of forgiveness. There were different kinds, shades and depths of betrayal. He'd conned her father for revenge. And probably slept with Stormy for the same reason, though with a different target. He'd lied from fear.

And I... Small decisions. Chance meetings at the beach. Talking and needing so badly to talk. Then, suddenly involved. Too late.

There were larger betrayals, and hers was part of that great complicated betrayal of Charlie and Joe and so many, the whole betrayal of the war. The crimes magnified each other. She would never ask him to take the blame for Mel's death. Not that. Not from a man who'd gathered the remains of his friend after that Ping-Pong game. ''Could you try to talk to him? Charlie, you can make friends with anyone you want to.''

''I don't want to make friends with your father.''

''Maybe that was always the problem.''

''Francesca. Eat some tofu.'' He settled at his desk and slit the envelope containing his bank statement.

"Please come with me. You don't have to come to Roy Jr.'s door, but if you'd just talk to my father..."

"Your father won't talk to me. I *have* talked to your father. I offered to buy back those mineral rights, and he sold them to me."

"Is that all? Is that all you said to each other?"

He spun the chair. "It's been twenty years. I can't remember what we said."

"I bet he remembers every word."

"Whose side are you on?"

She hesitated. A second or two passed.

He shoved back his chair, stalked to the door and grabbed his parka.

"You're coming with me," she said.

He shook his head, his face strange.

"Where are you going?" She knew. "You're not going to drink."

The wind blew after him.

She followed him out. "Charlie!"

He was walking, head down. Stopping, he gestured. Going to Joe's.

She said, "I love you."

With a nod, he hiked on, his mind clearly miles from her.

Francesca's throat knotted. *You don't have to talk to my father, Charlie. But would it kill you to say you love me, too?*

CHARLIE TOUCHED the wooden exterior of the frame hangar. The security light showed the snow-dusted reflection of his face in the window. But he wanted to see beyond. He only saw himself, making out with Francesca on that army cot, his hand between her legs. His blood rushed, and he smiled a little, relearning the meaning of bitter-sweet.

And walked on.

THE OLD MAN OPENED THE DOOR. Said nothing.

"Your daughter and I would like to invite you to Thanksgiving dinner."

"I'm afraid I must decline."

No surprises. Charlie clenched his fists in the pockets of his parka. "She hopes for a reconciliation with you, and apparently I'm the problem. So I want to apologize for being less than honorable in my dealings with you."

"Which dealings would those be?"

Charlie lifted his eyebrows. Roy Walcott wanted him to eat crow. Charlie was here for Francesca, as a gift—not because he owed her. He owed her nothing.

I love you.

At Roy Walcott's door and felt no love for Francesca, and that didn't surprise him. Love was not a steady state. Maybe she'd thought it was when she went to someone else's bed.

When he recalled the times on the army cot in his hangar it was with affection for past sexual feelings, delight in the power of them. Other times, he felt different things. He considered what Francesca had said her father thought he should've done, how he should have behaved. He had known it at the time, in a distant and unimportant way, something he'd decided didn't matter much.

He still felt the same way. He'd admitted to being less than honorable. He had apologized. The word "sorry" was not going to be spoken tonight. He wished to speak of other things. He wanted to tell Roy Walcott how it was, how it had been, to tell war stories that were not about war, and he knew better and had learned better a long time ago. He wanted to be drunk, and he knew better and had learned better a long time ago.

He didn't answer his former father-in-law.

And Roy Walcott's face said he knew that was how it would be.

As Charlie picked his way down the walk, he felt the other pilot's eyes at his back, and he felt the enemy's hate.

There was nothing more to say.

CROSSING C STREET, he saw her ahead of him and gave a wolf whistle.

Francesca wound her way back. "I changed my mind." She searched Charlie's eyes. He'd looked at her differently weeks ago, when she'd made love with him and run, then made love with him again. But this was normal, she told herself, normal and inevitable. She told him, "I don't want to have them to dinner. Not after the things Roy Jr. said about Stormy. Not after what Pammie Sue did. I try to tell myself there's a why, and the why is my father. It is him, isn't it? The way he won't let go of the business, won't forgive me, won't forgive you, won't believe Alan is Mel's son."

Charlie absently scooped up some snow from the roadside to pack a snowball. He would never have broken bread with Roy Walcott Jr., but he'd known Roy Jr. would save him the trouble of explaining that to Francesca. "Everyone's responsible for himself. Look at you, Cesca. He disowned you because of me, but you have a career, you've raised a great daughter. Your brother's over his head in ignorance and hate." Under the street-light, he pitched the snowball at a distant tree trunk. It hit.

"Maybe I was lucky to leave." *And it's not like I made such a success of our marriage, Charlie.* But he'd played his part, too, and he was playing a part now. "Charlie, I'm fifty-two, and I'm not going to pretend I don't notice that you refuse to say you love me. What are you doing?"

His arm had slipped under her coat, his mustache tickling her neck beneath her hair. "I'm not the best with words."

"Oh, yes, you are."

He sang "God Only Knows" under her hair, between her hood and her skin.

Francesca ached for the days, the years, she'd thrown away.

His far hand reached to cradle her face, to turn her toward him, to kiss her. He sang to her again, in his best Carl Wilson. His mouth pressed on hers, and she clutched the front of his parka with her gloves.

He murmured, "What do you say we get our daughter and that baby up here for Thanksgiving?"

Francesca considered. "She may have clients due. It would cost a fortune." But she had the money, and so did Charlie. What better use for it than seeing Tara. "I'd love that."

"We'll call her tomorrow. It's too late tonight. You can track her down with the answering service. She'll come."

"And we'll ask Tony and Gelsey for dinner—and Alan and Joe. And the climbers," Francesca concluded. "What? Why are you smiling that way?"

He bit his lip—and his tongue. No need to mention Hayley. "Joe—he's saved my life."

He meant because of his alcoholism, that Joe had been someone to talk to as he climbed from the pit. Charlie had saved Joe's life, too, in Vietnam, but he'd never said so. Francesca had learned it from another vet. "You've saved yourself, too. I didn't help." Not for want of trying.

They backed away from the trees to see the northern lights. "Want to go up and look?" Charlie suggested.

"Yes."

When he smiled this time, his eyes shone with love. She removed a glove to touch his face.

The trees reached over them, branches stretching skyward. They walked beneath them, past the yellow-glowing windows and the dark ones.

"It was a wake-up call."

He was looking at her, expecting her to understand. She did. He meant leaving him.

"But I could have come back to Alaska when you first asked," she said. "It might have been enough."

He shook his head, hands in his pockets.

They'd arrived at the house, and the dogs of B Street knew they were there. They listened to the howling. "I used to hate dogs," said Francesca. "That dog bit me the day before Mom died. I almost kicked it. But Mia loved dogs so much. When I rode in the sled, I saw how happy they were. They love to run, love to pull."

"I liked mine. But I love planes." His eyes had grown misty.

"I know." She'd never try to take it away from him. Not even flying climbers to Kahiltna Glacier next week and dropping them fresh fruit and rescuing them if they needed it and bringing them home. "I love midwifery. It's not dangerous, but I understand." Charlie loved flying even more, perhaps more than her or Tara, or perhaps it should never be measured, the question never asked. It

was who he was, and people were who they were first—
then they loved.

The keys were in the truck, and he kicked a path
through the snow to open her door. "Let's go."

COLORS SWIRLED IN THE SKY, making pink and green
snow and ice on McKinley. Even the crackling headset
and the engine lulled Francesca's mind. As they flew between spires, her pulse trembled and her body quivered,
so alive. This was the only way she could ever be here
in this beauty. She would trust her brother and she would
trust Charlie, but no one else. She was a daughter of
Talkeetna with loyalty in her bones till loyalty became
trust and an inner fidelity that was belief, utter belief that
Charlie was the best pilot in Talkeetna and Roy Jr. maybe
as good because he was her father's son. In the arctic
lights, she saw Mel's face and saw Roy Jr. younger and
not yet full of hate, and the lights blurred before her eyes.

Ice, rosy pink, stretched high to one side of her. The
plane banked around the mountain. Charlie knew the
landmasses; he watched and felt the air, prepared for
downdrafts and foehn clouds. Of so many things in her
life, Francesca was afraid, but not this, not flying with
Charlie.

They flew beyond the mountains, into open sky, into
lights grander than anything in her world, as birth was
deeper.

She spoke into the headset. "I'd give anything, almost,
for forgiveness, for love like it used to be, and it died
with my mother." The colors ran.

He sang a few lines from "Soul Kitchen" about wanting to stay all night, and the plane banked again, and she
knew they were going home. It was minutes later that
she realized he might have read something else into her

words, that forgiveness wasn't just about her family but about the two of them, as well.

THEY WERE IN THE FRONT SEAT of his truck, parked near the river with a view of the sky.

"Cesca. Don't stop," he murmured under the Beatles singing "I Want to Hold Your Hand," and her mouth caressed him, loved him, her fingers entwined with his.

The tape changed, and Smokey Robinson sang "My Girl," and she made love to him through Martha and the Vandellas and "Nowhere to Run" and a chain of music that was the past, a past untarnished and full of hope—the belief that he would never be drafted and the certainty that she would always know her brothers and the chance that her mother might get better and her father would accept Charlie, once the two of them were married. She knew the taste of him and sat up and kissed his mouth.

His eyes drained into her. "I love you."

She swallowed, hearing it for the first time all over again.

"Mr. Tambourine Man." Charlie's gaze, his head close to hers. "I'll make it right. The best it can be."

She held her breath. He'd always kept his promises.

Joe Burke's house

"YOU SURE YOU WANT to see these?" It was his photo album. Joe had asked casually, but the answer couldn't be casual. If she couldn't hear the stories, he didn't want her. The world was full of people who walked away.

"I do. I'm not American. I know this was important. I have no perspective."

Her voice was like Nicole Kidman's. "Well, I have no perspective on mountains," he said. He was used to talking to Charlie and other vets, which meant saying what was on his mind. "I haven't kissed a woman in—" *Say it, Joe* "—fifteen years."

"I'm surprised."

Good. Well, the kisses would keep. "So, this is me the day I got to Chu Lai. Creed Dalton, a crew chief, was always taking photos, so I got a camera, too. But I forgot to take it with me, and he always had his. There's Creed. Yeah. He died in…"

Here we go. Can you take this, Hayley?

She had a sweet face. His emotion didn't seem to bother her. Though she hadn't really seen emotion yet.

"It's late. I'd like to stay."

The back of the couch was under his head, timbers overhead, a woman in Talkeetna talking like Nicole Kidman.

"Sure. Want another beer?"

"Yes. Who's this?"

He smiled at the man whose head was tilted back, a cigarette dangling from his lips. *Someone who's still around.* "That's Charlie."

CHAPTER FOURTEEN

Hilo, Hawaii
June 30, 1978

"He's gone again, isn't he?"

What do I say to her? She's nine years old, and her eyes are ninety. We sit at the table. He's actually been gone two days, and it took our daughter this long to mention the fact. But Stormy has been around, and Tara and I never talk about him in front of anyone else.

Tara tilts her head, her eyes his, even the way her eyebrows arch. "He hardly remembers his mother. Do you suppose that's the problem?"

My little sage. The problem is, he's running, and there's nowhere to go. He's not just running from the fact that his mother disappeared from his life, from things he can't remember, but from what he can. To tell a nine-year-old the things he did is not right. They are his tales to tell, his life, his story. And she will never understand where he's been, and neither will I. *You don't get it.*

I get it, Charlie. You were human, and people you trusted failed you, and you failed others just by being human, by being in the wrong place at the wrong time doing the wrong thing, by being young, which you were and never will be again. You couldn't help it. But you can help failing us. I know where you are, not geographically, but otherwise. You are throwing-up drunk, and you will stay that way, live in it, retch in it, till you come home. You are killing yourself, and I've told you that, and you are so…so…

Tara asked me a question, didn't she? But I'm not completely here. How can I be present for my child in this chaos, this constant chaos? *Charlie, she wants to make you not drink. She wants it so badly, and I want it so badly, but I understand that we can't, and she doesn't understand. You are bad for her, Charlie. You're bad for all of us.*

Where did you go?

Talkeetna Village Airstrip
The next morning

CHARLIE WALKED THROUGH the empty hangar. Joe had pointed out an ad on the Internet yesterday—before Hayley arrived. Wouldn't it be fun to restore one of these?

No. Fun to fly it.

But he had the space for it here.

A sheet covered the frame of the army cot. Sheets on everything back here. He worked open the door and stepped into the snow. Trees hid the Walcotts' garden. He locked the door behind him and waded through snow. It soaked his wool pants. He had to leave for Anchorage at ten to collect the other climbers.

Roy Walcott was on his snowmobile in his drive.

Charlie said, "A minute of your time."

"You aren't worth it, that I recall."

"I'm sorry for my actions, which resulted in the death of your son." He'd told other lies. Sick from this one,

Charlie rubbed his fists against the lining of his parka pockets; the habit wore holes in his clothing. "I'm sorry I didn't behave as a gentleman in regard to your daughter."

He was big. He was huge in saying these things. *What a big guy you are, Marcus. You are the most generous creature on earth and the most honorable.* Yes. Honor.

Roy Walcott did not switch off his snowmobile. He watched the airstrip, no planes coming or going at seven-thirty this morning.

"I love Francesca. I've always loved Francesca. I carried her picture on my body every day I was at war."

The man had steely cold eyes.

Charlie rocked on the heels of his boots. "I'm going to Anchorage to pick up some passengers. Thought I'd stop and look at a Lockheed Vega that needs some work. You ever fly one of those?"

"She left you."

Charlie's chest tightened. "It was mutual. I'm an alcoholic. Dry now, but I wasn't then. Assume you read me right for my worth." *I'll just get on my knees and get it over with.*

"She never showed much character."

Heaving breaths. Charlie knew they were his own, the steam was his own. It was August of 1967, and Roy Walcott was showing again just how much his daughter meant to him. Charlie wanted to kill him, to kill him with words, knew he had the cutting words and he must control himself as he should have controlled the need to con this easy mark, to piss on his pride, to prove him the fool he was. He must control himself as he should have controlled himself when he put it on hot and fired and fired and fired and his voice told other men to fire and fire and fire. He must control himself as he should have with a

Ping-Pong paddle and ball that asked to fly to the perimeter, that asked for a dare. He was a pilot and he knew how to control himself. So when he spoke, he was deliberate and cruel and right, so right.

"Character? Character is a lie, Roy. That's a word insecure people use to feel they're better than everyone else. People use it to describe some trait they imagine they have, and you don't, when they haven't found out it doesn't actually exist. Because it's a lie. Like honor and courage."

Walcott switched off the engine.

"You do things or you don't, and it might have to do with how many aches and pains you feel when you get out of bed in the morning." *Try that on for size, Walcott.*

The garment would never fit.

"You're an empty man," Roy Walcott pronounced. "They say that the Vietnam War wounded men's minds more than most wars, but you were always empty, Marcus. I saw it the day you walked into town. Weak as a rotten timber and as full of holes. You had bad penny written all over you, and you've spent yourself on this family fifty times, and you just did it again."

"You got anything better to do with your final days than criticize the rest of the world?" Charlie's eyes burned. "I'm thinking of buying this Vega, wanted to ask if you'd like to see it with me, maybe help restore it. Your daughter wants you at Thanksgiving dinner. Have a heart, man. Mel's dead. Love Cesca. Love your grandkids. Sell your son the rest of that business. He's practically at retirement himself, and he's bitter. Not to mention that Pammie Sue's failure to report Mia's accident is costing you some business. Customers have taken note. And by the way, since you pride yourself on your own military service, you might pass on that I don't appreciate the spin Roy Jr. puts on my name." He had to give Walcott his back. Standing in the cold, ice beneath his eyes.

Breathe.

The snowmobile started.

Charlie looked.

A wrinkled chin pointed at him over a crumpled throat. "You conned me once, and you won't do it again. You haven't earned anyone's trust and definitely not mine. You come with an apology on your lips and then you tell me it's a lie."

"You aren't hearing."

Roy Walcott set his machine in motion and left at a calm and unhurried pace.

WITH HIS BOOTS AND HIS HANDS, Charlie dug deep snow away from the block someone had carved. He'd walked to the Village Airstrip, he'd walked here, he would walk to the airport.

Rooted before the uncovered stone, he sang into the frost and saw other faces, not just the Mel Walcott he couldn't quite remember. He sang "Imagine" and he was alone and knew that they all were, but he could imagine, he could imagine maybe better than Francesca, who wanted what could not be.

He sang to Roy Walcott and Roy Walcott, Jr., in anger and then to the sky in love, knowing every word, as he had known them since a month after he'd first heard them, standing in a downpour outside a hooch. Chilled, he sang, and his eyes ran, and his mind ran.

Mel standing beside his plane in '63 and Mel pitching a rotten egg at him in the depot and the Mel Francesca had described, the Mel whose postcard Charlie had burned. Mel who hadn't lived to hear this song and Charlie imagined, just imagined he could hear it now.

Trees rustled.

Another voice joined his. This voice sometimes sang to dogs who sang back.

Charlie stopped. "Hi, Alan." He faced his neighbor. "How are you doing?"

Alan indicated the puppy, King, running through the cemetery, lifting his leg on a tombstone. "Hanging out. He's a good dog. But he's not a sled dog."

Charlie's dog-owning days were over. He even thought twice about adopting broken Lockheed Vegas—and that was one perfect plane.

Alan. Alan, come to visit his father's grave.

Tell him, Marcus. Why carry it anymore? "You and I need to talk."

Wide blue eyes waited, and Charlie began storytelling. The story started with a girl who was much too young for the feelings that had been inside his seventeen-year-old body, but he didn't tell that part of the story, didn't tell that he'd seen the woman he loved broken with grief and broken again by her father over pride and jealous greed, didn't tell about control or controlled revenge, just told the outside, the shell. People only wanted the shell, as any man who'd tried to talk about war knew.

"I was never a good kid, Alan." He huddled in his parka and told Alan Smith the truth, and the truth was the shell, that simple, the truth he'd told Francesca and she'd understood. Though for Alan, for Alan he must explain deferments.

"Why did you do it? Con him about that mine..."

Unsentimental and puzzled at the world.

Charlie sympathized. "You've met the guy."

"That's it? It was a pilot thing?"

It was a love thing.

"You ask your grandfather what it was."

Alan shrugged. "My grandparents live in Hawaii. These people are poisonous."

Charlie thought of Cesca and Tara and Ivy, how Francesca and Tara had decided to adopt a grown woman.

"Alan. I can't do for you what Mel might have, were he alive." Charlie's throat was dry. Hot. *You could be sorry for this, Marcus.*

No. He wouldn't be.

"You're my nephew. I can— Look. I'm around. I live across the street." *Your mother wanted us to adopt you, and I said no.*

But Alan had parents who loved him. And he loved them. Things had worked out for him.

Shit. Shit.

Mia. Kid. I miss you.

Missed her more than he felt responsible for Alan. Missed her more than Cesca did.

Shut down. Shut down.

Outside the cemetery gate, alone, he hurried toward the airfield, studying the sky and a plane on final descent.

Marcus Aviation Office

"I CALLED THE ANSWERING SERVICE, and Tara's moved in with Beulah Ann. It's an apartment in the basement of her other midwifery student's house."

Francesca had waited until he was done talking with the climbers, Jon and Michael, who now huddled with Günther and Hayley, drinking coffee near the front window.

Charlie cast his dark-eyed gaze at her. "What's the problem?"

"She hasn't returned my calls."

"She does that."

"I just have a bad feeling, Charlie. I know. I know something's happening. That dream I had this morning..." It haunted her. Just the vision of Tara getting in Francesca's old Subaru with the baby, with little Laura. Terrifying. Somehow terrifying. *They're going to be in an accident.*

"Cesca. Dreams are disturbing. That's what dreams are."

"Sometimes mine are precognitive. Like when you were shot."

"I was grazed, and you dreamed I was shot in the head. You're a lousy psychic, Cesca."

"But it happened!" She eyed his passengers; Tony had come in and was showing them photos of the route they would take.

Francesca suppressed her sigh. "I'm going to the clinic, and I'm taking the truck to Wasilla to shop. Okay?"

"Are we making bread or buying?"

For Thanksgiving. "Let's bake."

The love of the night before, his promise, stayed her nerves, brought her to the present. She was going to work. She was going shopping. Tara probably wouldn't be able to come for Thanksgiving.

And perhaps, someday, there would be peace in her family.

HE STAYED AT THE AIRPORT LATE, working on planes with Joe, then strode past Roy Walcott Air Service in the dark and walked toward home.

Someone on Roy Jr.'s street was playing the Indigo Girls, loud. The music came from the Walcotts' house.

Kids must be home for the holiday. Roy's truck sat in the drive. The walk had been shoveled. Charlie hesitated on the porch before he knocked. Then it was too late.

Roy Jr. opened the door.

Charlie said, "What would it take for peace?"

The hard face changed slightly. He stepped outside and closed the door.

Charlie moved out of swinging range.

"What do you want?"

Once you tossed aside the fact that you were eating dirt for people you hated, once you told yourself you'd lied before, it didn't matter. "Let's get along."

"Why don't you get along out of here?"

Time to ask if his son had ever come home, but Charlie knew that Tony really hadn't. He talked to his mother and not his father.

There was nothing else but to go home. He had done everything he could, and Cesca would cry when she saw the northern lights and remember when her mother was alive and her family had loved each other.

He could stop in to see Joe.

He could stop at the trading post and buy a six-pack.

He continued toward B Street in the Alaskan dark. The winters were worse every year, and he longed for a beach. Maybe Hawaii. Could Cesca get away from the clinic?

The other trip, the trip he'd never taken, occurred to him.

He didn't want to go in winter, and summers were for flying.

Not yet.

But sometime. He needed to go sometime. There were other things to see there, too. The Smithsonian, the National Air and Space Museum...

Other things.

He didn't tell her what he'd done. He invited the climbers to Thanksgiving dinner, and they all accepted. He made love with Francesca, then listened to her worry about Tara, and when she slept, he saw Tara's swollen face and bruises after she'd escaped from Chile, her thinness. Gaps where teeth were missing. Then other images came, unrelated things, and he played tricks on himself until he'd won.

The following afternoon, his house filled. Charlie wished Tara—and Ivy—were there. Otherwise, it was perfect. Talkeetna hospitality. The table not big enough, with only room for the food, and Tony and Gelsey sitting on the kitchen counter, Gelsey reading her copy of *Spiritual Midwifery* and dreamy-eyed pregnant. Alan and Tony drinking beer, and Joe and Hayley, with got-laid-recently glowing around them like an aura, and Cesca and Günther picking out albums. Günther found Bob Dylan and asked, "Yes?"

"Go for it." Cesca grinned, looking for a second like their daughter, and Charlie's stomach was hollow.

What if something was wrong?

Forget it. Tara could go weeks without returning phone calls.

Tomorrow, he would take the climbers up to Kahiltna Glacier. The weather looked good. When they left here, later this afternoon, he and Joe would head for the airport, double-check everything. The weather looked good, but that could change at any time. The climbers expected to be up there for sixteen days.

Francesca edged over to him. "If anything happens to Tony, Roy Jr. and Pammie Sue—"

"Will never forgive me?"

Francesca caught his ironic look.

Charlie said, low, "Roy Jr. would fly him up there himself for the money."

Her mouth tilted slightly.

"I've talked to him. And to your dad. I apologized, Cesca." Easier to say it in the crowded room, where it sounded just like conversation.

Francesca read his eyes, then touched him, silently saying it was all right.

Beside the refrigerator, alone again, he opened a Surge. *I apologized, and it was a lie.*

PAMMIE SUE WALCOTT and two of her daughters came to the flight station the next morning to see Tony off. From the office window, Francesca watched the ritual of farewell. They hugged Tony, kissed him. Maybe prayed. While Gelsey waited, yards off to the side, wrapped in a patched down jacket and a madonna's smile.

Francesca had volunteered to answer the phones so Joe could be with Hayley. From the window, she watched Charlie walk around the Cessna, checking the plane. He'd take the climbers to Kahiltna in two groups. Seeing Joe help Hayley up into the plane, Francesca emerged from the office.

Tony said, "Bye, Mom," then stopped to embrace Gelsey.

Pammie Sue lingered, alone. Her daughters had left. Francesca tried to imagine the night of Mia's death. What would make a person fail to report the death of her sister's child? Afraid Mia might inherit...

Probably her sister-in-law would serve no jail time, but all of Talkeetna was horrified. Just two days ago, a patient at the clinic had asked Honeydew, "Is it true she shot at the dog?" A client had told Francesca, "I heard you're leaving town. Because of Pammie Sue." Honestly. At least, the weekly paper carried the facts, sandwiched between Talkeetna's unique astrological forecast and a personals column that was circulated as far away as Cheyenne, Wyoming.

Francesca sympathized with Pammie Sue now, as a mother with a mother's fears. Tara's style was Third World countries. And Tony... Denali had North Pole weather in June; in winter the cold had been measured at a hundred and forty-eight degrees below zero. Landing at Kahiltna International Airport, at seven thousand feet, Charlie would be safe in comparison.

Trying to ignore Pammie Sue, Francesca asked Gelsey, "Are you going to stay outside until they go?" The propeller on the Cessna slowly spun, picking up speed.

"Yes." She smiled, dry-eyed. Francesca did not yet know if she and Tony planned to be married or what their plans were.

Pammie Sue approached them, and drew back slightly and clasped her hands together. She rocked in her boots.

"Hello, Francesca. How are you feeling, Gelsey?"

"Fine." Her cheeks pinked. Happy to be pregnant, to be having Tony's baby.

Did I ever smile like that? Stormy had taken photos of her pregnant with Tara. *But I was always worried.* Could she take a page from Gelsey's wisdom and smile as Charlie left?

She waved. They all waved. The plane taxied.

Pammie Sue came to her side. "Charlie tried to get through to Roy Jr. I don't know what to say, Francesca. This has gone on too long, and I haven't helped. Roy Jr. has been so loyal."

To Pammie Sue, she must mean. "Good."

Gelsey said, "Well, I'm going to work."

"Take care of yourself," the two others said at once.

When Tony's girlfriend had walked to her car, Pammie Sue remarked, "She's very sweet. They came to tell us the other night, and at least Roy Jr. wasn't unkind to Tony. She plays the guitar. Did you know that?"

Francesca shook her head.

"I hated the things he said that night to my sister. I'm so used to not saying what I feel. It feels strange to tell you this now, but you were never a talker, Francesca. You've never gone around repeating things people say. It seems marriage is hating someone one day and loving him the next." She sighed. "I wish Roy Jr. and I had gone somewhere else and started our own business instead of throwing in with your dad."

Was it wrong to listen to a person who'd done what Pammie Sue had? Was it better to eternally show your disapproval and a visceral hatred that would come and go? Was loyalty to your childhood best friend more important than forgiveness?

But when someone didn't forgive...

The office of Roy Walcott Air Service sat box-like, a few hundred yards from where she stood. She would never try to speak to either her father or brother again.

"I think the worst sins," said Pammie Sue, "are the stupidest, the sins of weakness. I should know."

Francesca touched the snow with her boot. "Yes."

Nothing more to say.

Time to call Tara again. She'd try from Charlie's office. "Bye."

She went home before he returned from Denali. She still hadn't reached Tara and would try Isaac that evening or perhaps over the weekend. There might be a problem between the two of them—it was likely—but he could tell her where to find Tara.

Without Charlie there, she felt like a visitor in his

house. He'd invited her to move the furniture, hang things on the walls, and yet…

I brought so little.

She envisioned things she might do with the cabin, then dismissed it all. It was a house. She lived here.

She was using Mia's laptop to write a midwifery article when the phone rang. Tara.

She got up, picked up the phone. "Hello."

"Hi, Cesca."

Charlie. She waited, startled.

"Need me to buy anything on the way home?"

She saw through the request. He was telling her he was down.

Francesca knew better than to thank him. "Some of that ginger teriyaki from the trading post?"

"She, ah, went to Texas."

Isaac McCrea spoke with a slight accent that Francesca noticed and remembered even as her pulse sped. It was late Friday night, and the physician sounded tired. Charlie was in the bathroom shaving, a forever signal, a mating ritual.

"She was going to try and adopt Laura, but the birth mother showed up and wanted her back."

"Oh, God." The girl who'd abandoned her baby in Tara's car. "Isaac, tell me everything."

Charlie emerged from the bathroom in his jeans and stood motionless in the doorway, listening.

When she got off the phone, Francesca rapidly repeated it all—that Tara had given back the baby, that she'd gone to jail in El Paso, that the charges had been dropped and she was driving herself to Colorado.

"Why the hell didn't Isaac drive her?"

"I didn't ask."

He snatched up the phone. "I'll ask."

As he pressed redial, she cut off the connection. "Put down the phone. If any man is to blame for Tara's situation, it's you."

The receiver found its way to the cradle. He folded muscular arms across his chest, then dropped them. He returned to the bathroom for a shirt and came out, pulling it on. "It never stops with you, does it, Francesca? Everything she does is my fault, because of my inadequacies as a father."

"For once, I'd like to hear you admit your responsibility."

"She had a father in the home. The reason that changed was your decision."

"You were not in the home. Even when you were there, you weren't."

His smile lacked remorse or humor. "I'm sorry for my abundant inadequacies. I've apologized for them to everyone else in your family and now to you." He eyed the phone. "The asshole."

"You don't know Tara as well as you think you do."

"You think this is her fault?"

"I think she's capable of telling a man she doesn't want a relationship with him."

"A *man* would drive her back to Colorado, anyhow."

Francesca marched to the kitchen to put on the teakettle. "We just have to wait till she calls. And next time, please don't ridicule my intuition." Catching him rolling his eyes, she said, "I'm just a convenience to you, aren't I?"

He bent over to peer in the refrigerator, reaching for the bulb, which blinked. "Aren't there hormone supplements available? Isn't that what doctors do?"

"Shut up!"

Abandoning the job, he backed away, lifting his eyebrows.

She cried. That baby. *Damn it, Tara, why do you always get yourself in these messes? Why do you always hurt yourself?* "She's a glutton for punishment and, all right, it's because of me, too, because we were divorced. If that hadn't happened, she'd be different."

"Cesca."

"I can't take any of your pop psychology right now, Charlie."

"She's thirty years old, and you're not responsible for who she is, and neither am I. Sorry. Not taking the blame."

"We're not completely responsible, but we're partly to blame. You know it, too."

"Good night." He headed for the ladder.

"You're not even worried."

He didn't answer.

THE MORNING BROUGHT heavy snow, all-day snow. Charlie came home for lunch at two, and Francesca knew it was some kind of apology for the night before, for not holding her in bed, for a coolness that lasted into the morning. He was embracing her when the phone rang. It was Tara, her voice flat as she moved past the subject of Laura to midwifery and briefly to Isaac. Francesca and Charlie both spoke with her, and when they hung up, Charlie said, "Well. She's strong."

"She's in anguish, in agony. This is a nightmare, and I *warned* her."

He had no answer. He'd consistently failed to protect Tara, and so had Francesca.

The phone jangled again, and he picked it up. "Charlie here."

"Hi. They're in trouble. Radioed. They've got a climber in a crevasse."

"Who?"

"A male. Didn't say who."

Charlie contemplated the bending glass of the windows. "I'll come down." But the weather would be miserable on Denali, and he and Joe knew it, knew it might be hours or a day before anyone could do anything, even take off. "Find out where they are."

They disconnected.

"You can't fly in this."

"I'll have to see what's going on up there. Want to come to the airport?" He was already pulling on his parka.

She grabbed hers.

"IT CAN'T BE TONY. He wouldn't do anything foolish." Francesca spoke confidently. "Do his parents know?"

Joe Burke tuned in the weather and nodded.

"What about Gelsey? Has someone told her?"

Neither man answered.

Charlie was studying charts and listening to the weather, and he left the office abruptly. Joe grabbed his coat and zipped it.

"He's going, isn't he?" asked Francesca.

"He wouldn't go if it wasn't safe." Joe winked at her and went outside.

THE WEATHER BEGAN TO CLEAR, and by the time he took off, blue sky showed, and she could see the top of the Great One. She breathed easily and watched his red plane against the sky.

"Francesca!" Joe yelled from the door of the office. "Phone."

Tara? She hurried inside to take the call.

"Francesca, it's Honeydew. Taylor Whitney's coming in. She's been laboring at home all night and this morning. Can you get down here?"

To the clinic. A birth, planned as a water birth. *How I had Tara.* Everything else receded, everything but Taylor and her baby. "Yes. I'll be right there."

THE CLINIC BIRTHING ROOM was pale yellow with a birthing tub. Honeydew was Alaska's most enthusiastic advocate of water birth. She stayed in the tub with Taylor and her husband, Bill, as the mother labored.

Taylor was thirty-two, and wore her curly blond hair short. She and her husband operated a rafting and guiding business. In just two prenatal appointments, Francesca had grown to care about her and this baby, this child she so wanted. But she'd worried that Taylor's determination to have a certain kind of birth might interfere with the experience.

That wasn't happening. Taylor's moans were natural, her mouth loose, and Francesca provided support to brace her body during contractions. Everything was calm, flowing like the water itself. With no bright lights, only the single lamp Francesca had lit, Taylor ceased speaking. She had entered another realm, a private space.

Francesca couldn't help thinking of Tara—and Laura. Tara had wanted children with Danny but… *If only she could meet someone and have a baby.* She knew Tara longed for a child and not just for a child but for pregnancy and birth and breastfeeding and— *She'd be a wonderful mother.*

She had been. To Laura.

Honeydew listened to the baby's heart with a fetoscope between contractions.

The clinic phone rang in another room, and they ignored it. The clinic was closed. Honeydew's pager lay on the rustic table beneath the window whose wooden blinds were drawn. Anyone with an emergency would call the answering service, not the clinic.

Hours passed as Taylor's cervix gradually dilated, the room alive with the emotion of labor, of a baby on the way. Francesca's esteem for Honeydew increased as she watched the other midwife work, saw her rapport with the mother. How hard it must be for her to have lost Mia.

She glimpsed it in Honeydew's face from time to time. Remembering Mia. Feeling the absence.

As Taylor entered transition, as her moans became cries, the phone rang again. Honeydew soothed her with sounds rather than words, like the humming a mother makes with a child.

The phone stopped ringing, and the machine clicked on.

Bill told his wife, "You're so beautiful."

"I can't do it!"

"Yes, you can," Honeydew told her. "You are doing it. You have the best pelvis I've ever seen. This baby is going to come right out."

Her pager beeped, and Francesca checked it. The number was for Marcus Aviation.

"It's Charlie. I'll call him later."

Honeydew gave her a rueful smile.

"What?"

The other midwife shook her head. She focused on the mother, checking her. "You can go ahead and push, Taylor."

Francesca and Bill supported the mother. Taylor cried out as she pushed, a primal sound, unlike other cries, other human sounds, or perhaps sounding different to

Francesca because she was a midwife, because she *knew* this cry.

The pager beeped again, and Francesca asked Bill to turn it off. He did, and she didn't ask about the number.

"That's right. That's right." Charlie would never call back after receiving no answer.

A grunt. A cry.

"Here she comes. That's right...."

Sweating, Taylor screamed as she pushed and Francesca said, "Your baby. You can touch your baby." The reality of the repeated phone calls, the second page, intruded on her thoughts. She banished it, giving everything to the present, to the baby being born. Oh, beautiful baby. She let nothing else in, and she was on one plane of thought with Honeydew when the midwife said, "Taylor, the baby's shoulders are stuck. Let's get you out of the tub and on your hands and knees on these towels. Right here."

Shoulder dystocia.

Francesca and Honeydew had talked of this before. Mia was a miracle worker with shoulder dystocia.

Francesca supported the baby's head and reached into the perineum with a gloved hand and the shoulders turned and were born with the next contraction. Her eyes watered. The baby girl was alive and slippery, the mother and Honeydew both crying.

Bill said, "She's so beautiful. Taylor, you're amazing. Look at her."

The cord pulsed, and Francesca brought out the stainless steel bowl, looking only once at the pager.

The rescue hadn't involved landing on Kahiltna, but he'd known of another glacier. Very cold up there. Ice...

Twenty minutes later, the placenta came with too much blood. It was whole. Honeydew gave Taylor shepherd's purse tea ready for Taylor to sip while Francesca massaged the fundus. It was imperative to control the bleeding.

Another hour passed before she asked Honeydew, "Do you mind if I make a call? I just want to see if Charlie's back down."

"I hope the climber's all right," said her partner.

While Honeydew checked the mother for tears, Francesca went to their office, flicked on the fluorescent overhead and picked up the phone.

Joe Burke answered, "Marcus Aviation."

Shit. Shit. But Charlie could have stepped out.

"It's Francesca. Someone called."

"Right. Are you still at the clinic?"

No-o-o! "Yes. What happened?"

"He hit a bird. We've got three planes out looking."

"Is he alive? Did the ELT go off?" The emergency locator transmitter, his beacon.

Brief silence. "He doesn't have one with him. We took it off to… Anyway, he doesn't have it."

Francesca stiffened, eyes round in rage. "I'll be right there—as soon as I can."

Tony Walcott

"Günther's in Anchorage." I want to talk about the glacier, about being up on the ice, blinded by snow, and how Günther just slid away. But he's going to be all right. We're all down—climbers, that is—and I'm glad. It never feels like defeat to me when we don't make the summit. Death is defeat.

I don't know what to say to my aunt.

She's drinking coffee and sitting by the radio in

the dark. She ought to go home, but nobody's going home here.

And nobody's flying, either. It's snowing, and it's dark, and Charlie's out there, dead or alive.

I get up and hug her.

"Thank you, Tony." She seems to see for miles, see things we can't. "He's all right."

Does she believe in God?

Oh, here's Gelsey. She went to get me some coffee. "Thanks." She'd be happy I'm down but even when we hold each other, she looks worried for Charlie. That's the kind of person she is.

"Gelsey, I'm going next door. Hang here, okay?"

Outside, the snow's flying level with the earth, but it's not like the total white of the mountain, the closeness to death. I didn't want to come home; none of us did, and then Günther vanished.

The light's still on. Yes, there's Mom and Dad and Grandpa. Grandpa's got his coat on, ready to go home.

"Hello."

My father and grandfather lift their eyebrows the same way.

Grandpa steps around me, to reach the door.

"It would be decent to talk to her," I say.

He says, "Any other wisdom from the mountain?"

"What's the point in dying without talking to one of your children?"

My dad sighs. He rescued Günther today and flew him to Anchorage, and Art brought the rest of us down. Will Dad look for Charlie tomorrow?

My mother speaks. "He's right. Both of you should hear him."

Now it's going to be a war between my mother and my father, because she's told him that I'm right—and she's said it in front of me.

My grandfather tells me, "It's a pity you can't fly."

"Your granddaughter could." He still won't admit Mia and Alan are my uncle Mel's kids.

His lips tighten, and the weather hits all of us as he goes out.

"I hate this family. Charlie's my uncle. He's Alan's uncle. We're all family. What's the problem? Are you just broken?" I ask my father.

He zips his parka, too, and goes to the back of the office to shut off the lights.

"I'll come over with you, Tony," says Mom, "and sit with her."

Dad asks, "All night?"

I get out of there. I don't want to hear it. What my mom did with Mia makes me feel crazy, as though I don't know my own mother.

Snowflakes hit my cheeks. There's more snow up there.

The cold is much colder.

CHAPTER FIFTEEN

Hilo, Hawaii
February 10, 1980

He is unshaven, and his muscles are slack, and his brown, burned face reminds me of Barry, who sleeps on the beach. But his eyes are intelligent as ever, and that bothers me.

"Are you going to move in with him?" With Jay, he means.

"I don't know." I know only that I'm getting out of here, and I'm taking Tara.

Charlie licks his bottom lip and rests against the doorjamb. "Does she know your plans?"

"I've told her that we're moving and that I'm going to divorce you. You should be served with the papers soon—now that they know where to find you."

"You didn't think to tell me before you told Tara?"

"That would have been logistical. There's nothing you can say."

"Why." He is suggesting that this is something he could say, but he's not asking why.

It's not something I want to talk about.

His eyes are looking that way, reminding me how smart he is and what a waste it is and how much I loathe him. "Why?"

It's going to hurt him. The words come. "I'm in love with someone else, and it's been a long time since I loved you." It's revolting to say, and I am less when I say it. My life is broken.

Charlie moves just a little. Shifting.

He cocks his eyebrows. "Need help packing?"

"No."

He stands there. He stands there and won't go away, and I tell him, "I am packed. We're going to Stormy's. I was just waiting for you to get back."

"Here I am." And when I wish he would, he does not leave, and he doesn't open a beer. He just looks at me, plain as a Bible verse, contradictory as the -whole book. And just as deceitful.

Denali

THE RUBBER CUP HE'D TAPED over his nose beneath the ski mask felt warm and moist inside. He was likely to lose toes.

Charlie listened to the wind and watched the invisible daylight, the snow building a screen on the window. It had packed around the tarp he'd put under the cracked windshield. Snow was the best insulation, but it had already covered the plane's red paint.

He studied raven feathers and guts on the cockpit and saw other blood on another instrument panel in another aircraft in another land. Again, he checked his watch. Howling. No one could fly.

Snow cave? Fire? He'd played this over before, what he would do. He was doing it, but he was cold. Abdominal exercises again. Hold those feet up in the air. Water against his chest, melting. Drink it.

Another night.

Snow cave. Do like the Eskimo.

He retrieved the shovel.

Outside, the ice and snow made it easy. Stack up the packs and duffels, and the snow blows over them. Fire up the stove. Fingers. Really couldn't lose fingers. A few toes, okay.

Darkness and cold and the raven's feathers. He had brought two out with him. The walls of the cave thickened against the side of the plane, deep in its drift. A cocoon. In his sleeping bag, he could set the alarm on his watch. Doze. Beep. Dig out the door again. Cold. Back into the bag. Think hot.

Hot.

Sweltering beach.

Sleepy and smelling the rot and the latrines and diesel. Sand on his sheets.

The phone is going to ring.

No. It's freezing here. And black.

Dig out the door.

SHE DIDN'T WANT to be at home, even for the few hours she'd agreed to go, but maybe it was better. Except that she could smell him on his pillow, and she kept pressing her face there, kept trying to smell him, kept telling herself that her gut was right. She called no one. Tara had just lost that baby, and making her worry would be pointless. If her father was dead, Francesca would tell her. But nothing before that.

Oh, Charlie. This bed smells like you.

Get up. Turning on the lamp, she eyed his bookshelves.

Where were the things that were special to him?

There was a photograph album on a bottom shelf, but she didn't want to look at it because there would be no photos of her. Hers contained photos of him, for Tara.

Some of those albums belonged to Tara now, but Francesca had many of the baby pictures, the childhood pictures.

She eyed his scant collection of novels and opened his closet. Oh, here. This box.

She opened it.

With his medals were snapshots, and she had forgotten those. Hippie mother and baby. Protected in plastic, photos in plastic. *I looked damned good in a bikini. Half a bikini.*

Charlie, I love you. Hang on, man of my heart.

But she knew he wasn't carrying her picture now, to keep him safe, and his wedding ring was not on his finger, and their love had been stained by her betrayal, and everything was different.

Except that she loved him and wanted him safe.

Knocking interrupted the wind. Something banging the side of the house.

More knocking.

She gathered her nightgown about her and left the medals and photos and climbed down the ladder. "Coming." The lamp she'd switched on cast an orange glow on a small section of the room, leaving the other corners in shadow. She wasn't going to be sleeping well tonight.

She opened the door.

Snow flecked Alan's clothes, from hat to boots. "Did I wake you?"

"No. No. Come in." Snow blew over the carpet as he stepped inside.

She shut the door.

"Hey, I was wondering if I could sack out over at Mia's. My stovepipe broke."

"Sure. Or you can stay here."

He glanced about uneasily.

"Charlie's on Denali. His plane went down." As

Alan's face began to change, she rushed on. "There's been no radio contact. But I think he's okay."

His eyebrows drew together, and he collapsed on the couch. "Wow." He shut his eyes. "Hey, I need to bring some of my dogs in. Do you mind?"

Charlie would. "No."

"I'll be right back."

She returned to the loft and the closet and the corner where she'd stacked some of her things because she wasn't really living in this place. She remembered Charlie's jokes about maybe leaving her his house. A tear crossed her nose.

She put away the medals.

I'm so in love with you, and I want you to love me that way again. Can you ever really forgive me?

But he couldn't. He really couldn't.

"Come on. Come on, Sasha. Good girl."

She brought out one of her own photograph albums and opened it and saw him on the beach with Tara and closed it.

He's okay. He's not dead.

She pulled on leggings and two of his shirts and a pair of his wool socks and descended the ladder. Alan was putting an album on the stereo.

She heard Jim Morrison's dark and truest poetry, his lyrics, Doors' lyrics, breaking on through. No, not the other side.

Creed Dalton had listened to a tape of this album day and night, Charlie said. Seeing Alan, she wanted to tell him about the helicopter becoming a sunburst, about a game of Ping-Pong, wanted him to understand Charlie. "He's alive," was all she said.

The phone rang.

Her heart slammed, and she looked at the clock. Eleven. It would be Tara—or Ivy, Ivy's baby was due, and Tara had said she was coming to Colorado to have the baby, with Tara as her midwife.

"Hello?"

Alan searched the refrigerator and took out the orange juice. "Freedy, no." The dog removed his jaw from the table leg to meet Alan's eyes.

"It's Honeydew. Did I wake you?"

Francesca gave a short laugh. "No. Is Taylor all right?"

"Everyone's fine. Just—" Honeydew sighed. "Do you want someone to come over? I baked some bread tonight. But if you want to be alone..."

Francesca didn't want to be alone. She had a midwifery partner, a real friend, a growing friend, in Honeydew. Her nephew had brought his dogs over.

But I want you, Charlie. Oh, God, Charlie.

"Alan's here. Whatever..." She couldn't speak intelligently. "Joe's listening to the radio at the airport. I'm going back there soon."

"I'll be over. Hang tight."

Francesca went to turn on the porch light, but before she did, she stepped into the cold wind, thinking how much colder it was on Denali. He must be dead.

God, I'm afraid. Life shouldn't end this way. Love shouldn't end this way.

But it could.

HE TRIED TO CALCULATE the number of hours it was since he'd felt his toes. He still tried to move them regularly, and he drank hot chocolate and ate instant oatmeal without removing his gloves.

Altitude—maybe six thousand feet here. Tara lived higher in Colorado.

But not in this weather.

He felt for the shovel. Bent his fingers around the handle. This time the door was iced over. He jammed the shovel against it, against another place, and snow fell on him.

There. A hole. Make the opening wider. Blowing ice.

You have to be able to get out of that hole, Marcus. Flares. Right over there, in that can.

Digging.

Freezing hands.

Come on. Lighten up the weather. Lighten up.

But all was gray-white and blowing snow, and the plane would be invisible.

The flares were all he had.

ICE AND SNOW STACKED outside the office windows through the colorless hours of daylight. Francesca watched the clock hands, drinking coffee and eating the doughnuts Joe had brought in that morning. No planes searched for Charlie. The weather near the glacier was too severe.

Her rear end hurt from the office chair. It was Joe's. He paced and sometimes spoke on the phone, having helpless conversations. *Hey, remember when Max Larkin was down in that crevasse....* Trying to find information to help Charlie when they still couldn't say he was alive. Hayley and the other climbers gathered in the office with food, which Francesca ate without taste, without noticing what she consumed.

Tony and Gelsey came, and the slender, dark-haired girl sat against the counter beside Francesca. She said nothing, just brought Francesca things, remained vigilantly close.

I ought to be doing something. Isn't there something I can do?

It was two o'clock.

They won't go up if it gets much later.

She stood. "Excuse me." She zipped her parka.

ART TURNER was in the pilot's lounge of the flight station. "Can't go. I would if I could." He squinted at the window, then rubbed his forehead. "Well..."

Francesca prayed and prayed he wouldn't die trying.

He whistled under his breath, then edged to the door and slipped out. Beyond the windows, in the snow, he met another figure. Tall. She imagined the scowling face. But the men nodded to each other and set off toward their offices.

They are brave, these men. They are so brave. And Charlie would do the same for them and had, because both had lost their share of planes.

She stepped outside, and far down the field, the tall man was walking around his Cessna. A small spot in her heart was claimed for Roy Jr., because he would do this one thing.

AIRPLANE.

The sound.

Flares. Hands have to work.

Get out of the hole. Stand. Stand.

Shovel. Throw some snow off the plane.

A Cessna engine. Thanks, boys.

Can't see anything up there. Just her.

He judged distance and speed and knew the terrain above and around him. He lit a flare. He lit another.

They're not going to see these.

But they were up there, looking.

He stamped his feet and could not feel.

FRANCESCA HUDDLED ALONE in the office by the radio.

Another night.

Another night.

She'd taken a photo from the bulletin board in the back office, Charlie on Kahiltna Glacier, and she studied his face and shut her eyes and saw him many ways.

She wept. She had long since forgotten to call her daughter or anyone else. There was only this numbness. They would find him. It was just a question of hours and days. The plane had shattered on impact, and she saw this and sobbed.

HIS FEET.

You've really done it this time, Marcus.

Dark and blowing. Howling.

Move around, move around. Start the stove.

Take off gloves.

Light the stove.

Come on. Light. What's wrong here?

You're warm enough.

He did without the stove. In the sleeping bag, he grasped at thoughts, mostly that hindsight is always twenty-twenty. Don't sell the mine. Lose some altitude over Que Son Valley before the lightning hit, which he would've done if he wasn't chickenshit—even though he couldn't have known the lightning would hit the wing. Beg Cesca to stay because she loved him and wanted him. Get Tara some safe midwifery job in, say, France. Kill that bastard she'd married, Danny Graine.

Other stuff... He never looked back too far.

Life was full of what people called mistakes.

He eyed the raven feathers.

Mistakes were another lie, like character.

In the charcoal womb of the cave, he questioned her fidelity and if he should carry her picture in the future and if he wished he had it now and if he wished he was twenty-two again.

Funny. He didn't.

But he wanted all the time he had left, and he could put up with her wandering eye. Flame in his heart. She just burned there, burned....

The immense cold of the present touched him, and he found its brittle indifference beautiful and perfect.

Got to light that stove.

THE SKY WAS BLUE, and Roy Walcott Jr. banked close to the Cone, a spire they all knew, and his father, beside him, peered out the windows. "November three one-four-two Romeo, this is November two-four...." Art Turner.

Roy Jr. and his father listened to the report.

His father said, "...let's go back to the glacier."

A perfect day for flying. Funny how he'd wanted to kill Marcus. Now, it seemed a shame for the sister he really didn't like.

"That's a flare.... Can land on the Flat Glacier."

Roy Jr. spoke over the radio. "November two-four-six-one, this is..."

FRANCESCA HELD HERSELF, her breath hard in her throat. Setting a cup of coffee in front of her, Haylay grinned. "*Yes.* A flare. All right! A flare!"

Beside the radio, Joe shook his head and shook his head, half laughing.

He's alive. Francesca touched her face and couldn't drink any more coffee, couldn't do anything.

"LEAN ON ME."

Not a chance. He stumbled in the snow and picked himself up.

The spry and aged man said, "Suit yourself."

"He can't suit himself. Marcus, I've got to take off, and we're getting your ass out of here."

He let them hold him up. No getting into the plane without them.

"Here's some hot tea. Don't burn yourself." The old man buckled him in. Took the seat beside him.

Roy Jr. was on the radio. "...to Lake Hood."

They were taking him to Anchorage. He could peel off his mask and nose guard. "I haven't felt my feet for days." No one could hear him.

The old man pointed to the thermos.

Charlie drank and began to shake.

HER BROTHER AND FATHER were leaving the hospital as she arrived. Art Turner had flown her to Lake Hood, and she'd driven Charlie's car to the hospital.

They met in the hallway. For no reason, Francesca remembered Charlie telling Tara stories of the Red Baron. And his funeral. Buried with respect by his enemies.

"Thank you," Francesca said.

Her father nodded.

Roy Jr. said, "He's on the second floor."

HIS EYES WERE SCARED, and it was like talking with a child in that she had to wait some time to find out what was on his mind. If she was present long enough, he would bring it up.

"They're just toes. Joe lost his arm. And my hands look good. They're not worried about my hands."

Francesca met his eyes. "It'll make a good story."

"Better than Joe's."

Beside his bed, she breathed.

He contemplated his blackened toes. "Miss me?"

Francesca's chest tightened, some blockage in her throat. She wished she had a song. She wished she had a joke. She wished she had her rings on her left hand, but she'd given them back to him in Hawaii, and he'd thrown them in the ocean while she watched.

She leaned forward, elbows on her knees, face in her hands. If only she could start over. She tried to remember how to begin, how she had begun, and she could only see a boy in a white T-shirt and jeans, with cocky dark good looks, the best-looking guy she'd ever seen.

"Let me guess. In the absence of the best and most handsome pilot in Talkeetna, you've fallen for Dr. Bob."

Francesca blinked. Right. He'd asked if she missed him. Words failed her again, and he caught her expression.

"What is it, Cesca?"

It would be too hard, too painful, to say that she loved him and receive some surface answer, hear him talk around it or doubt it or accept it without reciprocating. She wanted more.

But the deeper things will come.

She opened her mouth and shut it.

He slipped into himself and away from her.

The words streamed, racing against the reopening of his wounds, which had been inflicted before she knew him, and the wounds she'd made and those she hadn't. "I lay on our bed—" our bed "—and smelled your pillow. I looked in your closet and found your medals. I wore your clothes. I sat in Joe's chair by the radio at three in the morning. I cried. I sobbed."

His eyes were straight and steady. He put his head against the pillow and closed them.

Anger surged through her as she waited for him to speak.

His eyelashes glistened.

She stood and shut the door, then returned to him. Her bottom still hurt from all the sitting. Her bones hurt, and she waited for words that would make everything right.

His eyes opened. Seeing his face, she put the bed's guardrail down and lay beside him, her calves and feet dangling awkwardly over the edge of the mattress and metal frame.

Charlie smelled her. Her hair grabbed his skin. The snow cave left him. He kissed her mouth, kissed her more. The photos in the box, the box she'd found, were of someone he'd loved and needed so deeply, so much. He thought he could carry her picture again.

But had no words to tell her so.

Roy Walcott

"I'm retiring. Right now."

Is my son pulling trump on me? I can get other pilots, even in winter. Marcus already has another pilot here, I notice, the kid from Eugene, Oregon—filling in while he's laid up. But without Roy Jr., it will be hard calling this place Roy Walcott Air Service. "Are you asking to buy me out, son?"

"No. I want to open an air museum in the Hangar. The building is mine, and it's a dream I've always had. I haven't got many more years of professional flying."

He doesn't seem angry, but this is just what Marcus predicted, and Roy Jr. doesn't play games. I take all this into account. "We'll need to find a buyer."

"Shouldn't be hard."

It's time to leave, time to walk out into this perfect flying day. Why feel pain over something that was lost on the Village Airstrip thirty years ago? This business has never been the same. My life has never been the same without her. I could've remarried, but she was special, and no one else has ever measured up.

There's the truck.

"Sir. Excuse me, sir?"

Those folks will ruin their luggage, setting it down in the snow like that. Nice luggage, too. They're nice people, though they seem dressed up for Talkeetna.

"Is there a taxi service to take us into town?"

Whose passengers are they, anyway? Someone without a lick of hospitality. "Where are you bound?" My truck sits three across, and I have nowhere to go.

"B Street. Do you know our son? Alan Smith?"

If Martha Storm was pregnant by Mel, she should have taken up the matter with him. Roy Jr. says she claims Mel was already in boot camp when she learned she was pregnant. I don't want to believe it, but I saw that young man just this morning, with his dogs, and he has the family look. And these are the people who adopted him.

I have behaved badly.

"I'll be happy to give you a ride. Roy Walcott."

"Bob and Colleen Smith. Thank you kindly, Mr. Walcott."

She has a little cross around her neck, and they have kind eyes. Naturally, I try to help them with their bags, but he'll have none of it, and I open the door and tell her to mind her clothes on the running board, it's a mite muddy.

I have Mel's things, and I never read his letters from girls, never wanted to. But if his son wants to, I suppose that's his business.

CHAPTER SIXTEEN

Hawi, Hawaii
December 23, 1994

"We're trying water births," says Solange, Tara's partner. "It's very exciting."

I really don't want to talk, and neither does Ivy, I can see. We're both watching Tara and Danny. As the bride and groom dance, I listen to the ocean and feel the sun and hope it doesn't rain. I'm surprised she wanted this band, but it's a very Hawaiian kind of wedding. It just doesn't seem like her kind of wedding.

Charlie fits himself onto the bench on the other side of Ivy. Nothing traditional about this arrangement.

But he says, as though Ivy is not between us, "You and I are up next, Francesca."

If he wants to talk to me, he'll have to do it without my daughter between us. As Tara dances on the patio, her face is perfectly happy. She giggles at Danny, and she's so beautiful. *Oh, darling, I want you to be happy.*

The bandleader says, "Tara and Danny would like all of you to join them up here."

I am not the first to get up.

Ivy's dress passes beside my eyes as she moves, and when she gets up, Charlie has already gone to get some punch, the nonalcoholic bowl. I'm glad he doesn't drink anymore. He looks good, better than I feel.

Oh, Tara, make something better of your marriage than we did.

I go out to dance, knowing that Charlie was a gentleman and I was not a lady and it has always been this way. When it begins to rain, the caterers rush about, and people head inside. From under an umbrella, I listen to the sound of it.

Someone hands me a glass of punch. I know the hand.

"Thank you. I didn't mean to not answer you back there."

He makes a derisive sound. All right, it was a lie, but does he have to point out my polite lies, the things I do to protect us from awkwardness?

He glares at the sea.

"Excuse me." I head inside, these moments casting a pall over my daughter's wedding. The pity is, we really did love each other once.

Talkeetna
December 1999

"MARCUS AVIATION. Charlie here."

"This is Isaac McCrea calling from Colorado."

Charlie shifted in his chair. He was wearing his boots again. Joe had said, *Some people have all the luck,* but he had his right hand on Hayley's hip when he said it. Isaac McCrea who didn't drive Tara back from Colorado? "Dr. McCrea."

"I'm sorry we haven't had the chance to meet yet. But your daughter is the most beautiful, the most wonderful—"

The man sounded a little choked up, and Charlie felt emotion collecting in his throat. The doctor he'd never met asked his permission to marry Tara.

Well, Isaac was going to have to ask Tara. Charlie told him so, and a minute later he replaced the phone. Outside, white flakes drifted down, fast and evenly spaced. He remembered August, so many years ago, touching down at the Village Airstrip with Cesca and knowing he should talk fast, ask her father the minute he saw him, make his intentions clear.

It wasn't easy to say quickly to a man whose wife had died the day before, wasn't easy to say while his son was cleaning a twenty-two and looking right at you.

I failed. I failed.

From the first.

FRANCESCA CLOSED HER EYES as she replaced the receiver.

It felt a bit like sneaking into Charlie's old hangar. Or telling her parents she'd had a great time at Stormy's when, in fact, she'd had a great time in his tent at Denali.

But now, she was keeping things from her child. Tara had asked if she and Isaac should arrange separate rooms for her and Charlie. She should have just said, *Tara, your dad and I are living together.* No. It had been more dignified to say they would make their own arrangements.

The phone rang again as she was stoking the woodstove, and she finished before she picked it up, breathless. "Hello?"

"Hi."

Francesca chewed her lip. "I think you'll like him."

"Hey. He asked. I do like him."

Francesca lifted her eyebrows, smiling some. "How are your feet?"

"I'm fine. I think I can dance at our daughter's wedding. If you'll dance with me this time."

Her eyes squeezed shut. "If you ask." She told him what she'd told Tara, and he laughed.

CHARLIE PARKED IN FRONT of the cabin at the edge of the Village Airstrip. That was Alan's truck, with his dog boxes. Maybe this wasn't the time.

But as he hesitated, the front door opened, and his nephew came out carrying a cardboard box.

Charlie switched off the engine and got out, carefully. Careful walking. "Hello, Alan."

Alan nodded. "He gave me my father's things."

One box? "Is that it?" Charlie had pictured a shrine to Mel Walcott, every belonging preserved for eternity.

"Just what he had in Vietnam."

Charlie felt enormously, eyes hot and watery. Mel had kept things with him, too, probably some girl's letters and photos, and Charlie hoped for Alan's sake that they were Stormy's. "Come over if…" He never finished the sentence.

Alan looked like he wanted to ask something, but he didn't. "Cool." He carried the box to his truck.

Charlie waited for the sound of the engine before he worked his way to the door and knocked.

It opened. "You forget some—" Roy Walcott stopped the question.

Charlie had already thanked him and his son. "Had something to ask you."

Francesca's father slipped back, out of the way.

The house was unlit, a cave. The man had lived three decades without his wife. Charlie dismissed that thought. "This may seem like a meaningless gesture at this point, but I'd like to ask you for your daughter's hand."

Roy Walcott gave him a look of sheer disgust, and

Charlie knew his own hypocrisy, knew self-hatred, and it was what the look in this man's eyes had always made him feel.

"I imagine she'll have you." Roy glanced toward the TV. *Wings* was beginning.

"I won't keep you from your show."

On the porch, Charlie weighed belated chivalry and feeling like a fool against the comfort of inaction. In hindsight, inaction won.

But the walk away from the Walcott home spun other thoughts. By the time he reached his truck, he realized deeper things, harder things. He hovered over the steering wheel while the engine idled, glad the truck was still warm. He shut his eyes. *It's never going to be what it could have been, Cesca.* The hard fact was, he could have lived with the infidelity.

He could have stood that.

A Cessna was taking off, and he followed it with his eyes and then edged out, to head for the airport.

Precipice, Colorado
December 1999

CHARLIE WATCHED HIS DAUGHTER dance with her tall doctor husband with snow falling on her hair. She'd smiled at her first wedding. But you couldn't fake ecstasy, and you couldn't fake tenderness, which Isaac showed her.

They'd married each other in the snow by a frozen waterfall, and even the judge nodded in time to the ghetto blaster music. The song ended, and there was a slow rhythm and the promise of sunshine. *Where is My Girl, anyway?*

Her hand in his. Dancing slow. He sang to Francesca, and her blue eyes flashed at him and then avoided him.

He ignored the tightness inside him, thought of other things. Tried to.

Cullen and Ivy handed their newborn to their daughter, Gabriela, for the next song. Cully was a good baby. Maybe Tara would have a baby now.

Well, she had three others, partly grown. Isaac's kids were just fine, smart and handsome.

"It's a nice wedding," he told Francesca.

"You're not too cold?"

"Come to think of it, if you could hold me a little tighter…"

He felt her tears against his neck and knew it wasn't for what Tara had gained as much as for what they had lost.

The Springs Spa and Resort
Precipice, Colorado

MOONLIGHT REFLECTED off the frozen snow on the nearby peaks, keeping Charlie awake. Or maybe he couldn't sleep because she kept tossing. They'd been here three days since the wedding and were leaving in the morning.

The jeweler had needed every day.

And Charlie needed more time still, much more.

He didn't have it. Neither of them did.

The ring was in his pillowcase, and he grasped it, with tragedy in his heart for all the things he could not blame—her father, her brothers, her mother's death, the war, alcoholism, infidelity.

Just himself.

He snuggled behind her, drawing her against him, and set the ring on its chain on the sheet in front of her. She'd always worn her rings on a chain, because of her work.

Francesca moved. She worked the clasp on the chain

he'd picked out, and he took the ends from her and fastened it beneath her thick hair. Kissed her white skin. "I love you, Francesca."

Her body shifted until she faced him in the moonlight.

"Now's your chance to say that I'm the best pilot in Talkeetna and you've always wanted to marry me."

"You are by far the best pilot in Talkeetna. You're the only man I've ever loved. And I've been married to you since I was nineteen."

He knew lies, and this wasn't one.

Their faces were close, and a tear or two wasn't bad. Not these.

"I've never made love with another man, since... you."

"If you say, 'Please, Charlie. Please,' you might get lucky tonight."

"Luckier than this?"

He told her how lucky.

"Please, Charlie. Please."

"Cesca, if you could shut your eyes and moan it would sound more...persuasive."

"Let's not tell Tara just yet. I want to be married in Talkeetna in the summer. Oh, Charlie. Oh, Charlie."

That was more like it.

Washington, D.C.
April 3, 2000
Dalton, Creed Price

THERE YOU ARE.

There you are.

More than a name. So many he'd found, each more than a name.

More than a memory.

"THEY'RE STILL down there." Hayley adjusted her yellow sun hat.

Francesca held her lips tightly closed. Yes. It was time. She and Hayley had walked around the Capitol for three hours and stopped for cappuccino. "I want to go down myself."

There were names she wanted to see, men she had met and photos she had seen and a brother she had loved.

But she didn't move. "I really didn't expect it to be so big."

Or to feel so much. So many *W*s.

So many boys.

Mel… Oh, dear Mel…

There was a blindness and an emptiness. She turned away, leaving the names. Joe stood talking to a vet in a wheelchair and another vet with him, while Charlie read names he must have already read.

Francesca touched him.

He kept reading, but he groped for her hand, and his fingers locked with hers.

THERE WERE NO SMOOTH WORDS that night. Just the honesty of a rough voice in the night in a strange hotel room and the body she knew best, as she knew his hands and his voice. "I took you with me. Everywhere."

"I know."

The truth jammed in his throat. The self-evident truth. It hurt. It hurt. When he was a child, he'd learned to expect hurt, so much that he often didn't feel it when it happened.

But at some point, he'd stopped expecting hurt from her.

When it happened, he felt.

The trust was back, wrapping around him. Dangerous. The Wall had loosened things, and he was afraid, afraid to be the person she'd cast away. Afraid to be himself. He'd cried down there.

But there was crying. And there was the thing he felt coming on now. Total, head-losing unraveling.

He sat up, stripping back the sheet. Where could he go?

"Are you all right?"

"Sure." A lie. The depths of love and loyalty had not happened in his marriage, had not happened where they should have. He'd met them in a strange world where their opposites had coexisted, as well, day holding hands with night. It came, washing, breaking in waves.

"Charlie."

She took him to her, and much later her breasts were wet, beneath him. He remembered the sensation, just barely. It crept into the fringes of consciousness. He wanted to ask her, wanted his memory confirmed. He saw why he'd forgotten.

Day after day, night after night, even the nights like this. She'd said once that the smell of alcohol on his breath made her ill. Charlie had never quite believed that.

Maybe he should believe it.

She'd said to someone else, in front of him, that drunk men were the world's worst lovers.

And this. This half memory, that he used to lie with his head against her and cry.

The loosening deepened.

The depths of loyalty and love were in a woman's breast, bearing the weight of a soldier's head, his head and everything inside. His shoulders shook beneath her hands. If he'd asked her to stay, said one word, she would have. He rolled to his back, his hand over his face, broken as he never had been by the past.

"It's clear up there. Think about the blue, Charlie, and the snow."

Her hand touched his hair.

He listened. She showed him the other past, the past he'd chosen, they'd both chosen, and she knew the words to use and knew how it looked and felt because she was one of them, the flying people, and their history was hers, as his was.

She felt good. Good to hold. He saw Denali and brought Francesca closer and let many other things float away, carried on a wind he didn't even feel. There was only now.

He said, "I need a picture of you."

EPILOGUE

Hilo, Hawaii
November 22, 1968

"That's just the cawl over her head. It's all right."

"Look down, Cesca."

I see her in the water, and my vagina burns as our daughter is born, Charlie's hands following her, catching her, in the water.

So many hands bring her up to me, to my arms.

"My baby."

He holds me, holds me up, his wet skin against mine. "She's pretty. God, she's pretty."

Talkeetna
February 2, 2001

Tara has never said the words that she can't do it.

It has been a hard posterior labor, and Isaac is soaked with sweat. He's afraid and not showing it to her, just looking in her eyes, and she probably hasn't noticed that he's sweating, even in the water. I see this but have tuned out the other people in the room, this circle of birth. All but Charlie, on the chair beside the tub with his head down. So much has gone wrong for Tara, and this must go right.

"Push again, Tara. You're so strong, honey."

She cries as she pushes the head out, and Ivy's hands are there.

No cord.

"We're fine, Tara. Gentle."

"Oh, God!" She sobs, my sweet daughter. I love her so. "Oh, God. My little girl."

She holds her up, and I suction her, and the baby yawns.

Precious, precious baby.

Ivy is crying over this child.

I lift my head. Charlie's eyes are open and good. The tiny baby, the new creature still slippery with vernix, has just come to us, remembering still the world from which she has come, which is not only my daughter's body, nor Isaac's sperm, but somewhere beyond, and she has brought that place to earth again, healing us all.

SUPERROMANCE®

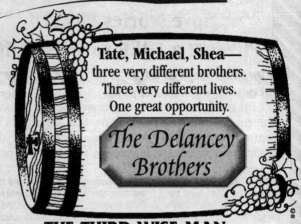

Tate, Michael, Shea—
three very different brothers.
Three very different lives.
One great opportunity.

The Delancey Brothers

THE THIRD WISE MAN
by Muriel Jensen

It's Shea Delancey's turn to find love. Well, strictly speaking, he found it some time ago, with Samantha Haskell. But he put an end to the relationship when he found himself in financial trouble.

Now he learns that Samantha's in trouble. And he learns that she has a baby. *His.* The only solution is to persuade her to come to Oregon…with his son.

She agrees to come for Christmas—and Shea figures his large, loving family will do the rest!

On sale December 1999 at your favorite retail outlet.

*M*akes any time special ™

If you enjoyed what you just read,
then we've got an offer you can't resist!

Take 2 bestselling love stories FREE!

Plus get a FREE surprise gift!

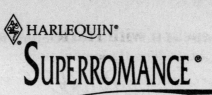

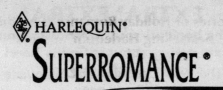

HARLEQUIN®
SUPERROMANCE®

Three childhood friends dreamed of becoming firefighters. Now they're members of the same team and every day they put their lives on the line.

They are

AMERICA'S BRAVEST

An exciting new trilogy by

Kathryn Shay

Available wherever Harlequin books are sold.

HARLEQUIN®
Makes any time special ™

EXTRA! EXTRA!

The book all your favorite authors are raving about is finally here!

The 1999 Harlequin and Silhouette coupon book.

Each page is alive with savings that can't be beat!

Getting this incredible coupon book is as easy as 1, 2, 3.

1. During the months of November and December 1999 buy any 2 Harlequin or Silhouette books.

2. Send us your name, address and 2 proofs of purchase (cash receipt) to the address below.

3. Harlequin will send you a coupon book worth $10.00 off future purchases of Harlequin or Silhouette books in 2000.

Send us 3 cash register receipts as proofs of purchase and we will send you 2 coupon books worth a total saving of $20.00 (limit of 2 coupon books per customer).

Saving money has never been this easy.

Please allow 4-6 weeks for delivery. Offer expires December 31, 1999.

I accept your offer! Please send me (a) coupon booklet(s):

Name: _____

Address: _____ City: _____

State/Prov.: _____ Zip/Postal Code: _____

Send your name and address, along with your cash register receipts as proofs of purchase, to:

In the U.S.: Harlequin Books, P.O. Box 9057, Buffalo, N.Y. 14269
In Canada: Harlequin Books, P.O. Box 622, Fort Erie, Ontario L2A 5X3

Order your books and accept this coupon offer through our web site
http://www.romance.net
Valid in U.S. and Canada only.

PHQ4994R